A STRANGLED
CRY OF FEAR

A STRANGLED CRY OF FEAR

B.A. CHEPAITIS

WILDSIDE PRESS

PROLOGUE

"I didn't do it," Francis Durero said.

Jaguar Addams sat on the other side of the interrogation table from him, her hands folded, her gaze fixed on his broad, dark face. If he was standing, he'd loom over her like a mountain. Even seated his form cast a shadow across her.

"Did you kill the others?" she asked. "Mathias, and Lopez, and—"

"Yeah," he cut in, waving his large hand as if swatting an irritating insect. "I did those women. My brother told me to. But I didn't do Diane."

Jaguar, an empath who was as expert at reading faces and voices as she was at reading minds, watched his expression, listened closely to his tone. His cheek had an intermittent tic, and his skin glistened with sweat, but not from anxiety. Both came from the meds he took to control his schizophrenia, just one consequence of his exposure to chembombs during the Killing Times. And if the courts had named him a murderer, the blue birthmark around his left eye named him something worse.

Francis was a mutoid, his marred genetic code telling its tale in his many health problems.

His family lived in Manhattan during the Killing Times, when the level of violence in North American cities reached critical mass and became, in essence, a domestic war. But he wasn't injured by the killers who roamed the streets. His mother was pregnant when she belonged to a vigilante Safety Squad formed to kill the killers. They used homemade nerve gas and biochem bombs and grenades, whatever they could make or get their hands on. Her work, the work of others like her, left a legacy of genetic injury that still appeared in the children and grandchildren of those exposed, one that was written on Francis's face.

His condition and the murders he'd committed landed him on Prison Planetoid One, which specialized in rehab for mutoids and the criminally insane. He'd been there only a year when he was convicted of killing again—this time a Planetoid Teacher. Now Jaguar was one member of a committee reviewing the rare order of execution Planetoid One had requested. This was her last interview with him before confirming his death.

"I didn't do her," Francis repeated, swinging his head in a wide arc back and forth. His shoulders, massive mountains on a massive frame, moved with his thick neck, with his words.

"Why did you kill the others?" Jaguar asked. She knew what the files said, but she wanted to hear how he told the story.

His glance moved over her. "The ones in green. Like you. My brother told me kill them."

The sage green of her dress was associated with those who practiced the empathic arts—telepathy, empathic contact, precognition and more. People like her and her supervisor, Alex Dzarny, who wasn't too happy about her being on this assignment.

"Does your brother want you to kill me?" Jaguar asked, keeping her voice neutral

"No," Francis said flatly, just stating a fact. "He don't talk to me no more. Now I make things. That's what I do." He hugged a stuffed bear to his chest, made in his work program.

"Do you like that?" Jaguar asked.

He licked his lips as if tasting the question. It probably wasn't one he heard often. Who would check into his likes and dislikes? "I like it," he said, and the tic beat its rhythm in his cheek. "I like making things. I like it."

"Do you like Planetoid One?" Jaguar asked, pressing on.

Francis shook his head hard.

"You don't like it?" she asked.

His eyes went wide. "I like it," he said loudly. "I *like* it."

"Okay," Jaguar reassured him. "It's okay, Francis. Everything's okay."

The tic in his face danced, and Jaguar wondered why they couldn't fix that. Planetoid One laid claim to the most advanced treatment for mutoids. Of course, Jaguar thought, they had to say something to maintain their funding.

They were the first prison planetoid built, and they still used bubble-domes instead of mass generated atmospheres like Planetoids Two and Three. They had no VR system, no replica cities to create the kinds of programs Jaguar could use with her prisoners. Instead they staked their reputation on long-term programs for the criminally insane and mutoids. That made Francis about the worst PR they could get. Jaguar wasn't surprised they wanted him dead.

But she wasn't sure why Board governor Paul Dinardo requested her for this committee. Neither was Alex, who knew the laundry list of reasons that made her a bad choice. She was an empath, just the kind of woman Francis once enjoyed killing. She was against the death penalty. She had history on Planetoid One, none of it good. And she had an ambivalent past with the Teacher Francis was convicted of killing. Diane Lasher, friend and enemy. Enemy and friend.

"Tell me about Diane," Jaguar requested. "Was she good to you?"

"She was nice," Francis said immediately. "Let me do things. The garden. The food."

Jaguar smiled, memory of Diane's better side returning to her. She was kind to the prisoners, kind in general, her light blonde hair framing bright blue eyes full of energy and enthusiasm.

She'd been both kind and enthusiastic in welcoming Jaguar, her reclusive and suspicious new Teacher, to Planetoid One. They became friends, Jaguar drawn to someone who was as much unlike her as possible. In looking back, she wondered if she'd used Diane, feeding off her light at a time when the world looked pretty damn dark to her. The Killing Times weren't that far behind her, and she hadn't come close to healing what they'd done.

But Diane also seemed to get something from her. Maybe she needed shadows to mark her light. Or maybe she liked the way Jaguar saw her as something rare and wonderful, a person who hadn't been damaged. If so, she'd outgrown it. They'd been friends only a year when Diane reported her for employee misconduct, a euphemism for using the empathic arts.

"Everyone thinks you killed her," Jaguar noted. "She had slash marks on her chest, like you made on the others."

Francis hugged his bear until its black button eyes bulged, then pushed a fist against the table. "I told you," he hissed. "I *liked* her."

"Okay," she said. "Okay."

He receded into his chair, closed his eyes and hummed softly to himself. Jaguar sighed.

Francis was a sorry case. A nasty mix of physical and mental illness, with the strength of a few football players. He'd murdered seven women, all empaths, after his brother was killed by a woman suspected to be an empath. And now an empath was to sign his death warrant. She wondered if this completed the circle of violence, prejudice, and vengeance.

She rose to leave. "Thanks, Francis," she said, and left him sitting in the white-washed room, hugging his bear.

* * * *

Supervisor Alex Dzarny waited for Jaguar in the hall outside the holding tank, pacing between office doors, ignoring the people who passed by on their daily rounds.

"You look like someone who's about to have a root canal," Jaguar said as she walked to him.

The tension dissolved from his face and he managed a rueful smile. "I didn't like the set up," he said. The other interviewers had guards and a laser fence, but Jaguar insisted on unprotected contact, calling it a moral prerogative. Though she used her red glass knife as needed and never regretted a necessary killing, she thought state sponsored execution was a bad idea, allowing all involved to deny personal responsibility. She preferred full contact, and the burden of full knowledge. If Francis died, she would know she killed him, and why.

"Because he's a mutoid?" she asked.

"Because he's a killer," Alex replied.

Mutoids were troubled with ailments ranging from blindness and twisted intestines to mental illness and impaired cognitive functioning, but evidence was clearly against them being violent by nature. They were just easy to blame because they were easy to pick out of a crowd, as the color sage green was during the Killing Times. Our eyes betray us into prejudice, Alex thought.

Looking at Jaguar's profile—her silken mahogany and honey hair, the angles of her amber-toned face, her Native heritage written in her skin—he knew she felt that in a more personal way than he did. That might be why she accepted this committee assignment without a fuss. But he'd still been uneasy about the interview.

She raised an eyebrow at him. "I've dealt with murderers before. That's my job."

"And you know how Francis killed the other women? He snapped their necks. The last one in front of five witnesses who weren't quick enough to stop him."

She shrugged it off. "They weren't me. And I can't stand those laser shields. They interfere."

Interfere. She meant they made empathic contact difficult. "You didn't—" he held up the first two fingers of his right hand in the gesture of the empath. He'd warned her not to attempt that.

"Just a surface touch here and there," she said. "Nothing he'd notice."

Of course, Alex thought. She was the most skilled empath he knew, able to move into the thoughts and experiences of others as smoothly as water into dry stone. She'd done that to him more than once.

He let his hand drop to her arm, ran it lightly across the folds of green silk she wore. "Why'd you wear this?"

"He claims he doesn't kill empaths anymore," Jaguar said. "I wanted to see if he meant it."

"And?"

"No anger, no fear. In fact, not a molecule of reaction. He says that's all over."

"Huh," Alex said.

"Yeah," Jaguar agreed. She let out a long breath, and moved forward.

They walked down the corridor in silence, but he stopped her at the door to the meeting room where she'd confirm execution. "Jaguar," he said, "you can still beg off this one."

She eyed him coolly. "Paul requested me. What'll he say?"

"To you? Nothing. I'll tell him Dr. Addams finds herself incapable of rendering a decision in this matter. I'll catch some heat, but not enough to burn."

"And I'd let you, if it was true. But it isn't, so let's get this over with."

"Wait," he said, and then he spoke subvocally.

Look at me, Jaguar.

She lifted her sea-green eyes to his dark ones. He moved across the surface of her thoughts, feeling his way within the emotional complexity that was Jaguar. All was serene, without a hint of static, and only a lingering sorrow. In response to it he gave her a memory of his hand on her face, his mouth on hers. She moved to him, then quickly withdrew.

Careful, Alex. People will say we're in love.

People rarely speak the truth, Jaguar.

He felt her laughter before she broke contact, and then they were looking at each other in no way that would raise an eyebrow. They weren't ready to make their relationship public. Too many consequences. Too much unnecessary trouble.

"Ready, Dr. Addams?" he asked out loud.

"Let's go," she replied.

He opened the conference room door, and they entered.

The others—Teachers and Supervisors, legal reps and Board governors—were seated around the gleaming black table, waiting for them. Paul Dinardo, governor for Alex's zone, shifted his slouch and raised his heavy eyebrows at Alex as they took their seats. He always anticipated trouble when Jaguar was involved. Alex shrugged, and he leaned back.

"Since we're all here at last," Governor Richard Tremont said pointedly, "let's begin."

Everyone settled in. This was a *pro forma* meeting, a public voicing of an inevitable decision, and therefore the protocol was weightier than the substance. Richard would review trial transcripts and victim statements, forensic evidence and investigative procedure, breaking every ten minutes to ask for questions. It would be a lengthy and tedious meeting.

But in this prison system the order to execute was contained within the most cautious of routines. The Planetoids were established to replace a punitive system with rehabilitation and restitution, based on the premise that all crime grew from fear and therefore criminals could be rehabbed by facing their fears. An order of execution was a distinct departure from that concept. In 20 years they'd had only four cases of prisoners convicted of premeditated murder during their programs. That and a credible prognosis of incorrigible were required for execution, with unanimous agreement from four other Planetoid voices.

Richard droned on, expecting no questions and receiving none. They'd had weeks to go over the material he reviewed. When he concluded he turned to the Planetoid Two interviewer.

"Samuel Barry," Richard said, "How say you in the matter of Francis Durero?"

He stood. "I speak for execution," he replied, and sat again.

"Laura Less, how say you?"

She stood and repeated the formula, as did Rinaldo Scott.

The others shifted into motion, closing up notebooks and looking at watches to see how late they were running for dinner. One more Teacher, a closing speech, and they could leave.

Governor Tremont turned to Jaguar. "Dr. Addams, how say you?" he asked.

She rose and faced him. "I speak against execution," she replied, and sat back down.

Alex jerked his head up hard. No one else reacted.

Assuming her assent, expecting it, they didn't hear what she'd actually said. Richard nodded somberly and began the ritual speech absolving them of guilt in Francis Durero's death.

Jaguar stood again. "I *said*," she cut in, "I speak *against* execution."

A collective gasp rose in the room. Alex leaned his elbow on the table and pressed the palm of his hand to his forehead. Across from him, where Paul Dinardo sat, he heard quiet laughter.

Jaguar, dressed in the colors of the empath, her complicated history known to everyone there, scanned the faces around her. She held one long hand palm up, let her shoulder lift and fall.

"He didn't do it," she said.

CHAPTER 1

What happened next was administrative meltdown. Never in the history of the Planetoids had a Teacher spoken against execution at this point in the proceedings.

Richard Tremont had to consult the codebook to find the proper protocol, while the other Teachers and governors each insisted on saying something about it. As they yipped on, Jaguar made the most discrete exit Alex had ever seen from her.

He was glad of that. If she stayed, there was no telling what she might have said or done. And he should have known there'd be trouble. She was far too relaxed going in to be confirming an execution order. While he was trying to discern what, exactly, made her decide as she had, Richard discovered that in a case where consent wasn't unanimous, the next step was to thank the committee for its time and dismiss them. He did both, expeditiously. Paul cast a look at Alex and made his own quick exit.

The remaining governors gathered to fulminate around Alex, asking repeatedly what the hell was wrong with Addams this time. He had no answers, but that didn't stop them from pounding away at the question. When he finally extricated himself he made his way to the holding tank, hoping Francis was still there. He had some questions of his own to ask before he went home.

Francis was *in situ*, and the conversation Alex had with him took a good deal of time because he wanted to be thorough. It was past nine when he got back to his apartment, but his telecom was buzzing as soon as he walked in.

He hit the answer key and once again saw the perturbed face of Richard Tremont, this time on his viewscreen.

"Alex—did you talk to Addams yet? What the hell is she playing at?"

"In general," he said, "Dr. Addams only plays when she's hunting."

"Then what the hell is she hunting for? Never mind. It doesn't matter. We've called a meeting. Tomorrow afternoon. Four o'clock, in the boardroom."

"You want her there?"

"Absolutely not," Richard said. "But you'd better be."

With that, he signed off.

Of course, Alex thought. Administratium, the heavy element. When in doubt, it called a meeting. He put his telecom on silent mode and took a moment to contact Jaguar empathically.

She was open to him, but her mood was similar to that of a cat poised either to strike or run away. He got right to the point.

You could've warned me, he said into her.

I thought you knew, she replied.

Thought I knew, or thought it would be more fun to surprise me?

Thought you knew, came the definite reply. That, however, was followed immediately by an even more definite mischief. *But it was fun, wasn't it?*

A smile formed on his face, against his better judgement. She was right on all counts. He should have guessed. And it was fun, in its own way. A Jaguar kind of way.

He let her feel his laughter, and then he filled her in briefly on what she'd missed after she left. He didn't mention his conversation with Francis, but he did tell her about the upcoming meeting. Her response was brief.

I'm not going, she told him.

They don't want you there, he replied.

He sensed her surprise, felt her thoughts moving through the possible implications. Her relationship with him had changed, and she herself had changed in some fundamental ways, but she hadn't lost her suspicion of the bureaucracy. That, he thought, was a good thing.

How bad is it? she asked.

We'll figure it out. Lay low. We'll talk tomorrow.

She offered the thought of her hand pressed to his face, and her stubborn insistence that she was right. With that, she left him, and he made his own way to bed. He was asleep almost as soon as his head hit the pillow, not at all troubled by this. They'd survived much worse, and gone on to see their escapades become nothing more than local legend

* * * *

When Alex entered the boardroom the next afternoon the first face he saw was Regina Hawthorne's, the Planetoid One governor responsible for Francis Durero's zone.

"Alex," she said. "Sit by me."

Alex raised an index finger to indicate he needed a minute and moved around the table to where his own governor, Paul Dinardo, sat.

Paul gazed up at him, his long, basset hound face looking even glummer than usual. "You gonna say I told you so?"

"I don't have to, do I?"

Paul ran a hand over his balding pate, then looked at his palm. "Y'know, I had a lot more hair before she started working here."

"I don't think you can get her on that one," Alex noted.

"Yeah. Go see Regina. Maybe you two can work something out."

Alex patted Paul's shoulder, then moved around the table and took a seat to Regina's left.

"Alex," she said. "How are you?"

"I'll be better when this is settled. You?"

"Perfectly sanguine," she said. "This, too, shall pass."

Alex could see she meant it. Her face expressed only calm. It was, in general, a calm face, her short and curling silver hair framing wide blue eyes in a circle of fair skin with soft lines that seemed as if they'd been etched in at birth. Unlike many governors, Regina always looked as if time was her friend.

She gave the impression that she'd seen all the world and could cope, which might explain why she was the untitled Uber-governor for Planetoid One. She never panicked, and she had a way of sharing her quiet energy that made her popular. She was often in the hot seat, the one called on to give press conferences for controversial cases with home planet interest, the one asked to address legislative funding meetings. And she was responsible for the programming Planetoid One had now, with its emphasis on medical intervention, and its work programs.

Alex didn't necessarily agree with everything she did, but he admired her personal integrity and valued the peace she could bring to a volatile situation. He hoped it would work at this meeting, attended by many of the same people from the execution committee, with a few additions from Planetoid One. Most were talking quietly to each other or using their cellcoms to make last minute contact with people in their zone regarding other important matters. Alex kept his attention on Regina, whose voice was most important here.

She would moderate, the source of reason and calm. And though she operated on a consensus basis, if she was against any of the suggestions raised they just wouldn't fly.

She looked around, taking in the moods and agendas of those in attendance and processing them all through her fine mill. Alex, who'd seen her testing run, knew she wasn't positive for empathic skills, but her social intelligence was unrivaled. He had no doubt she'd long since classified him in her master schemata and decided how to manage him. Now she turned a smile his way. "How's Jaguar?" she asked.

"Doing well," he said. "You should go see her. It's been a while, hasn't it?"

"It has," she said. "We keep in touch, though."

Regina was the only person from Planetoid One Jaguar still spoke with. Though they were miles apart in their vision for Planetoid work, they had a deep respect for each other. As the first female governor, Regina had claimed power within a very male dominated system, and so she'd been a role model for Jaguar. She was also, like Jaguar, a study in contradictions.

Though she didn't approve of using the empathic arts with prisoners, she also didn't believe empaths should be fired. That, for a brief time, made her Alex's ally. When Jaguar faced dismissal for using psi capacities Regina supported his request to have her transferred to Planetoid Three instead. She was adamant about treating empaths without prejudice, but she was equally adamant about Jaguar leaving One. It wasn't, she said, a direction they wanted to take.

"I wanted Jaguar to be here," Regina said now. "The others made such a noise about it I decided it was more of a risk than a benefit."

"Really? I'd think they'd welcome the chance to pound away at her."

Regina tilted her head at him. "Don't you know?"

"I don't even know why I'm here," he said. "What happens to Francis has nothing to do with us, once the decision not to execute is rendered."

Governor Richard Tremont approached Regina, touched her shoulder lightly. "Shouldn't we begin?"

"Yes. Of course." She turned her attention to the other occupants of the room. "If we could all be seated?"

There was general movement, followed by a general stillness as everyone settled in.

"This meeting," she said, "will determine the best course of action to take in the matter of Francis Durero. First, we'll hear suggestions. With any luck, discussion will lead to consensus."

Alex bit back on a smile, thinking of what Jaguar said about consensus—that it was a way for one person to manipulate many others into their point of view. Regina, she admitted, was very good at it.

"We have no precedent," Talek Malor from Planetoid Three said. "The codebook doesn't say what to do if a Teacher speaks against execution. Just that the execution doesn't take place, and governors should use discretion in determining what happens with the prisoner."

"All the better," said Susan Eideler, a Planetoid One Supervisor, and someone Alex knew as the ultimate conservative on a Planetoid of conservative thinkers. "That means we can do exactly as we please."

Richard turned to her. "But what do we please?" he asked.

"That's easy," Susan said. "Send Dr. Addams to Planetoid One and let her figure it out."

"Interesting," Richard mused.

"Not a bad start," Talek agreed.

Murmurs of approval went around the table and Alex suddenly understood why they didn't want Jaguar here.

"Wait a minute," he said. "This is about Francis, not Dr. Addams."

All eyes turned to him, then back to Susan.

"He's got a point," Talek said.

"Yes," Richard agreed. "We can't let this look like it's about her."

"It won't," Susan said. "As the dissenting vote, she'll assist in follow up investigation, conduct interviews, review evidence and so on. If she spends some time with Durero she'll see what a killer he really is."

Alex turned a shocked face to Regina, who shook her head lightly. This, too, shall pass, her expression said. All well and good, he thought, but he wouldn't let Jaguar pass with it. He turned away from her and toward Paul Dinardo, who looked as shocked as he did.

"She's under no obligation to resolve this," Alex said. "She volunteered for the committee and rendered her considered opinion. If you want an investigation, hire an investigator."

"I see your point, Alex," Regina said softly, "but we really don't want outside involvement in a matter that's strictly internal."

"Absolutely not," Susan agreed. "You know how that goes. They're way too ready to think *we're* the mutoids and freaks."

"And empaths," Governor Karis from Planetoid Two added, looking at Alex.

"Well, I said freaks, didn't I?" Susan said, and small laughter rolled around the table.

Alex sent a glare to Paul, who grimaced. Then he turned to the others. "Let the investigation come from Planetoid Two," he said, looking at Karis. "You're a neutral party."

"It's not our problem," Karis said. "We spoke *for* execution."

"Then this isn't a meeting about procedure," Alex said. "It's an opportunity to pressure a dissenting voice into recanting. Is that it?" He surveyed the faces around him. "Is it?"

All eyes avoided his.

"Christ," he muttered, "Almighty."

"I would hope not," Regina said firmly. "It would be an egregious error to do so."

"I agree," Paul chimed in. "Absolutely eg—what Regina says. And Alex is right. It's nothing to do with her. Besides, you don't really want her running around loose on One, do you?"

There was some uncomfortable shifting. Paul hit the nail on the head with that, Alex thought. But to his surprise, Regina intervened, and not in a good way.

"Alex, it *does* makes sense to have the dissenting voice investigate," she said. "Dr. Addams saw something we missed. Perhaps she could clarify the situation."

Everyone except Paul brightened at her words. Alex felt a sinking in his stomach.

"Not in these conditions," he countered. "She'd be off her turf, working with people who are upset at her decision and her attitude about policy on your Planetoid."

Everyone here knew about Jaguar's disapproval of the work programs. More than once, with her usual preference for honesty over tact, she'd called them sanctified slave labor.

"Her attitude isn't the problem," Susan said. "It's her mouth. She keeps talking when she doesn't know anything. Maybe if she goes back she'll learn better."

"That's ridiculous," Alex said crisply. "She doesn't need to be educated."

"Dr. Addams isn't someone to be blinded by personal prejudices," Regina concurred. "But we all have our feelings in these matters, and hers run high. Alex, do you think that's an impediment to her investigation?" She turned toward him, held his gaze.

He was in a bind. If he said yes, that would reflect badly on her. And while Jaguar didn't give a rat's ass if the gathered governors of all three Planetoids sneered at her, he didn't want to give them any new excuses to do so.

"I think there's better solutions," he said. "For instance, you could have Durero transferred temporarily to Planetoid Three, let her work with him here."

Take that, he thought. Now you're in a bind. Unfortunately, one of them found a quick and dirty way out.

"That won't work," Richard said, "She can't investigate without viewing the crime scene."

"Then I'll bring her to One, and we'll take Durero back to Three," Alex offered.

"You sound like you're afraid to let her out of your sight," Susan purred. "Is that a professional concern, or a personal one?"

He brought his gaze to hers and held it. Okay, he thought. Here it is.

People had gossiped about the two of them being lovers for as long as she'd been on Planetoid Three. In the past they'd both simply ignored it, but the gossip had recently become true, and there were rules against such interactions between Teachers and Supervisors. If anyone made a fuss they were up the creek. In the absence of paddles, he'd have to use his hands.

"Both," he said. "Personally, I'm concerned at the tone I'm hearing about someone whose well-being I value. Professionally, I have prisoner programs to run, and she's the best Teacher I've got, in case you've forgotten her success rate."

"Nobody," Susan said, "could ever forget what she's done." She counted on her fingers. "Blown up a shuttle, destroyed a VR site, helped a prisoner escape. That's just her public record. Should I name the rumors, too?"

Soft laughter moved around the table. "You left out a few things," Alex said. "Stopped an Apocalypse on the home planet, kept the Planetoid from being turned into a wasteland, uncovered an illegal moon-mining operation, and—let's see, saved my life more than once, if that matters."

The laughter quieted.

"Nobody's questioning her talent," Regina said. "We're just trying to decide what to do with this case."

Murmurs of assent followed. Alex sat back and drummed his fingers on the table, waiting for what came next.

"I think she should go to One and investigate," Talek said, "since she's so talented."

Governor Karis spoke. "For the record, Talek, you're suggesting that Dr. Addams engage in follow-up investigation on Planetoid One in the matter of Francis Durero and the murder of Diane Lasher. Is the rest of the group in favor of this?"

All hands raised in the affirmative except for his and Paul Dinardo's. The others ignored Alex and turned to Paul. He cleared his throat and spoke. "I'm against it," he said. Alex cast him a glance equally composed of gratitude and surprise.

"Why?" Susan asked, just as surprised.

"Let's be honest," he said. "We all know how she is. She'll be pissed as hell if you send her, and either she won't get a damn thing done or you won't like what she comes up with. Believe me," he added sincerely, "I've tried that kind of thing with her. It don't work."

"She has to do her job just like everyone else, doesn't she?" Richard said sharply.

"Refusing would be grounds for dismissal, I'd think," Karis added, sounding hopeful.

"For anyone else, yes," Richard said, "but Dr. Addams often gets preferential treatment." He looked hard at Alex.

"What's that mean, Dick?" Alex asked, emphasizing the last word.

"My name is Richard," he replied curtly.

"I'm being friendly. What's it mean, Dick?"

"Just what I said."

"Say it again," Alex suggested. "This time in English."

Richard puffed up his thin chest and pushed his narrow face toward Alex. "Everyone knows Dr. Addams crosses all lines of protocol, blatantly ignoring code, using methods only her Supervisor countenances, and she gets away with it because…" He paused. "Do you really want me to go on, Alex?"

"Yes," he said distinctly. "I do. For the record."

"I don't," Paul jumped in. "And neither does anyone else."

Alex made a fist and hit it against the table. Everyone jumped except Regina.

"Let him talk, Paul," he said. "I won't be held hostage by innuendo and supposition."

How, Alex wondered, would he respond when Richard said something about empaths always covering for each other? Of course they do because no one else will? Or what would he say when Richard asked point blank if he and Jaguar were lovers? Yes we are, and I'm damn proud she wants to be. And then what?

In this moment of white-hot rage, he didn't care. He'd quit. Go to the home planet with Jaguar and have something like a real life. They'd always be welcome with her people in New Mexico. He stared at Richard, daring him to say what was on his mind.

Richard stayed quiet. Alex had a low-key demeanor which made people forget he was over six feet with a build to match, but those in the room who'd seen his rare displays of anger didn't want to be on the receiving end. And regardless of how they viewed the empathic arts, everyone there knew he'd gone head to head with a Telekine and won. They didn't want to mess with someone who could do that. Especially now, when they saw the anger flashing in his dark eyes.

Regina was the first to break the silence.

"This meeting," she said firmly, "is about Francis Durero, not Supervisor Dzarny or Dr. Addams, both of whom have gone above and beyond their duty, risking their own lives more than once in service to this system. Everyone here knows that. And any question of professional misconduct is a serious matter to be dealt with through official channels, not casual slander. That," she added, her voice full of reprimand, "is very bad form."

The others looked down at their folders, away from Alex. Regina turned a reassuring face his way, but it didn't matter. The main point was already lost.

"At any rate," Susan said, speaking his thoughts, "she's going to One. Right?"

"That seems to be the consensus," Regina said hesitantly.

"What about backup?" Alex asked. "I could release a worker. Two workers. She should have someone there to help out."

"Kind of you to offer," Regina said, "but it's not necessary. We'll provide what she needs."

The others nodded. Alex bit at the inside of his mouth to keep from screaming at them. It would obviously do no good.

"There's still one thing you haven't considered," he said.

"What?" Talek asked.

"That she's right," Alex said.

There was no response. They didn't seem to understand his words. He continued. "Look at her record. She's difficult, she blows things up, but she has a 100 percent average of being right. In fact, I already assume Francis didn't kill Diane Lasher. And I'll back her on that."

A long pause followed as they absorbed his words. Alex turned to Regina. "Even if you don't believe it, we have to assure her safety in an unresolved murder investigation. You've already had one Teacher killed."

Susan whispered something to Talek and he laughed uncomfortably.

Alex whipped around to them. "Please share," he said. "I could use a laugh."

"Oh, Alex," Susan said. "Stop being so portentous. I just said maybe we could kill two birds with one stone, so to speak. Gotta love a happy ending."

"Susan," Karis said, over the general response of shock.

"I was *joking*," Susan said. "I mean, it's a joke, what Alex says. If Durero didn't do it, that means—well, it's ridiculous. Jaguar—*Dr.* Addams—is just being contrary. Give her some time with Durero and she'll see that."

"Don't give her too much time," Alex suggested mildly. Everyone turned to him, and he smiled. "It took her about ten days to shred the VR site. How long do you think it'll take her to deconstruct a bubble dome?"

"I hope that isn't a threat," Susan said.

"Not at all. But if there's anything at all to find, Jaguar will find it."

To his surprise, her face blanched. She turned decidedly away from Alex and to Regina. "I won't waste any more breath on this. Are we done?"

"We are," Regina said. "This meeting is dismissed, and I thank you for your time."

Alex sat in a state of smoldering anger as the others packed up to leave. Regina leaned over and patted the back of his hand. "You'll tell her, won't you? It'll be better coming from you."

"Sure," he said. "Throw me to the big cats."

Regina laughed, looked around. The only person still lingering was Paul Dinardo. She cast him a smile. "Could we have the room for a minute, Paul?" she asked.

He shrugged, got up and left. Regina turned back to Alex. "Alex, just so you know, I hoped this would happen. I want Jaguar on One."

He raised an eyebrow. "Why, Regina?"

She looked around, as if suspicious of listeners. "There's been a big push for this execution, but people don't realize how bad it makes us look. The media's always right on top of this kind of thing. I'm hoping she'll find some way to get us out of it. If anyone can . . . "

She left the sentence unfinished, but Alex knew how it ended. If anyone can, it's Jaguar. Any impossible task, any difficult, dangerous or unpleasant job went to Jaguar, who would see it done. That was, unfortunately, pretty damn accurate. She'd earned a reputation for taking on the worst of the worst with success. Sometimes he felt pride in her ability to do so. Other times it bugged the hell out of him.

"That's not exactly fair to her, is it?" he asked. "Make her go back to a place that can only hurt like hell, on a highly vexed job, with as much resistance as possible?"

"But that's where she's in her element, Alex. We both know that. And don't worry about what Susan said. I'm sure she'll be perfectly safe with us."

"Will you provide the bodyguard?"

"Would she trust any bodyguard on One?"

He shook his head. Of course she wouldn't. Rightly so.

"I'll keep an eye on her," Regina said, "And if she establishes a presence for a while, they'll all be satisfied. Frankly, I think they just need some time to get over themselves and do the right thing. Tell her that, will you? It's just a little tedium, then she'll be back to you."

"Back to work, you mean," Alex amended.

"Yes. Of course," she agreed, but her smile said something else. She also assumed they were lovers, though she seemed pleased about it.

That was the best he could hope for, he supposed. He continued to sit, collecting his thoughts while she made her exit. He rested his face in his hands, considering his own next moves, until he felt another presence at his back. He knew who it was.

"You gonna stay here all night?" Paul asked.

Alex lowered his hands. "Consider the alternative," he said. "I have to tell her."

"Yeah," Paul said. He took a seat next to Alex. "Look, I didn't want this to happen. You know that, right?"

"I saw your face. I'd like to know why, though. You never bothered about her before."

Paul glanced around as if someone might be listening. "What Richard said about you and her—there's a lot of that talk going around."

"Always has been."

"From what I can tell, now it's true. That makes a difference."

"It sure does," Alex agreed. "At least, we like it better this way."

Paul grimaced. "Jesus, Alex. What the hell are you thinking? There's rules."

"I'm familiar with the protocols. There's also loopholes."

"They get used or not, depending. And with her…." He blew air out through his lips, sounding like a horse. "You two better keep a low profile."

"Not our strong point," he mentioned.

"Don't I know it. Listen, personally, I don't care what you do after hours. You're one of the best supervisors we got and I'll back you."

"What about Jaguar?"

Paul waved a hand in the air. "She's like hornet spray. Nasty stuff, but you're glad it's there when you need it. And between you and me, she's got a few senators in her pocket after that whole moon mining thing, so she's probably safe until the next election. 'Course, if she changed her vote, she'd be off the hook on this one."

Alex made a derisive noise.

"That's what I thought," Paul agreed. "But maybe it's a good thing. There's something I want to know about One, and she'd be doing me a big favor if she found out while she was there. She does kinda owe me about now. Come to think of it, so do you."

Just a few months ago he and Jaguar had both resigned so they could go after a Greenkeeper on the home planet. Paul had deliberately failed to hand in their letters, so they'd been able to return to their jobs with nothing on their records. Of course he'd cash in on that sooner or later, but why now? Why with this?

"What's up, Paul?" Alex asked.

"Something you're not gonna like," Paul said. "And for once, I'll agree with you. Let's go back to your office and I'll tell you."

Consensus was clearly against Jaguar today, from all quarters. Alex pressed his hands against the table and pushed himself to stand. "Okay," he said. "We'll finish the day like it started. With bad news."

CHAPTER 2

Planetoid One

A man in a blue suit sat at a desk inside an office on Planetoid One, staring down at a message on his personal notepad. As he read it, he smiled.

He looked remarkably like any other office worker on the Planetoid in that he was unremarkable. He was an adult white male, tall and bulky, his features not memorable for attractiveness or lack of attractiveness. His suit hid his rather demure tattoos, a series of special codes written small that ran across his shoulders and down one side of his back. Each code named a client whose identity was decipherable through a document left with his lawyer, to be used in the event of his violent death. With each successfully completed job, he had a new tattoo inscribed. All his clients knew that. He was not a man who willingly relinquished control.

But here and now he was just another Planetoid One worker, and those who met him had a hard time describing him once he was out of view. That was due partly to his eminently forgettable looks, and in part to a trick he'd picked up while working with military Psi Ops. It was easy, he'd found, to blur the memory of those who met him. Clowning, it was called. Creating situations that distracted the eye, distracted the mind from the truth. And he was a master Clown.

He'd also earned a reputation as a solid Collector, bringing in information, important objects or, when requested, people. But his primary work was as a Cleaner, tidying up messy situations, getting rid of messy people. He earned most of his money this way, contracting with both government and private sector clients, all of whom referred to him simply as The Cleaner.

His current job required all three skills, and he'd been on retainer for it for a few months, working a cover job while here. So far much of his work involved Clowning, making sure certain procedures within the system remained invisible, but he'd also completed one Cleaning job. He'd been paid well, the money waiting in his very private home planet account, and his cover job was interesting without being onerous. He'd also been able to gather data he knew he could sell elsewhere. All in all, it was a pretty good gig.

Today, when he touched his personal notepad screen and opened the file for this job, it had a new message, which is what made him smile.

A new subject was coming his way and he was to begin a D and D order on her. She needed to be both discredited and dead.

He liked D and D's much better than straightforward cleaning. They required a subtler approach, a longer set up time. They were almost like writing a script, needing artistry and finesse rather than just brute force, and he prided himself on his artistry.

When he saw the subject's name, he felt a special thrill. He knew something about her. Quite a bit, in fact, since he kept up with the who's who of empaths, and she was a big one. He remembered some rumors about her giving the pentagon a hard time, and thought of one of his other clients, one who might be interested in doing some collateral damage, or at least gaining some collateral information on her. That client would also be interested in the data he was collecting in his spare time. Whenever possible he liked to double up on his jobs.

He considered possibilities. He was scheduled to go to the home planet tomorrow as part of his cover job. While there he could check with that client, see if he wanted in on this.

In the meantime, he already had some ideas on how to manage the D and D, and he could start some set up right away. He reached into his desk drawer and removed a small data retrieval unit designed to pick up specific energies of interest to this job. He pocketed it, got up and left his office. He'd walk the halls and check the environment, see what possibilities arose from the combination of subject and scene.

He had a pleasant job ahead of him, and he might as well get to it.

CHAPTER 3

It was evening by the time Alex finished with Paul, made what progress he could toward setting up what would happen next, and got himself home. On and off he'd tried to contact Jaguar in as many ways as possible—telecom, belt sensor, empathically—to no avail. She was following his advice and laying very low.

He decided to go home for dinner before he went to her apartment, but when he opened his apartment door he felt her presence. He adjusted to it, tried to catch a scent of her mood, but all he could smell was incense burning.

There.

She was sitting in his rocking chair, staring out the bank of windows that overlooked the shores of the replica of Lake Ontario, one of the nicest parts of this replica city of Toronto, built specifically for Planetoid Three. He closed the door softly behind him and walked across the room, stopping just behind her.

"Where've you been?" he asked.

She ran a hand through the curls of smoke rising from the incense on the table next to her, playing it like a cat played thread. "Here," she said. "Waiting for you. They want a report, I suppose."

"Jaguar—"

"It's a pretty simple one. He didn't do it."

"Listen to me—"

"You want it in triplicate? He didn't do it, he didn't do it, he didn't—"

"—I *know* that."

She turned and regarded him cautiously. "Say more," she suggested.

He ran a hand through his hair and let it rest at the back of his neck. Though they were lovers, in their work relationship she remained difficult and disturbing. If their work was a dance, he thought, it would definitely be a tango. Argentinian tango. Fortunately, he was as good a dancer as she was.

"It's a long story," he said, "but it starts with Regina."

He filled her in on his conversation with that woman, and Jaguar listened, nodded.

"That sounds like her, though it's a helluva thing to throw in my lap," she said.

"I said the same thing. But she's just where it starts. After her, there's Paul Dinardo."

"Paul? What's he got to do with it?"

"He stopped me after the meeting. Wanted to have a talk."

She waved a hand at him. "Take it at your own pace, Alex. I'm in no rush."

"You're not, believe me. And I will, since it takes some telling. First, just so you know, Paul stood up for you in the meeting."

She narrowed her eyes. "What's he want?" she asked.

"He has concerns about Planetoid One, and he was talking to Diane Lasher about them. That's why he put you on the committee. He figured if there was trouble, you'd sniff it out."

Jaguar rose from the chair and went to the window. For a moment she stood looking out, perfectly still. Then she whirled on Alex.

"Great Hecate's cloak," she said. "Dinardo decides there's trouble and *I've* got to take the heat, without a clue what's happening? How'd that work for him last time he tried it?"

"It's not like that, Jaguar," Alex said, though he remembered how angry he was when Paul had Jaguar working blind in a Pentagon Blackout operation that could have been the end of her.

"Then what is it like? Bubonic Plague? Hemmorhoids? Why don't they just kill me and get it the hell over with?"

"They won't. They'll just dangle swords over your head to get you to cooperate."

"In what? State sanctioned murder of a disabled and defenseless mutoid, who happens to be innocent?"

"No. Going to Planetoid One."

Her expression shifted from anger to tension. "Xipe totec flay them," she whispered.

"I wish," Alex agreed.

"They want to transfer me back? Permanently?"

"No. Just go and investigate in the matter of Francis Durero. That's how they put it."

Some of the tension left her, but the anger remained. "I don't do investigation," she said. "They want me there so they can pressure me to rescind."

"If that's all it is we're lucky. There's a lot of anger on One about your objections to the work programs."

She made a sound like growling. "Warehousing prisoners for slave labor. Their economy's dependent on the population they're supposed to serve. Francis—that bear he clutches so assiduously—they make them for export sale, right? Pay their mutoids ten cents an hour, take the profits and call themselves saviors. And how much of their population is mutoid now?"

"A little more than half."

"Most of them there for life. They're taking in lesser crimes, too. Assaults, petty theft, public pissing. Great scam. I still can't believe Regina's supporting it. I've been talking about it for years and nobody listened."

Alex understood her anger. He'd studied management psychology, and knew the tendency of organizations to promote those who served the profitability of the organization rather than its mission statement. Over time, without careful watchdogging, any organization could fall into the trap of forgetting what its original purpose was. Right now, Planetoid One was tilting distinctly in that direction, and needed a tap on the shoulder to turn it around. Jaguar, he knew, was an expert tapper.

"They all listened," he said. "They just didn't like it. But Paul listened for a more personal reason. His little sister was exposed to chembombs in the Killing Times. About two years ago she had a baby. Born with a blue patch."

Jaguar's face expressed the same interest a cat might on seeing a wounded mouse. "How interesting," she murmured.

"Retract the claws," Alex commented. "You won't be using them. Paul started watching the mutoid programs on One. Diane got word of his interest and put a call into him. She said something was wrong, but she wouldn't talk on the lines. She wanted a meeting."

Jaguar's forehead creased in thought. "About what?" she asked.

"He never found out. She was murdered first. She did say if anything happened to her, he should audit their exports."

"Shit. It wasn't Francis. I was right."

"Like I told them, you almost always are."

"Almost?"

He shrugged. "I made it always, for their benefit. Paul suspected a smuggling operation. They've got some high risk pharmaceutical manu-facturing, stuff that gets sold illegally on the home planet. Citrozine's worth the most." That particular euphoric was very popular right now, recreational users willing to pay a great deal for it. He rubbed an invis-ible powder between finger and thumb. "Diamond Dust," he said.

"Pretty," Jaguar said, "and expensive. Who's running it?"

Alex shook his head. "Paul couldn't find any evidence. He did the audit and they were clean. Inventory stable, and their shipments pass inspection by every means."

"Then what?"

"I don't know. Paul is hoping you'll find out."

"He's asking me to do that?"

"Yes. But asking, not telling. He said he'd consider it a favor."

She ran a finger down the tip of her nose to her lips and tapped them thoughtfully. "What do you say about it?"

"I say it's a high risk venture. One woman's already dead, and if there's something illegal going on you'll be next on the hit list. Even without that, Susan Eideler's out for at least a little of your blood. Any idea why?"

Jaguar shook her head. "I didn't have much to do with her when I was there. She was a team member, and I never requested her."

"She's moved up the ladder. She's a Supervisor now."

"She looked like she wanted to be a suit. What's Regina say?"

"She says go and keep a low profile, let everyone get over their snit, and she'll watch your back. But they won't let me send back-up and no-body's naming the limits of your time there, so I'm not very impressed."

"You're saying I shouldn't go?" she asked.

"I'm saying I'd rather you didn't," he replied carefully.

"What's my alternative? Retract my vote?"

He shrugged. "That would work."

She turned her lucid eyes to his, reading for the feeling behind his words. She spoke to him subvocally.

Is that the kind of woman you want in your bed?

Better than a dead woman.

Not much.

He held a hand out to her. What could he say? They'd been through all this before. He had a heart filled with passion for her, and for the job at hand. She felt the same about him, and the job. It was a tension they'd learned to negotiate.

Call it, Jaguar. I'll back you either way.

She broke contact and looked away. "Paul knows about us, doesn't he?" she asked quietly.

"Yes."

"Anyone else say anything about it?"

He nodded. "They don't want to push it. They just want to use it to push us."

"That sounds right. You're sure Dinardo's not trying to get rid of me?"

"Not this time," he said. "Apparently you have some senators in your pocket."

"I don't have pockets," she noted. She mused some more. "If I do this, he'll owe me in a big way, won't he?"

"He already does," Alex pointed out.

"But this time he'd have to acknowledge it."

"Jaguar, what're you thinking?"

"That it might be good to get a pocket and put him in it."

Alex shook his head. "We can manage without that."

"Maybe *you* can," she said, "They won't transfer you. They'll transfer me, and who'll they put me with? Galentas, the petty fascist pig dog who substitutes a gun for the deficit of a tiny prick? My ass is on the line either way. And yours isn't." She turned her back to him and gazed out the window.

She'd named a truth he couldn't deny. Her profile, her gender, the color of her skin, the bent of her mind, all testified to it. She was at risk. He was not. He walked to where she stood.

"We could call it quits," he offered. "Temporarily at least."

"And I could retract my vote on Durero. Which do you think is more likely?"

He put a hand on her shoulder, but when he touched her, a shiver ran through him. Crows walking on his grave, he thought. That's what Sophia, the old lady who taught him his arts, had called those unexplained shivers. And since he was an Adept, skilled in precognition, she also taught him to pay attention when they came.

"Something happening, Spider Magus?" Jaguar asked quietly. Though the art of the Adept wasn't hers, she always sensed its particular tingle in him.

He was silent as he attended the feeling. No vision accompanied it. Just a sudden sensation of being dropped into emptiness. A loss of earth. An unboundedness, encompassing more than him and Jaguar. It held a presence larger than time, a part of everything that would happen on Planetoid One. He breathed in. Breathed out. Let go of Jaguar's shoulder.

"Something," he said. "I don't like this, Jaguar. I think you'd feel the same if it was me."

She turned to face him. "I'm sure I would," she agreed. "And I'm sure that wouldn't stop you."

She had him there. "You're going, aren't you?" he asked.

"I am."

"Why? All expediency aside, tell me why, Jaguar."

She took a step away, turned toward the window. "Diane was my friend. I want to know what happened to her."

No surprise there. Though others saw her as a maverick, inconsistent and unpredictable, she had the most persistent loyalty of anyone Alex had ever met.

"She wasn't your friend when she knew the truth about you," he pointed out.

"When I find out the truth about her maybe I won't be hers anymore. Then we'll be even. In the meantime, she's dead and Durero didn't kill her, and I want to know who did."

There it was, he thought. "Then we've got a job ahead of us," he said.

She shifted, turned and faced him again. "I notice you haven't yet asked *why* I think he didn't kill her. And that you agreed with me."

"You're very observant," he said coolly. "What do you make of that?"

"I'm thinking you saw the forensic report, which says Diane was hit from behind before she was strangled. Francis always approached face first, going for the throat without any blows."

"That did seem important to me. Anything else?"

"You're pretty thorough, so I'd guess you had a talk with Francis yourself."

"An accurate guess. And?"

"And you saw the same thing I did. He's not a paranoid schizophrenic, like they say. He's carrying an ephemeral. One that only kills empaths, which Diane was definitely not."

Alex sighed. That confirmed what he'd found. An ephemeral. The term empaths used when someone was possessed by a ghost, either as shadow memory or an actual spirit. Not a term recognized by the penitentiary system, but one he and Jaguar both considered when they worked with prisoners. And something he'd seen in Francis, just as she had.

Long before Francis was arrested, his brother Damon was killed by a woman who was, by all reports, an empath. She'd beaten the charge, claiming self-defense, which may well have been true. Damon had two previous assault charges, and was known to have a temper. Now his restless spirit was still with Francis in some essential way, perhaps seeking revenge, or perhaps protecting the little brother he'd left behind. But Alex hadn't determined if he was there as memory or spirit.

"Any idea if it's shadow, or a true ephemeral?" he asked.

She shook her head. "I didn't go deep enough to determine that, on advice of my Supervisor. But maybe my Supervisor went against his own advice and dug a little deeper"

"He didn't," Alex said. "Not the right place, and there wasn't time. But he agrees with you. Diane wasn't an empath, Francis isn't paranoid schizophrenic, and he didn't kill her."

He saw the small muscles around her neck and shoulders relax. Brief time had passed since they'd become lovers, since he'd stood with her on the mesa and shown his willingness to give his life for her. They were both adjusting to a new emotional order, and she was still relieved when he believed her.

"There's more, Alex," she noted. "I think Francis's meds suppress the ephemeral, no matter what kind it is. He showed no antagonism toward me when I was obviously there as an empath. And I think he could be cleared pretty easily, if he was in the right program."

He heard frustration in her tone and wondered once more at her contradictory nature. She wouldn't hesitate to kill Francis if she had to, but she would still rather see him healed than dead, would rather see his brother's spirit at rest than punished. She held firmly to a core belief that healing was a better solution than revenge, and she hated to see a job botched.

On both counts, he agreed with her.

"I know, Jaguar," he said. "And maybe we'll get him here when this is over. For now, that's absolutely *not* your job. No trying to find the ephemeral, no attempts at empathic contact with Francis."

"I'll get nowhere without it," she said.

"You'll get dead if you try it on your own," he replied crisply. "In fact, I want you to do as little as possible until I send back-up."

"You said they won't give me any."

"They won't, but I will."

"Who could you get?"

"Rachel's already looking into that," he said. Rachel Shofet, former prisoner and now good friend to Jaguar, was the best researcher and hacker on all three Planetoids. "She'll get the right person. You know she will. I'll follow as soon as I can."

"You? Alex, everyone knows you there. You can't possibly—"

"They can't possibly stop me. Don't you get that by now?"

She showed him a scowl. "I've dealt with worse than Francis. And I don't want special treatment just because we're lovers."

That. Of course. It was bound to come up sooner or later, and he knew how to meet it. "Special? You call it special, being thrown into that lion's den? Listen, Dr. Addams, if Paul asked for any other teacher I'd forbid it out of hand. I'm only allowing it because I know you can manage it."

Her scowl subsided into furrows on her forehead, but she wasn't quite ready to relent. "I'm just saying I know the people and the place. I don't think I need a team for this one."

"I say you do. You'll be investigating potentially explosive problems, under constant surveillance from people who may want you dead. Or at least a little less troublesome than usual. And we can't be in touch since the bubble domes block outside empathic contact, in case you forgot. So you'll keep it low to the ground until you have back-up, and absolutely no empathic contact with Francis until I get there. That's a direct order from your Supervisor, who happens to be a very skilled Adept."

She didn't trust flattery, but when he played the Adept card she knew he meant it. "Okay," she said, only a little grudgingly. "When do I leave?"

"First morning shuttle," he said.

He saw her tense, then deliberately relax. She turned to him, and in her expression he read her sure knowledge of risk as well as her confidence in her own capacity to get the job done. She studied him, and put a hand to his face.

"You're really nervous about this," she said, quiet now, his lover rather than his co-worker. "What exactly did you see?"

He smoothed her hand under his. "Nothing specific. Just—I have to be there. That's all I know. And the lack of contact bothers me. I don't like being separated that way."

"We won't be," she said. "Not really. My people have a chant for lovers like us." She spoke inside him, her words moving soft as grass in the wind.

If we were robbed of time and hope and flesh, still I would find you with thoughts that move too swift for any harm to chase. In all the universe of light, I will turn to yours and follow. In all the universe of light, you will be drawn to mine, familiar and strange as your own.

He leaned over and kissed her hair, breathed a thought into it.

Wait for me. Wait for me. Wait for me.

He put his mouth on hers and kissed her, breathing the thought into her as he pulled her down onto the thick carpet at their feet. He impressed it into her body as they moved together in their pleasure, in their love for each other, which was stronger than time or distance, and which they'd found would not suffer separation for long until one of them called the other home.

In all the universe of light, she would turn to his. In all the universe of light, he would find hers.

Wait for me, he breathed. *I will be there.*

* * * *

After she dressed to go back to her apartment and pack, he walked her to the door and watched her lean and muscular frame recede down the hall from him. Her long dark hair, the streaks where it seemed to be dipped in honey, the particular pride of her carriage, so familiar and still so surprisingly miraculous, pulled at him, lunar and inescapable.

"Jaguar," he called.

She stopped, her back to him, head lowered. Then she turned to face him. He could see she'd already begun focusing her concentration on the task ahead.

She tilted her head at him inquisitively. "Did you want me?"

Did he want her? Yes. Always.

"Be careful," he said. "Wait for me to get there. I'll find a way."

He could feel the questions she didn't ask as she turned away and disappeared from his view.

CHAPTER 4

Home Planet, Virginia, USA

The Cleaner was on permanent retainer with the military and had worked for General Matthew Durk in the past, so he was admitted into his office without delay, his retinal scan giving him priority status. When he entered the office he walked across the very good Pakistani rug, the only personal item in the room besides a photo of the General's yellow Labrador Retriever, to the desk where the General sat. He nodded politely, took a seat in the chair on the other side, and got right to business.

"I'm on Planetoid One for a while. You want anything done there?"

Durk didn't ask what his job was. He knew better. "Is there anything worth getting?"

"I can grab some post-mortem data from their infirmary," the Cleaner said. "They've got a lot of activity."

"Point of Death?" Durk asked. His unit was researching heavily in that area right now. They'd found that post-mortem energies carried a punch in deltas unlike the living human energy field, and they wanted to study it further, though they didn't yet know what they'd do with the information. But much of Psi Ops was speculative, and they didn't mind dropping a dime to add to their store of information.

"That, and long-term. They've got a way of keeping the energy stable and present."

This earned the Cleaner a small frown. "How?"

"A new vent system. It works off a laser field, and seems to do the trick."

Durk nodded. That made sense. The energy also blocked empathic contact, a similar field and range. But he had another question about it. "Why would they want to?"

"I'm looking into ways they might use it. See if they can access it to up the ante on their own energy system. They're always interested in saving a buck on One."

Durk's frown deepened into a look of derision. "You think you're dealing with lab rats?" he asked. They'd tried holding onto post-mortems in Special Ops, and got nothing but trouble. For reasons they couldn't explain, they created turbulence in all their equipment.

"Not that different," the Cleaner said. "I shifted my equipment to accommodate the overload, take care of the glitches. I'm guessing I can figure out the rest. You want me to bring you some data on it?"

Durk considered, tapping his wooden hand against his desk. He doubted it would work, but the Cleaner was good at that kind of thing. It was, he said, a hobby he enjoyed. Psi ops might as well look at his numbers. "Do so," he said. "The usual rate of pay. Anything else?"

"A Dr. Addams is paying a visit," he said. "For a Planetoid investigation. I hear she gave you some trouble once. If you want, I can do a cleaning on her." He had no objection to getting paid twice for doing the same job.

"No," he said, definite and without room for negotiation.

The Cleaner let it go. He never pushed these things. The client was either interested or not. "Data retrieval on her?" He could work that in somewhere between Discredited and Dead.

Durk waved his wooden hand in dismissal. She used psi capacities his unit couldn't even name yet, and from a past incident he knew her knife could slit a throat in under a second.

"You couldn't shine her shoes without getting a heel in your eye," he said. "Leave her alone. Get the post-mortem data. That's all."

The Cleaner rose, shook down his pant legs. "Sure," he said. He turned and walked away. He didn't waste time, and neither did the General.

But as he put his hand on the doorknob, Durk spoke. "Wait," he said. The Cleaner did so.

"Are you already cleaning her for someone else?" Durk asked bluntly.

The Cleaner kept his hand on the doorknob, didn't turn around. "Do I kiss and tell?"

Durk grunted, and his wooden hand went tap tap tap on the desk. "If that's your job, you're in deep shit. Better men than you have tried and failed."

The Cleaner shrugged. He'd heard that about her. It didn't bother him. "Maybe better," he said, "but not smarter. And I have the best toys."

He opened the door and left the office.

One of Durk's guards, standing outside the door, watched him leave, and then was surprised to hear a sound not often associated with the General.

From within the office, he was sure he heard that man laugh.

* * * *

Planetoid One

The shuttleport on One was noisy with the motion of machinery, goods, and people. Jaguar stood inside it, listening to the announcements of arrivals and departures, to the low and constant hum of the ventilation system, the cacophony of voices that always sounded louder here.

She stared up at the translucent ceilings, then around at the people walking by or being driven in the shuttleport carts. They all looked busy, many working their cellcoms or pressing one hand against an ear and speaking rapidly to whoever was on the other end of their earpieces. Most of them wore suits and carried briefcases, a very different fashion sense than that on Planetoid Three. She sighed and picked up her bags, scanning for the sign pointing to Tunnel 10, which led to the bubble dome housing she'd be staying in. When she found it, she walked.

She'd last been here six years ago—or was it seven? Seven years. Not, she decided, long enough.

She saw a flash image of herself, a memory from when she'd first arrived, new at the job but with a head full of her own ideas about how to manage prisoners. She'd been prepped for her work by both the intense Planetoid training and by the work she'd done with Jake and One Bird, her guardians and mentors after her grandparents were killed during the Serials. They'd worked her harder than the Planetoid ever could, putting her through a series of sweat lodges, testing her empathic boundaries by every means possible. They knew the risks she'd face, and knew her well enough to realize she'd go beyond even the ones they could imagine.

She'd done so more than once, and she supposed she would again. That much hadn't changed, though other things had.

Now she carried more confidence and a great deal less pain than the young woman who'd walked these corridors seven years ago. At that time the first person to greet her was Diane Lasher, who came up to her, extended a hand and said, "Dr. Addams? Welcome. Glad to have you with us."

She clasped Jaguar's hand firmly, smiled as if she meant what she said. Jaguar, doing a quick read on her, realized she did. She had very little dishonesty in her, and even less complexity. She was as she presented herself—warm, enthusiastic, high energy.

Her native warmth went far to thaw Jaguar's naturally cool exterior, and her capacity for laughter reminded Jaguar that happiness still existed in a pure form for some people. Diane had been with her historian parents in the protected boundaries of a small village in France during the Killing Times, helping them research the Little Ice Age of the 1600s while Jaguar was struggling to survive on the streets of Manhattan. She was the first person Jaguar knew who was unscathed by that event, unscathed by the world in any real way. All she'd ever known was love and support, and that was what she extended to others.

Diane, whose light she drank like a promise, offered the possibility of other truths than the ones she'd lived. Through her friendship she'd been taken under Regina Hawthorne's broad wings, and her soothing influence worked its magic as well. They had changed her. They had, she thought, been more than friends.

Jaguar's mother died in childbirth, and she'd been raised by grandparents. When they were murdered, she'd gone to the New Mexico village of Thirteen Streams, where Jake and One Bird, contemporaries of her grandparents, had taken over her guardianship. But Regina was more of an age to serve as a mother figure, which was different. And Diane had become the sister she'd never had. They were, she thought, the closest she'd ever get to a nuclear family. Unfortunately, they reached critical mass, for all the wrong reasons.

Diane's betrayal came as a physical shock, the hand that always supported her knocking her flat instead. Even worse, she knew Diane was acting in accord with her most deeply held principles, part and parcel of who she was. Jaguar couldn't hate her for being exactly who she was after she'd learned to love her for that same reason. To this day what she held in memory of Diane was a sense of her light, which had given her hope. Because of that she'd returned to Plaentoid One. But a different Dr. Addams was here today.

Planetoid One was also different in some ways. When she was last here they didn't have half as many mutoids, and the work programs were still just a concept Regina was trying to realize. Now most of their population was classified either mutoid or criminally insane, and the work programs were central to their operations.

However, their attitude toward empaths remained the same. The regulations that once prohibited hiring Teachers with empathic capacities were gone, but Planetoid One still strictly enforced the rules against use of psi capacities with prisoners. On Three and Two the unwritten rule said a skilled empath could do their job as they saw fit, if they didn't make a noise about it. That, Jaguar knew, was largely because of Alex, the first Supervisor to quietly allow his Teachers to use the arts, always backing them in their choices and discreetly offering his own empathic skills in ways that proved too useful for the governing entities to give up.

That wasn't the case on One, where they stuck to psychotherapeutic and medical programs, their people trained in using neural probes and medications more than anything else.

"Technotoys and drugs," Jaguar mumbled to herself. "New names. Same old shit."

Of course some prisoners needed medical intervention. They had more illness than fear. But the Planetoids weren't the place to treat them, and the home planet didn't need more excuses for not dealing with them. Planetoid One was becoming a warehouse for the unwanted, exactly what the system was supposed to prevent. Soon they'd be stocking up on empaths so the home planet wouldn't have to deal with that issue, either. Maybe, she thought, they were starting with her.

She followed the pink glow of surveillance lights to the entrance of her bubble dome, and at the gate she put her face to the retinal scan and waited. The station guard read it and told her someone was coming to meet her. She should stay put. As if, she thought, there was anywhere she could go.

She gazed up at the translucent dome above her, feeling the waves of micro and radiant energy it took to maintain the structure, the laser fencing surrounding all facilities. It made her neurons crackle, made it impossible to establish empathic contact outside its boundaries, disturbed her perceptual field in subtle ways. She wasn't good at dealing with massive energy incursions. She wondered how she'd put up with it for the year she'd worked here. Of course, the last time she was here she wasn't trying to contact anyone empathically outside of the domes, or worried about someone trying to kill her.

"Someone'll be here for you soon," the guard said, eyeing her restless motion. She made herself still and waited until she saw Regina moving toward her on the other side of the gate. She was dressed in long skirt and soft blouse, her usual attire. Jaguar always wondered about it. Such soft clothing for a woman with such secure control over her particular realm. But it probably put others off their guard, made them suspect she was herself soft, until it was too late.

"Jaguar," she said warmly as she approached, "I hate to say it, but it's good to see you."

Jaguar smiled and let Regina hug her briefly, returned the squeeze and released her. Regina kept her hands on Jaguar's shoulder and surveyed her, her face full of sympathy.

"I know," she said, "it's horrible for you. But selfishly, it'll be nice for me to spend some time with you."

"You'd be the only one here who feels that way, Regina," Jaguar said.

"You're probably right. But we'll make the best of it." Regina nodded at the guard. "Have someone bring Dr. Addams' bags to her room," she said. "Harris corridor, room 131." She took Jaguar's arm and led her forward. "Much better," she said. "Now we can stroll unencumbered. You remember Harris corridor?"

"I was there for three months when I first got here."

"You'll find nothing's changed, except there's a new coffee shop around the corner at Jenkin's Market. But how are you, Jaguar? Not just now, but in general, I mean."

"Outside of this, I'm fine Regina. Work's going great, and all's well with the world."

Regina smiled, bringing up dimples in her round face. "I believe you. You seem. . . .relaxed. Even here. But work's what you think of first. What about the rest of your life?"

Jaguar paused, smiled at her blankly.

"Social life, love life, personal growth, family and friends—the rest of your life, Jaguar," Regina prompted.

"Oh. That. Well, that's fine, too. I'm singing a lot with *Moon Illusion*—when I can, of course. Gerry's pretty upset when shit like this happens and he has to do his own singing."

"And?" Regina asked.

She was fishing for something, and Jaguar thought she knew what. Regina, perpetually single, always encouraged her workers to establish solid relationships, even to start families, though more often than not that meant they left their work here. Jaguar tried to take the conversation elsewhere.

"My people on the Home Planet are well. I was there recently with—" she stopped herself, realizing she was about to say with Alex. "With an assignment," she amended. "You really have to let me take you to Thirteen Streams sometime. You'd love New Mexico."

Regina laughed. "Don't try your evasive tactics with me. I won't let you wiggle out of this. The grapevine says you've taken a lover."

Jaguar offered a cool smile. "Do they think that's a first for me?"

"Oh, Jaguar. This is *me*. You and Alex—are you together now? At last?"

She wanted to say yes, wanted to take advantage of the opportunity to share her joy, especially with Regina, mentor, model, and the closest to a mother she'd ever had. Her example showed Jaguar how a woman might find her power within this very male system. She and Diane spent quite a few nights sitting at Regina's table after hours, drinking wine and arguing with enthusiasm about various theories of rehab for prisoners. They'd come to be seen as a triumvirate of powerful women, some of the men referring to them as the three witches, asking how their last cauldron had gone, the sharpness of their fear cloaked within a jovial, joking manner.

And Regina, who'd seen her pain at Diane's abandonment, also saved her ass from being fired altogether. She'd sent her to Alex, and would certainly be glad of her happiness with him. But Jaguar was reluctant to give up any secrets here. Too many ghosts, and all of them listening. Too much knowledge might put Regina in a bad position at some point. That was either paranoia, or her finely honed instinct for danger, her capacity to pick up on the smallest signal of it in a face, in a gesture, in the air. Either way, she'd listen to it.

"People have been talking about me and Alex for as long as I've been on Three, Regina," she said. "I'd think they'd get tired of it by now."

Regina showed clear disappointment. "Then it's not true?"

Jaguar was a lousy liar, but she had a talent for evasion, and she used it. "I can get sex anywhere," she said, "but a really good supervisor is hard to find. You think I'd risk it?"

Regina sighed. "I've said this to you before, Jaguar. Love is worth a risk or two."

Jaguar grinned. "Yes, Mother. I remember. And our work should be part of that love, caring for the prisoners as if they were our own children."

Regina laughed. "I remember saying that. Vaguely. How much wine did we drink that night?"

"Too much. And some tequila got in there somehow, I think."

"Those were good days," Regina said, sounding wistful. "But—well, if you're happy, I'm happy for you. Are you? Happy?"

"I'm happy to be alive," she said. "Happy my hair is looking as good as it is. Happy about a really good tequila. How's everything with you? Anything interesting going on?"

"I'm getting old, Jaguar. The most interesting thing in my life is waking up in the morning."

Jaguar laughed. "Not this week."

"You may be right. Ah—here's the scanning station."

They passed into a small grey room, where red lights blinked as they were scanned for weapons, drugs, any suspect object. Jaguar's glass knife passed through undetected, as always. For as many new sensors that were invented, humans came up with a way of sneaking past them.

"That's fine, then," Regina said, when the lights all turned green.

They moved through the open space beyond the entrance checks, and from there into what served as the streets of the bubble domes—broad corridors banked by housing facilities. They were the equivalent of hotel suites, row upon row of numbered doors that all looked the same except for the small decorations some people put on their doors to help them find their own rooms after a night of carousing at one of the pubs or lounges.

"Do you need anything before we get to your room?" Regina asked. "We can stop at the market."

"I just want to settle in. I can shop tomorrow—I mean, I think I can. What's my routine here? Has a schedule been set for me, or am I supposed to wing it?"

Regina chuckled. "Nobody would dare let you improvise, Jaguar. No, we've got a pretty full schedule laid out. Piles of records to go through, tours, interviews with Diane's co-workers, sessions with Francis. And you'll be attending daily meetings so you'll understand our system as you investigate."

She stifled a groan. Alex was right. They wanted to kill her. Death by meetings. "Great," she said as heartily as she could. "What's first on the agenda?"

"Tomorrow is orientation, and a training on our new psychotropics. You'll find that interesting. We've seen some great results with this generation of Alitrans. They lower mutoid anxiety levels considerably."

Without thinking Jaguar opened her mouth and let some untactful words fall out. "Nice to know the miracle of science can relax the slaves," she said dryly.

Regina stopped walking and regarded her with pained courtesy. "These are my programs, Jaguar. I've developed them very carefully, with our prisoners' welfare in mind. "

Jaguar regretted the sharpness of her words, though she continued to believe they were true. It was something she'd argued about with Regina in the past, and she would continue to do so.

"Sorry," she said, "I'm tired and my mouth got ahead of my brain. And don't get me wrong. I like work programs for prisoners."

"I know. We talked about it often enough. But you've been making lots of noise against these. Frankly, it's troubled me."

"It's not your vision that's wrong," Jaguar said. "It's the connection between the prisoners and your economy. The Planetoid's getting dependent on what they do. Last time that happened—well, we both know what came next."

Before the Planetoids, prisons on the home planet swelled to house millions, most of them poor or mentally ill, racially or geographically disadvantaged. They became an industry, a complex system of economic interdependency. When they were no longer supportable the states started release programs, but they let all the wrong prisoners loose while cutting social welfare programs that might help them adjust. Those prisoners began the ritual killing that became the Killing Times. The Planetoids were built to make sure that never happened again.

"We both also know there's lots of people who believe empaths started the Killing Times," Regina noted.

Jaguar paused, looked to her. "You're not one of them, are you?"

"Of course not," Regina said. "I'm saying your sight may be limited by your experience, just as the vision of other people is limited by theirs."

"Or maybe I'm the voice crying in the wilderness, making sure your model doesn't go to bad places. I don't want home planet legislators thinking we should all be dependent on our prisoners to support us. They're way too inclined to take the easy way out in these matters."

"I wouldn't worry about that, Jaguar. You have some funding advantages," Regina said. "A few Senators to call your own."

Jaguar cast her a quick glance, saw her mouth pinch in and quickly release. The tiniest expression of resentment, flashed once and swallowed into a smile. Jaguar had the high regard of Senator MacDanials, who was on the budget committee. A Senator in her nonexistent pocket, and Regina resented it.

"If that's true," she said, "I think we earned them."

Regina ducked her head down, brought it up again. "Did I sound petty? I apologize. I just hate grubbing for money. Very tiresome work. But really, Jaguar, don't you ever worry about what you do on Three? So much opportunity for abuse of the system. And the prisoners there are so toxic."

"Francis was no slouch."

"He's mentally ill. It's different than someone who—who eats their husband with a stir fry."

Jaguar grinned at this reference to one of her assignments. "You heard about her? She's actually doing fine. Got through her program and went on to work in a battered woman's shelter on the home planet."

Regina tsked softly. "She worked out, but what about the ones who don't?" she asked.

Jaguar shrugged. "Next life cycle."

Her success rate was 98 percent, but Regina knew her failures usually ended up dead. The consequences of failure on Planetoid Three were clear and high. Jaguar had no illusions about that. Neither did her prisoners.

Regina shook her head. "You say that, yet you voted against execution for Francis."

"My prisoners have a fighting chance," she said. "Putting a mutoid in shackles and killing him when he's defenseless—that's a bureaucratic meat grinder."

"Hm. I happen to agree. But what you do—I still think it's cold. And I sometimes worry it'll make you cold—cynical and bitter. You always had a tendency for—let's call it primal detachment."

Jaguar smiled at the term, and the worry. Much had changed, but Regina still took the mother hen position with her. She found it felt good.

Reassuring. She never had the chance other children got, to be both rebellious and loved, by parents whose wisdom you eventually incorporated into your own complex worldview.

"No, Regina," she said. "The exact opposite. If I can flip a pedophile or a murderer, even just one, it makes me less cynical. And I've flipped quite a few of each. Plus drug dealers, con men, cult leaders—well, you know."

Gerry, Rachel, Adrian, Clare, and many other former prisoners now brought their store of good to the world because of her work. Watching a prisoner move from murder to remorse to compassion wasn't easy. It left her feeling skinless, vulnerable to hope, that most terrifying of energies. But cynicism was the position of rationalists and disappointed romantics, and she was neither.

"What about the ones who don't make it?" Regina asked, and Jaguar heard real concern in her voice. Something personal there? She cast her a glance, saw something like turbulence behind the calm in her clear blue eyes.

"What is it?" she asked.

Regina shook her head. "Nothing. Just—I'm wondering."

"Some of the prisoners don't want to go on. They can't figure out how to be different, and they don't want to keep being who they are. And they all know the score by the time they get to me. They live with risk, and make choices. So do I." She thought of her last conversation with Alex. "Not always comfortably, but always with full awareness."

Regina looked around. "It's different here. Our prisoners are productive and content without risking their lives."

"But most of them never leave. These days, at least, your population doesn't heal. They just—maintain."

"It's still a goal I'm more comfortable with."

"No concerns that the home planet is using you as a dumping ground, a way to get rid of all the mutoids they can't be bothered with?"

"If that's the case, they're better off here, where we can be bothered."

"Yeah," Jaguar admitted. "You may be right about that. But it's just not what I do."

Regina's face brightened. "Then, as usual, we'll have to agree to disagree, with mutual respect, yes?"

Jaguar smiled. The mother and daughter bond, unbreakable except under the most extreme circumstances. We are different, but we are still connected, in the most essential ways. "It's always worked before," she said.

"Yes. And since we're on that subject, there's something I'll need from you."

"Tell me."

Regina held her hand out. "Your knife. No weapons allowed here."

Jaguar felt her smile freeze in place. "Teachers here have weapons."

"You're a visitor, Jaguar. Not a Teacher."

"I'm investigating a murder. I should have the means to defend myself."

"From what? Meetings and reports? Your knife won't get you out of that. And if I let it through, there'd be hell to pay. Susan Eideler's already been very clear about that."

Jaguar's jaw tensed. Without speaking, she unstrapped the mechanism that held the retractable blade close to the skin of her wrist. A shiver washed through her, then she put her hand out and let it go.

"Thank you," Regina said. "And don't worry. I'm keeping a good watch on everyone while you're here. They all know that."

That, Jaguar supposed, was something. Regina was kind, soothing, but she allowed for no breach of her rules, and she'd shown herself to be protective of Jaguar in the past. Still, there was a murderer abroad. Jaguar wasn't about to forget that.

"You think Diane's killer will care what you think?" she asked.

Regina startled. "But—well, Francis killed her." She stopped walking, looked to Jaguar. "You know that, don't you? Alex told you, right? I know the protocol leans toward execution but, well . . . ."

She let the sentence trail to silence and thought of Alex's conversation with Regina. "You hope I'll figure out a way around the protocol?" she asked.

"You are very good at that," Regina admitted. Then, she sighed. "I'd much rather let Francis live out his natural life here. We'd keep a better watch on him, of course. Adjust his meds and so on, but I don't want him executed. I spoke against it, but others pushed for it. Quite vocally."

"Who was the loudest?" Jaguar asked. That, she thought, would be a good place to start digging. And it would be better to dig while Regina believed she was merely trying to prevent an execution.

"Susan Eideler was one. She was good friends with Diane. And of course Diane's ex-fiancee—Ned Tackerson—had a lot to say. Do you remember him?"

"I don't think he was here when I was. I didn't even know she got engaged."

"You're right. He came right after you left. They had quite the affair, and then they broke it off, but they stayed friends. He's not a Teacher, though. He works in our PR department."

"You have a PR department?"

"Something else we started after your time. Our production programs grew, and we had a lot of interaction with the home planet, selling our wares, so it proved useful. In fact, our PR director and the production manager are on the home planet now, setting up marketing and distribution for our Big Bear exports."

"Like the bear Francis clutches?"

"That's right. It's a very successful export. Francis used to work in production, stuffing the bears, and Derek Rhinehart, the production manager, lets him keep one or two. He's a lovely man. You'll interview him when he comes back. Him and our PR director, Clyde Holmesby."

Jaguar bit back on some words she knew she shouldn't say. Instead, she considered Regina's stance, and how to make use of it. "So you won't mind if I gather enough evidence to establish reasonable doubt for Francis? At least, enough to get rid of the execution order."

"You'd be doing us all a favor," Regina said. "Aside from the humanitarian considerations, executions don't do our reputation any good."

"Okay," Jaguar said. "Then let's start with the fact that Diane was strangled from behind and Francis always attacked from the front."

"No good," Regina said. "His defense lawyer tried that, but Francis made those marks on her, and everyone knows that's his signature."

Jaguar sighed. That was all she had. That, and the ephemeral Francis carried, but she couldn't even mention that here. Regina wasn't one to see the spirit realm as a solution to mundane problems. "Then I'll need something else," she said.

"Like what?" Regina asked.

"The most logical thing is finding someone else who *might* have killed her. Someone with motive, means, opportunity."

Regina frowned. "I—I hadn't considered that, oddly enough. An interesting denial on my part. But I'm not sure you'll find anything. Everyone liked Diane very much. Even though. . ."

"Even though what?"

"Well, there were some accusations about a relationship with a female prisoner—a pretty young schizophrenic woman, here for aggravated assault. She wasn't responding well to medication, and we had trouble with her before Diane took over her case. Then, of course, she had to be removed from it. The girl didn't make the accusation, though. Susan Eideler reported an incident she thought was suspicious."

Susan again, Jaguar thought. She was everywhere. "I thought you said they were friends."

"They were. Thick as thieves. But Susan's a stickler for the rules, and she felt obligated, she said. There was a thorough investigation, but it came to nothing. You knew Diane, so you know how unlikely it was.

It broke off her engagement with Ned, though. Or, something did. They broke up just around that time."

"And you think it was this accusation?"

"I'm not sure. It could be just one of those things. In a closed system like ours relationships get heated fast. Sometimes too fast to realize they won't work. But Susan and Diane patched it up, somehow. Diane respected what it took for her to make the report, thank God. You can imagine how difficult that kind of fight makes things. Here's your room."

Regina stopped and opened a door, one in a long row that all looked the same. These rooms were for visitors and new workers. No point giving them the better housing until they looked like staying. She handed Jaguar her key card, and the two women stepped inside.

Jaguar looked around. Her bags were already there. Other than that there was a bed. A desk. A bathroom. A kitchenette with a tiny refrigerator, a toaster oven, microwave, and a hot plate. She remembered the set up from her first six months here. That, at least, hadn't changed, except for the small black circle on the ceiling she recognized as surveillance equipment, and a black box on the wall she knew as an intercom.

"Cozy," she said.

"I know it's not much, but you can take your meals in the dining halls, and this way," she pointed at the circle, "we can keep an eye on you."

"Right," Jaguar said. "What's that for?" she pointed at the intercom.

"So you can reach security quickly, or for security to reach you if they see trouble headed your way."

"Can I turn it off?"

Regina raised her eyebrows. "Why would you want to?"

"So I can get some sleep."

Regina closed the door behind them. "It's for your safety, Jaguar. Alex was concerned. I think he's overly cautious, but I didn't want to take any chances, so I had this installed. It was the least I could do."

"I always thought that was a funny phrase," Jaguar noted.

Regina folded her hands together and regarded Jaguar thoughtfully. "There were other precautions I wanted to take. I wanted a guard or a laser fence for your interviews with Francis, but you wouldn't have them at your initial interview, so that was voted down. Especially since you said he didn't kill Diane."

"Hoist by my own petard?" Jaguar asked.

"If there's ever any hoisting around you, that's usually what does it," Regina noted dryly.

"Yeah. And I'm guessing Susan was also loud about it."

Regina shrugged.

"You couldn't fight that? And here I thought you could do just about anything."

"Jaguar. That's silly."

"No," she said. "I really did. Especially when I first came here and saw how much you did get done."

Regina smiled, obviously flattered, but she was not an arrogant women. She brushed it away with a wave of her hand. "The moment of disillusionment comes to all students. All good students, that is. I'm glad our friendship could survive it. Someone will send your schedule of meetings by morning, but I'll stop by and bring you to dinner tomorrow night. We'll eat in the common lounge and I'll introduce you around."

"As long as I'm not the first course," she said.

"Audiences don't eat their entertainers. You provide a little thrill of adventure. Much needed on these sky islands."

"I suppose," Jaguar said. "Though I could do with less adventure and more dancing."

"Well, on Saturday nights, in the Terra Lounge, we have that, too."

Regina left Jaguar unpacking her bags and wondering who would ever dance with her here.

CHAPTER 5

Planetoid Three

"Sir," Scott White said, "I've got the monthly expenditure data for you,"

Alex looked up from his computer, where he'd been scanning Rachel's list of possibilities for Jaguar's back-up. He stared up at the young man standing in front of him. With his angular face and clear blue eyes, his taut physique and close-cropped hair, he looked more like army than Planetoid—which made sense, since he was a former Navy SEAL.

He was also exceptionally bright, impeccably trained, and very low profile. And his testing run showed clear telepathy, with all the bumps in alpha waves indicating he used it regularly. No surprise there. Before he joined the SEALS he'd worked under General Durk, who ran the Psi Ops unit of the special forces.

Alex made Rachel dig deep to get that information. Durk kept his people very private, and Scott never talked about it, which told Alex he was neither a braggart nor a fool. But when his resume came over the transom, specifically requesting this zone, Alex suspected he was a pentagon plant, so he insisted on a thorough background check, along with his own empathic look-see. Both said Scott was no longer army, and he'd gone to the trouble of confirming this with some people who were in a position to feed him accurate information.

All agreed that Scott left Psi Ops to join the SEALS well before he left the military altogether. And according to all reports, he'd never looked back. He wasn't working for Durk anymore. He wanted to be exactly where he was.

Now Alex considered him as possibly the very best person to bodyguard Jaguar. His telepathic skills would be useful, and his SEALS training would equip him to handle any situation she faced.

But the last assistant Alex sent to watchdog Jaguar ended up dead, and he still felt the pain of that. With all his training, Scott had only been working here a few months, and Alex wasn't quite ready to throw him off a bridge, straight into Jaguar's lap.

"You don't have to call me sir," he told Scott.

"Yes—Supervisor."

He said it with such discomfort Alex reneged. "Sir is fine, if you like it best. I'll take the data, and thanks."

He handed it over and left the room. On his way out he held the door open for Rachel, who was incoming.

She stood in front of Alex's desk and put a file folder down on it. "Here's the second list," she said. "All the new personnel, and their specialties."

"From here and Two?"

"Like you asked."

"Good. I'm not finding anyone on the first list." He turned his attention to the material while Rachel watched, a smile on her soft, round face, and her brown eyes lit with anticipation.

"Waiting for something?" he asked, pausing to look up at her.

"Yup," she said.

"What?"

"You'll see. At least, I'm pretty sure you'll see. Just read."

He turned back to the file. He wanted a face no one would recognize, but someone whose record showed they could manage complication, and someone who didn't mind working with an empath. The new list had twenty names on it. He scanned it quickly, then read it again, stopping halfway down.

"I'll be damned," he muttered.

"I thought you'd say that," Rachel replied.

He looked up and stared somewhere over Rachel's right shoulder, thinking it through. "It could work," he said. The man in question had just finished training for Special Team Work, which meant he was willing to play a variety of roles in a Teacher's program, on request. And he had some special skills all his own, learned well before he started training.

"He knows his way around a firewall?" Alex asked. Besides watching Jaguar, they'd want help in digging into Planetoid One systems.

"He got into some secure sites in his previous line of work, so he's a *pretty* good hacker," Rachel said, the implication being he wasn't as good as her. "And—well, you know the rest."

Alex nodded, remembering this man from their past association. He made a decision. "Get him. You can bring him up to speed, and we'll give him an earpiece to communicate with you. Because he can't hack as good as you and might need your help."

"I'll be on call, then."

"Twenty four and seven, until this is over."

"I don't mind that. Only, I wish you'd send me."

Alex shook his head. "Too many people there know you. It won't work."

"I know. I just wish it would. I want to do something."

"You already did, finding the perfect back-up. And trust me, you'll do more. I'll want a bodyguard for Jaguar, so you can cast around for that. And start the paperwork on this one. Slide him quietly through Personnel, into their systems programming. I'll let Paul know."

"Then what?"

"What you do best. Dig. Find out anything you can about Planetoid One. Specifically, anything that might be related to Diane Lasher's death, or systemic corruption. And figure out a way to get me there."

"The first part's easy. That last bit—if I can't go, I don't see how you can."

He lifted a hand, turned it over. "Then you'll have your work cut out for you."

Rachel gave him a smile and exited, and Alex pushed his telecom button, getting Paul's home planet office. When his face appeared, he didn't waste time.

"Go secure," he said, and waited to hear the appropriate number of buzzes and beeps.

"Okay," Paul said. "What?"

"I found someone for Jaguar's backup," Alex said. "A new team member, with the right background and some knowledge of the subject. Or at least the most important subject. The paperwork's on the way."

Paul nodded. "When does he go?"

"ASAP. Tomorrow at the latest. I don't want her alone there."

"You need to tell me any more about it?"

"Not unless you want to know."

"Then roll it along. I'll sign off on it."

Alex said he would, and ended the call.

When Paul's face was gone from the screen, he swiveled his chair around to look out the window and contemplate other possibilities. What bothered him most was not being able to communicate with Jaguar empathically. And he didn't even try to give her an earpiece, knowing they'd check her for that kind of equipment.

Except for telecom and computer, neither of which allowed them to speak with any privacy, they were cut off. And crows were walking over his grave.

He needed to be there, too. But as he stared out the window, he couldn't yet determine how to do that.

"Wait for me," he murmured into the night, knowing that even if she did, events might not wait for either of them.

Planetoid One

The Cleaner walked through the orderly space of the Infirmary, admiring what he saw. In the outer rooms, which housed patients with less serious illness or simple injuries, nurses and doctors moved with quiet efficiency from bed to bed, speaking to a patient now and then, reading charts, checking monitors, administering medications. Patients rested under the influence of the best combination of drugs available. Not a moan of pain or distress could be heard.

He reached into his pocket and pulled out his personal recorder, started it going.

He had one small projection amplifier and two recorders—one for personal use and one for Durk. The recorders both compiled a complete digital analysis of Electromagnetic fields, Human Energy Fields, thermal anomalies and more. He'd use his personal one to take readings here for comparison with corridor and meeting room readings. The second recorder would go back to Durk with all its gathered information and his report after he had a week's worth of readings.

It was important to establish a baseline for each one before he began the next part of his assignment, since that would affect the workings of his projection amp, which he'd use to create the illusion of ghosts for Dr. Addams, as part of the Discredit portion of his work.

Today he'd test the amp's reactiveness to energy levels in the infirmary, since the near presence of death sometimes interfered with very sensitive devices such as this one. If his battery lights started draining he'd have to calculate the difference between readings here and in the hallways and rooms where he'd do the main part of his work, and make adjustments as necessary. He walked up and down the room, moving close to some beds, then stopping to check his equipment.

Nobody questioned his presence. He was a familiar sight, often stopping by to visit with sick mutoids who worked in the Big Bear export program, bringing them gifts and chatting with them. Sometimes he'd sit with the dying while their bodies gave up the ghost, and the nurses admired his compassion, not realizing it was just a great opportunity to collect the most lively data on pre- and post-mortem energy.

He had ample opportunity to do so here. They had more death in this infirmary than the other two Planetoid prisons combined, and he was one of the few people who knew why. Not that his client, who played all cards very close to the chest, wanted to tell him. But he'd insisted on the full picture or he wouldn't take on a job. Of course, he assumed there were some lies still being told. Clients always lied about something and if you didn't get that, it could get you.

He'd already caught them lying about the vent system, but when he pointed out how that problem was actually a possibility, they'd come clean and even paid him extra to go ahead and look into the ways he could use it. That was turning out to be an interesting project, so he didn't mind. He only hoped that would prove true for any other lies he caught them in.

He moved to the next area of the infirmary, where more serious illnesses were managed, but he didn't linger long there. HIs interest was mainly in the room beyond ICU.

As he entered ICU the space grew even quieter, most of the patients unconscious, many on the fast track toward a permanent state of sleep. The only sound here was the whirring of equipment that breathed for those who couldn't, and the tidal sound of hearts beating through monitors. The staff was efficient, and mostly silent.

His recorders showed no imminent deaths, and his projection amp stayed steady, so he moved on. At the far end of ICU a guard was stationed in front of double doors that led to an area very few people were allowed to see. The blood donation unit. He flashed his pass at the guard and was waved through. When the doors clicked shut behind him he stood and surveyed the room.

In front of him were row upon row of beds, each one holding a mutoid, each mutoid connected to an IV that let their blood flow into a bag hooked nearby. Each one finally giving something back after a lifetime of taking. That, at least, was the way he saw it.

He'd brought himself up in the world by virtue of his wits and his strength, never asking anyone for help since his parents were killed in Los Angeles during the Serials, victims of the same biobombs that created these mutoids. He'd roamed the streets along with thousands of other children, scrounging for whatever they could eat, sleeping briefly in dumpsters that smelled of rotting flesh while another child stood guard, knowing even there they weren't safe from the killers, from those who killed the killers.

He'd made it through, and lived to see these twisted mutoids receive special educational opportunities, special funding for their unending medical problems, special dispensation for being broken, while he got nothing at all, not even a pat on the back for being smart and strong. Seeing them here, each one of them offering their blood to save other lives, to support the system that supported them, was a particularly rich source of satisfaction for him.

He took it in, sighing deeply, feeling all his molecules settle into balance as the world was balanced through this act. Of course, he knew many of them wouldn't survive. Their systems were fragile already, easily tipped toward death. A few pints of blood could send them into kidney failure, heart failure. But that was, to him, a justifiable risk, no different from the risks he'd taken to stay alive. The world wasn't meant to be easy. Not ever. Now they had to live that truth, just as he had.

To his mind, they contributed much more with their deaths than they had with their lives. Their deaths were even useful for him, creating an environment where he could gather a great deal of unadulterated post-mortem data, for which he was well paid.

He checked his recorders and saw the readings had gone off the charts. And of course, his projection amp battery was draining fast, its yellow indicator lights flashing. He touched the button for the back up system, something he'd installed recently, and the yellow lights reverted to a steady green.

"Good stuff," he murmured. He'd been hoping that would work. He'd certainly need it for this job.

He noted the time and let it run, wanting to see how long it would last. He continued his walk up and down the rows of beds. When he passed one where a mutoid was actively dying he noted the fluctuations in thermal waves on his recorders, the weird wobbling of static energy and EMF always accompanying this moment. Durk would be pleased, he thought. He stayed here for a few more minutes, sitting by this mutoid's bed and patting his hand while a nurse gave him a smile of approval. When he'd gotten all he wanted, he stood and made his way toward the far end of the room.

Here, just a little beyond the beds where mutoids gave blood and life for the system that kept them, he could get data on the post-mortem energy that lingered well beyond immediate death. In this place, and in certain other hot spots on Planetoid One, that kind of post-mortem energy, one month old or older by his reads, was readily available for his equipment to read. He was one of the people who understood why.

He scanned the ventilation system built into the walls and ceiling. It was put in just before Diane Lasher was killed, and it was the ultimate in energy and air conservation, recycling both at a rate of close to 95 percent, operating off a solar cell placed on the roof of the bubble dome.

The system was a real money saver for Planetoid One, but the Cleaner had found an unexpected corollary effect, which engineers and installers hadn't considered. It also retained or recycled the exact kinds of energy he was taking readings on. Post-mortem energies.

When he told the client this, it was clear they already knew about it, and didn't give a rat's ass. Nor should they, except that it might be another way of saving money for them. After all, it was just energy, and as he'd told Durk, he had a few ideas on how he might tap it.

Of course, it wasn't necessarily easy. It created aberrant readings—too strong, too high, too meaningful, the EMF off the scale, the HE thick and full of static, the thermal reading showing shapes that were vaguely human instead of the usual bar graphs. The kind of readings one would expect to see emanating from a true ghostly presence.

Not that he believed in any of that. He'd just read enough of Durk's research to know what they used as evidence of ghosts. Or, more accurately, evidence of TE's—True Ephemerals. Durk liked euphemisms, the more syllables the better. In ordinary terms, TE's were real ghosts, with human consciousness and ephemeral form. Specific dead people rather than just lurking energies remaining from the process of death. He wondered sometimes if finding proof of that, real proof, would make Durk happy. But he doubted the general had the capacity for anything like real happiness. Satisfaction, maybe. Not happiness.

For his part, he figured long-term post mortem was the same energy as point of death, but the equipment read it differently. He couldn't imagine a scenario that would make him see it any differently. Ghosts, hauntings, poltergeist activity—all that was stuff he created with his projection amp, for clowning or cleaning purposes. As far as he was concerned, they didn't exist outside of the technology it took to make them appear. Dead was dead. If it wasn't, he'd have quite a few angry ghosts haunting him, but none of his cleanings had ever returned to trouble him, or talk about what he'd done on a witness stand.

However, the event of death released subtle energies, and the new vent system was apparently keeping that energy from dissipating so that every death from the time it went in lingered in the air. He'd been calculating that into the formulas for his upcoming job, and he hoped it didn't present any surprises.

On the other hand, his speciality was taking situations that others saw as problems and turning them into opportunities. Already he'd thought of a few good ways to use this one.

He nodded at one of the nurses, who greeted him brightly, with a smile that said she'd be glad to have a drink with him any time he was available. He returned the smile, though he wouldn't take her up on it.

Mixing business and pleasure was a bad idea. When he got back to the home planet he'd use his pay for a few weeks worth of real pleasure. Right now, he had work to do.

He flipped off his machines and went on his way, satisfied with his day so far.

CHAPTER 6

Jaguar was still in her robe, just out of the shower, when she heard a knock on her door. "Oh, hell," she groaned. "Another meeting."

She'd had two days of meetings already. They'd brought her here to investigate and were giving her no time to do so. A pretty neat trick, she thought. A way of wearing her down, making her do what she hated most. And, she thought, it might just work. Every meeting she attended made her feel like she was chewing on aluminum foil. Another few days of it and she'd run screaming from a conference room to execute Francis herself.

Her first day orientation consisted of hours of inconsequential lecture about the history and functioning of the bubble domes, followed by a complete tour of the facilities, as if she'd never seen them before. That evening she had to sit through a presentation about changing laws and their effect on use of mutoid genetic material in research. Her second day was spent filling out forms for personnel, who felt compelled to explain everything three times, in elaborate detail. After a bad dinner in the cafeteria she'd gone to another mandatory meeting, this one with a less than scintillating presentation about privacy and sexual harassment issues. She wondered what new joys today would bring.

She went to her door and opened it. On the other side stood a tall, slim woman with curly dark hair, dressed in an expensive suit and holding an arm full of files. Her features were sharp, her narrow eyes were alert, as if she hoped the world would make a mistake she could call it on.

Susan Eideler.

"Dr. Addams," she said brusquely. "Good morning."

"I'm not calling it good yet," Jaguar replied. "How've you been, Susan?"

"Fine," she replied, and from the way she said it Jaguar thought it must be a new definition of the word. "I brought these for you."

She held out the burden of her arms. Jaguar took it, found a balance just before she dropped the whole thing, and went to her desk and deposited it there.

"Thanks," she said. "What are they?"

"Durero's files. Work program information. Trial transcripts. The works."

"You could've sent it digital."

"It's confidential."

"And I'm not?"

"Not even a little bit," Susan said.

"Right," Jaguar said. She glanced down at the pile, and back up at Susan, who still stood in the doorway. "Did you want to come in?"

"No," Susan said bluntly.

Susan was blunt. Tall, attractive, brutal and blunt, were the words that came to mind when Jaguar looked at her. Jaguar was not quite as tall, and she hoped not as brutal, but she could be even more blunt. "Then why are you standing there?" she asked.

"Regina instructed me to see if you needed anything else," she said tersely.

"Right," Jaguar said. "Just following orders. Good for you." She shifted some of the material in the pile and looked at folder titles. "Where's Diane's personnel file?" she asked.

Susan shook her head. "That's more than confidential. That's classified."

"This is a murder investigation. Didn't the original investigators see it?"

Susan looked up and down the hall, then took a step into the room and closed the door behind her. Her face stopped being professionally cool and tightened into anger. "This isn't about Diane. Don't make it about her."

"She's the one who got killed. You know we always go over victimology."

"She wasn't a victim. She was a Teacher, working with Durero. That's what got her killed."

"Would I be here if I thought so?"

Susan glowered. "I'm not authorized to give her file to you. You want it, you'll have to get it from Regina."

"Then I will," Jaguar said. "Well, you've done your duty, so you can go away."

She opened a file and started to read. After a moment, she realized she hadn't heard the door open and shut. She turned and saw Susan still standing there, her arms folded across her chest.

"What now?" she asked.

"It's—it's disgusting. You, of all people, poking through Diane's life, digging through it for dirt. She would've had you fired, if your lover didn't stop her."

"You mean Regina?" Jaguar asked.

"You know who I mean."

"No I don't," Jaguar said, just to be contrary.

"Alex wanted it. Wanted you on Three. That's a fact."

"Here's another one—you wanted me here," Jaguar said. "It wasn't my choice."

"You chose to vote against execution."

"Because Francis didn't do it. And I'll find out who did, with or without Diane's file."

Susan unfolded her arms and took the few strides necessary to get close to Jaguar and point a finger in her face. "Be careful," she hissed. "Very careful."

"Back at you," Jaguar said cheerfully. "You're aware there's a security camera in my room?"

Susan's gaze darted around, landed on the surveillance camera on the ceiling. She reined in her face. "What I mean is you'll be interviewing Durero," she amended. "And you better be careful with him, because he's a killer."

"You say that as if I haven't dealt with worse," Jaguar commented. She kept her gaze steadily on Susan, holding her still, brushing her thoughts with some of the cases she'd seen.

Susan stepped back and held a hand out as if to ward her off. Jaguar retreated, and grinned. "By the way, I'm scheduled to interview you at—" she glanced over at her schedule, "Two this afternoon. Don't be late, and don't tell any lies. Is that careful enough?"

Susan turned and left the room, banging the door hard behind her.

Jaguar took in breath and let it out. So much for keeping a low profile. It might not be possible. She glanced at her schedule for the day and saw that her next function wasn't for another hour. That would be her first interview with Francis. Alone. Unguarded. Unmonitored by any camera whatsoever.

"Every day has its own unique pleasures," she muttered, and proceeded to get dressed.

Before she left her room she put a call in to Regina to ask for Diane's permanent file. "Susan seems reluctant to give it to me," she mentioned dryly

"Oh. Well, Susan," she said, as if that explained all. "Anyway it's with HR. I'll have to get you clearance for it. Could take a day or two."

"That long?"

"We have our procedures. In the meantime you can see her public material down in the main computer banks."

"What'll that get me?" Jaguar asked sharply. It was ridiculous to expect her to conduct an investigation without information on the victim.

"Quite a bit," Regina said, staying upbeat. "Diane organized and ran lots of specials—one time events for her people—and that's all there.

Also any of her awards, any grant applications or funded research—and so on."

Jaguar bit back on a comment about PR ruling all. Their mutual respect compact wouldn't last long if she kept snapping her teeth at it. "Thanks, Regina," she said.

"Just let me know if you need anything else."

Jaguar closed her telecom. "I need my knife," she muttered. "And a shuttle back to Planetoid Three." She sighed, and made her way down the hall toward the computer banks. She might as well do this now.

* * * *

One of the things she disliked about Planetoid One was the feeling of enclosure. The place was, in reality, nothing more than an oversized space station, and you never got away from the walls. Even the greenhouses and the scattered forest areas that provided oxygen eventually led only to another steel wall. The forest areas had the advantage of plexi ceilings, though, and if she ever had a free hour between meetings she'd go and see them again. She'd spent a lot of time in them when she worked here, staring up at what would be darkness if they hadn't included a projection of sky that mimicked the natural course of a home planet day.

But here, where temporary workers were housed, when she left her room she was in a hallway no more than 15 feet across—just wide enough for any equipment to drive through, as she was told in her orientation session. On her side of the hall were rows of rooms just like hers. Across the way were more of the same. The linoleum floor was neutral beige, the walls painted a green referred to as 'Postal' because it was supposed to ward off the anxiety that made people go crazy with a gun.

The better accommodations were reserved for long-term workers. Each year you stayed bumped you up to a nicer place so that Regina, for instance, lived in a small house right next to the forest, and her corridor, wide as a city street, with sidewalks included, also had a plexi ceiling. Susan had half a duplex in the Lexington Market area, near a theater and one of the more popular pubs.

Jaguar's corridor eventually opened up into the larger lobbies of offices if you turned right, and further out from there were shops, some specialty restaurants, the Terra Lounge. On the same level but isolated by secure gates was the area where prisoners were housed, some in open rooms, and some in cells. It took special clearance to get into them, clearance Jaguar hadn't been given. She would eventually be allowed to see the morgue, where Diane's body was conveniently found.

She already had clearance for the computer banks, on the lower level. She turned left and headed toward the stairs. As she did, she had a clear memory of walking this hall with Diane, the two of them talking over a case. Diane had tucked a hand in Jaguar's arm, a gesture nobody else could have gotten away with.

Regina had joined them. Jaguar could still see her coming from the other direction, waving at them. She and Diane had moved forward to meet her. They'd all gone on together, stopping for coffee. What were they talking about? Jaguar couldn't remember which case. She only remembered Diane's contagious enthusiasm for her work, her innate hopefulness that all problems could be solved if you brought enough energy to bear on them.

Soft sorrow moved through her, and she allowed it. Nothing wrong with feeling this sadness. Nothing in it that would cause her undue harm. It was, simply and without complications, grief. Grief at her death, and grief at what had happened between them.

Jaguar's last case on One was with a woman convicted of twenty counts of fraud and grand larceny, plus attempted murder of the police officer who tried to arrest her. Though the testers said her fear was of poverty, to Jaguar's sharp eye her deeper fear was of betrayal. She'd started a program that involved taking her empathically through every instance of betrayal she'd ever had, letting her re-experience them, making her sit still with them and connect them to her crimes. She hadn't talked about what she was doing, because in those days she never discussed empathic work with non-empaths, but she hadn't gone out of her way to hide it, either. She'd used the arts before, and would use them again because she thought the ruling against them was ridiculous, and assumed nobody was really following it if they had any sense.

But this time, for reasons she never found out, she was only a few days in when someone went to Diane and reported her for this code infraction. When Diane called her on it, she responded directly and honestly. Yes, she was an empath. Yes, she used the arts, and used them well. Why did Diane think her success rate was so high, anyway? She figured Diane would scold her, tell her to be more careful, and let it go.

Instead, Diane viewed her with frank repulsion. "You're fired," she said. "There's no room for empaths in this system, or in my life."

No discussion. No take backs. To Diane, Jaguar was worse than a mutoid. Mutoids couldn't help what they were. She could.

Between Alex and Regina, she'd been transferred to Planetoid Three instead of fired, but Diane was true to her word. She never spoke to her again.

At the time it hurt like hell. Though Diane had sometimes expressed a kind of shuddering fear about the empathic arts, Jaguar hadn't realized how profound her prejudice was. She didn't seem like the type of person who would nurture something that unreasonable.

For a while, she took it personally. When the hurt went away she began to wonder what fear lived under Diane's bright exterior to make her feel that way. In fact, she still wondered.

"Diane, I wish we could've figured it out," she muttered to herself.

She was so deep in her thoughts she didn't see the two women standing in her path until she was on top of them, at which point she pulled up short.

"Sorry," she said, and made to move around them.

To her surprise, they moved with her, continuing to block her. She frowned, stared at them, then blinked. She knew these faces. She'd seen their photos in Francis's file. One was Sarah Lopez. The other Gertrude Mathias. Two of the women he'd killed.

Okay, she thought. That's interesting. She'd dealt with ghostly presences in her time, but usually she didn't see them this clearly. Her grandmother, who had a gift for dealing with the dead, perceived them as solidly as a living person, but it was rare for her granddaughter to do so, so this was a surprise. Something to do with the bubble dome energy?

She moved her hand at her side, feeling for the energy around them. Static, and plenty of it. And a heaviness, a sensation akin to dread. The women continued to stare at her. She did as she was taught to do by all the very skilled empaths who'd guided her in her arts. She talked to them.

"Did you want something?" she asked.

No response. They just continued to stare, sorrowfully.

"If you've got something to tell me, I'm listening," she continued.

A hand touched her shoulder and she whirled on it, grabbed it by the wrist, an instinctive move.

The security guard who stood behind her opened his eyes wide with shock. Apparently they weren't as reactive here as on Planetoid Three. She released him quickly.

"Sorry," she said. "You startled me." She glanced over her shoulder, saw that the women were gone. She sighed, turned back to the guard and flashed her visitor's pass. "Dr. Addams. Here on Planetoid business."

The security guard rubbed at his wrist. "Yeah. I thought maybe you needed something."

"What made you think so?"

"Well, you're standing here talking to yourself."

She twitched out a smile. "Bad habit. But I'm just peachy. You?"

"Fine," he said. "Have a nice day." He ambled on.

She turned around and kept walking.

Not good, she thought, in so many ways. The guard would put this in his daily report, and he'd talk to all his buddies about it since gossip was one of the favorite sports of Planetoid One. Before the day was out word would be everywhere that she stood in corridors talking to herself.

And he didn't see what she saw, which meant either he couldn't perceive ghosts, or they didn't actually exist and she was seeing things. The many different energies bopping around the bubble dome might be affecting her perceptual field, making her project what was in her own mind into the air around her, something that had happened to her on the Virtual Reality site once.

Certainly she hadn't felt anything like real ghosts in the vicinity. All she'd picked up on was static, and the heaviness that came from increased Electromagnetic Field energy. That could easily come from the energy rich environment of the domes.

"Rat fuck," she muttered, then caught herself, looked around. No more talking to herself. None at all. And no more talking to apparent ghosts. Next time she'd just walk through them.

As she made her way to the stairwell something new came along to brighten her day. This time it was a presence at her back. Someone behind her. She didn't slow down, but she opened empathically to check on it.

A definite presence, and it was interested in her. But it lacked the static or heaviness of what she'd just seen. Quite possibly, she thought, a real live human was following her.

She wouldn't be surprised if Susan had someone on her tail. That was within the boundaries of reason, a rational explanation for what she felt. She checked the reflective surfaces ahead of her—windows and metal walls all around—to see if she could spot anyone.

There were people walking the hall, but none were Susan, and none were obviously tracking her. She kept her glance on glass and mirror that she passed, but she saw only a shimmering of motion that seemed to skip from one surface to the next behind her, a small bird made of light, flitting in her wake. As far as she knew, pieces of light had no conscious intent, and no reason to follow her.

Still, the feeling of a presence continued. More perceptual field trouble? She hoped not. She'd rather deal with a very real killer than that. Some kind of tracking device, giving off the same signals a human tracker would? Or maybe it was an empathic tap, someone here who didn't mind breaking the rules to get information on her. She got to the stairwell door and opened it, turning slightly and glancing behind as she did.

Nobody and nothing was behind her. She moved into the stairwell, let the door shut behind her. If anyone followed she'd know right away.

Down one flight, then another, and she heard nothing, felt nothing. She breathed out in relief. The place was making her twitchy, she thought. What she'd felt was just nerves, after a strange sighting of dead women who weren't ghosts at all.

She shook herself and kept walking. By the time she got to the door on Ground Floor 1, she felt the presence again.

She paused, checked in with herself. Since the Killing Times, and the year she'd spent on the streets of Manhattan trying to stay alive, her capacity for detecting a tail had been infallible. If she felt someone behind her, someone was there. She should trust that here. And she felt someone. Or something.

But whoever or whatever was following, they wouldn't learn much. She was here, doing what she was supposed to do. "Carry on," she muttered before she could stop herself, and she opened the door.

As soon as she did so she was flooded with sensation, tossed into the vastness of an unbounded area charged with boundless, sparking energy. Then, a hesitant reaching toward her, followed by a whispering inside her, the voice thin and delicate as morning mist.

Go left, it said.

She stood and waited for more. Nothing came. The vastness receded and she stood with her hand still on the door, staring into the even narrower corridors in this part of the bubble dome.

A woman in a suit passed by and smiled at her. She smiled back, let go of the door and peered at the signs posted on the wall across from the door. The woman would assume she was checking where she was going rather than crazy. So she hoped.

As she stared, part of her brain tried to work out what had just happened. The other part noticed that the signs told her if she went left she'd be heading toward the infirmary. If she went right she'd be at the computer rooms. She had no clearance for the infirmary, and not a lot of time to look at Diane's material before her interview with Francis, so she went right instead. And she felt a distinct nudge at her shoulder, pushing her back toward the left.

Go left. The infirmary.

Following the imperatives of her arts, which included listening to sourceless voices and being receptive to the demands of trailing bits of light, she turned left.

When she got to the doors labeled *Infirmary* she pushed at them and found them locked. She saw the slot for a key card, the groove for a thumbprint, and considered. As she did, the voice whispered within her one more time.

Hurry. Save us.

That, she thought, didn't sound good. She resisted the urge to respond and focused on her task instead. In general, she was good with a lock, and she knew these kinds. She held her hand over the thumbprint, focused her thoughts on opening, and waited.

There was a click, immediately followed by a sharp alarm going off. She pulled her hand back and stood still. "Huh," she said. "Must be something I missed."

She was walking away when a voice at her back barked out a stern command to stop. She turned to the voice.

A security guard had a stun gun pointed at her. No, she thought. Not a stun gun. Laser fire. Set on high. A lot of trouble to go through for the infirmary, she thought. They must be very protective of their sick people here.

She smiled. "Hi there," she said as he approached. "I'm Dr. Addams, here from Planetoid Three. I thought I'd tour the infirmary now, while I have a little time. Didn't mean to raise the militia."

He twisted his lips around. "Clearance?" he asked.

"Planetoid pass," she said, holding it up.

He shook his head. "No good. It's a special clearance area."

"You got something contagious in there?"

"No, ma'am. Nothing to worry about. Just sick people. Not to be disturbed."

"Then how do I get clearance?"

"Your supervisor'll get it for you."

"Or Regina? I mean, Governor Hawthorne?"

He shrugged. "That'd work."

"Then I'll see you again," she said, and she meant it. Clearly this place needed investigating. In the meantime, she turned back and made her way to the computer rooms.

This time she felt no presence behind her, but when she entered the computer room she was still deep enough in thought that she almost missed the next surprise of the day. In fact, she clipped right past, then stopped dead in her tracks.

Seated at a desk and working a computer was someone she knew. Someone who had no business being here. Before she could decide whether he was really there or not he whispered, "Act natural. Don't turn around."

She turned around.

"Adrian?" she asked.

He grinned. "Guess I forgot how good you are at taking directions. Next time I'll tell you to come here and give me a kiss."

She moved to him, grabbed his shoulder, pressed it hard, then let it go. "Hecate," she said. "It's really you."

"You think I was a ghost or something?" he noted. "Or maybe you hoped that?"

"If you only knew," she said, grinning at him. He'd been a prisoner of hers on Planetoid Three a few years ago, a convicted con man. Facing his fear of being unimportant had led him to risk his own life to help her save Alex. He'd been one of her favorite successes, and she still appreciated what he'd done for her.

"But why are you here?" she asked. "You're not a prisoner again, are you?"

He laughed. "No. I work here."

"Since when? I thought you were on the home planet."

"I was. But it was boring as hell." He swiveled his chair back and forth, sent an appreciative glance up and down her form. Some things, she thought, didn't change.

"Boring?" she asked.

"Very. One day I found myself coming up with a new scam, just for fun. Then I remembered my time with you, which was anything but boring, and I applied for work on the Planetoids. I just finished my training on Two."

"And you didn't let me know? I would've gotten you onto Three instead of this rat trap."

"Thanks, but I'm pretty well situated. And by the way, Rachel says hello, and stay out of trouble. I told her as if."

She eyed him. He moved his hand to his ear, tugged on it lightly. She moved her head in the slightest possible nod. She got it. Alex had sent him as her back-up, and he was in touch with Rachel. Not a bad idea, she thought. Trust a con man to sniff out a con game. And she'd already broken him in, so there'd be no learning curve.

"We should talk more," she said. "Catch up with each other."

"Love to, but not right now. I'm busy." He glanced around at the people, and the cameras.

She grinned. "Me, too. I'm having a helluva time trying to get a personnel folder on a murdered woman."

He paused, listened to something she couldn't hear, then smiled. "Maybe you'll get lucky with that," he noted. Then, more quietly. "Your friend Rachel—she's kinda special. You know that, right?"

"Don't get any ideas, Romeo. She's got a girlfriend."

His face showed chagrin. "Hell. Why're all the good ones taken or—or taken."

"A question nobody's ever answered, my friend. You can console yourself by taking me dancing. At the Terra Lounge, tomorrow night."

His face brightened at the prospect.

"Incorrigible," she said, and walked away, thinking of the next disappointment he'd have to face.

* * * *

Jaguar had another twenty minutes before she met with Francis, and she decided to use it selfishly. She went back to her room and telecommed Alex. They couldn't say a lot, but at least she could see his face. But when her viewscreen opened up, it wasn't Alex she saw. It was Rachel.

"Hey—didn't I call Alex?" she asked.

"He's at a meeting, so his calls are being routed to me. He didn't want to miss anything important."

She knew what that meant. If there was any trouble at all, Rachel would get him. He wasn't taking any chances. "Nothing important. Just let him know I got the package you sent. And I appreciate it."

Rachel grinned. "I thought you would. There'll be more. And your other request is en route."

"This is getting interesting," she said. "How's everything there?"

"As usual. Three new cases today. One you might like—a woman who tested high for psi capacities in the Adept range. Convicted of felony theft from a casino with the highest possible security, but only got caught because she killed a guy who tried to rape her in the streets as she was leaving."

"Rat fuck. And I'm stuck here. Listen, tell Alex to call me later. After ten, I guess. I should be done with all the meetings by then."

"Sure," Rachel frowned, looked somewhere over Jaguar's left shoulder.

"Something wrong?" Jaguar asked.

"Nothing. Just—should we talk when your company is gone?"

"Company?"

"The woman standing behind you."

Jaguar turned. Saw no one. Turned back to the viewscreen. Rachel's frown had deepened.

"That's funny," she said. "I could've sworn I saw her. . . ."

Jaguar let this roll around her thoughts until it settled down. "How many women?"

"Just one. Must've been a shadow or something."

"What's she look like?"

"I'm—not sure. Just. . . well, now that you ask, it wasn't like I *saw* her. I just—I just *thought* her."

"Right," Jaguar said. "So what did she think like?"

"Oh. Um. Blonde? Worried?"

Jaguar smiled hard at the screen. "Skip it," she said. "Bad connection, probably. Listen, do me a favor. Get Diane's file on the computer. Check on her place of birth for me."

"What? But you—"

"Just do it," Jaguar cut in.

Rachel turned half away from the screen as she worked the computer. Her expression went through a variety of changes as she pulled up Diane's file and gazed at the photo of her.

"I'll be damned," she whispered.

"Not you," Jaguar said. "Myself, I'm not so sure."

Rachel turned back to the viewscreen and opened her mouth to say more, but Jaguar held up a hand to silence her. "Place of Birth?" she asked.

Rachel caught on and traded her confusion for a bright smile. She was, Jaguar thought, one of the worst liars in the world, but she tried. "Carlisle, Indiana," she said.

"Okay. Thanks. Alex thought there might be a record discrepancy but he was wrong. Let him know what you saw, or thought you saw, okay?"

"Yeah," Rachel said. "I most certainly will."

CHAPTER 7

Planetoid Three

"What're you trying to say, Rachel?" Alex asked.

"I'm not *trying* to say anything. I'm just telling you what happened, which Jaguar said I should do."

She'd duly reported the small and inexplicable incident of the telecom, which was beginning to remind her of an Edwardian mystery novel, and Alex was staring at her with his brow knit, his dark eyes sparking with frustration.

He smoothed his desk with his hands as he thought it through. "Okay. To reiterate. Jaguar called, and you spoke with her. While you were speaking, on your telecom screen you saw a blonde woman standing behind her, in her room."

"Thought her," Rachel corrected. "In my mind, only like she was in the room."

"Right. The woman disappeared, and Jaguar asked you to get Diane's file, and when you saw Diane's photo in it you decided it looked remarkably like the woman you'd seen—I mean, thought."

"Correct," Rachel said.

"But what does it signify?"

"Figuring that out is your realm, not mine. I'm just reporting."

Alex sighed. He wasn't in a good mood. He'd wasted two days exploring different ways to get on Planetoid One, from stowing away on an InterPlanetoid shuttle, to getting in by Senatorial fiat. Nothing he came up with was close to possible, but his Adept vision was pushing at him more imperatively each day to be where she was.

And he wasn't happy with what Rachel reported. Most likely it was residual image, an energy called up by Jaguar's presence, empathically projected because it was very much on her mind. That kind of thing had happened to her in the past. Put enough technology around her and she started spitting out some interesting stuff.

In spite of that cogent explanation, he found it disturbing. He knew Jaguar, and she wouldn't even mention it unless there was something else going on as well. And it meshed in some indefinable way with what the Adept space was poking him about.

"I'll file it for later," he said. "Let's get back to something less cryptic. I need to get to One. Can you get me onto a shuttle with a different ID?"

She rolled her eyes at him. "You know I can," she said. "But it won't help you any. They'll still recognize you."

"I'm pretty good at not being seen, Rachel," he said.

"You can't stay invisible forever. I mean, that's what Jaguar told me. And where will you sleep? How'll you eat?"

"Sleeping and eating aren't particularly on my mind right now," he said.

Rachel regarded him kindly. He didn't like that. It was a recognition of his desperation that he was even thinking in these terms.

He tapped a finger on his desk. She was right about a few things beyond the sleeping and eating problem. He wouldn't be useful to Jaguar unless he was mobile. He'd have to stay close to her without being noticed. But the only other option he'd thought of so far was to get permission to do the investigation with her. He'd contacted Paul about that, and he was willing to sign off on it, but when he asked Regina she said, courteously and firmly, that it was best if Jaguar managed alone. His presence, she said, would only raise more hackles.

He kept pushing, saying neither of them cared about that, and she continued to politely decline. Apparently she did care. He sensed other agendas below the spoken one, and considered an empathic check on her, then decided against it. She'd notice and take offense, something he didn't need right now. Instead he gave Rachel the extra assignment of digging into Regina's past and present more thoroughly. As if she didn't have enough to manage.

"Alex," Rachel said now, "if I could think of something I'd do it. You know that."

"I do," he said. "Anything from Adrian?"

"Nothing yet, but he's just started. I've got him going through all kinds of files—fiduciary to personnel. He'll spot anything suspicious."

"He will," Alex agreed. Con men had a bloodhound's nose for a scam. But it wouldn't help him get where he needed to be. He swiveled his chair around and glowered outside his window. Something. There must be something. Some way to get to her.

Rachel, watching him, made a clucking sound of sympathy. "Too bad you're not a mutoid," she said. "Then I could get you in easy."

As she said it, he caught sight of his own face reflected in the window. He imagined it with a blue patch across the cheek and eye. Imagined his hair a different color, his nose slightly altered with plasticene. Possibilities began to mill and seethe within him.

"Oh, really?" he asked. He swiveled around and turned a smile toward her. "You could?"

Her smooth forehead creased into a frown, then her face lit up like a Christmas tree. "Oh," she said. "Oh. Yes, I could."

Alex's mind began ticking off items of protocol. Mutoids with smaller charges were sent almost immediately into work programs. A day or two of orientation, then they worked in the production facilities, in the cafeteria, in maintenance. But getting a prisoner onto a Planetoid was a different process than workers. He'd need a governor to sign off on it.

"Is Paul on the home planet, or here?" he asked.

"Here," she said. "For a meeting."

"Staying at the Governor's Inn?"

"Yup."

Alex pushed himself to stand. "Start the paperwork on a new mutoid prisoner for One. A small charge—something that lets him go right into the workforce. Maintenance would be best. Can you get that?"

Rachel was already at the door. "Done by morning. Can you get—"

"—Paul's signature. That's where I'm headed."

He followed her out the door and they went their separate ways.

* * * *

Alex called ahead to Paul, saying they should meet in the bar at the Governor's so he could catch him up on events to date. Though Paul had been amenable so far, he anticipated some resistance to this move, and wanted to set it up right.

When he entered the bar he saw Paul seated at a table, already nursing a beer. Alex gave him a wave, signaled that he was getting his own beer, and then joined him.

"What's up?" Paul asked him as he sat.

"Not too much yet," Alex said. "We're still digging through files."

"You got someone good on that?"

"Two of the best."

Paul took a long sip of his beer. "If you got nothing else, what's this meeting about?"

Alex leaned in. "Do you have any photos of your nephew?"

Paul startled. "Yeah. Why?"

"Can I see one?"

Paul pulled out his wallet, showed a small photo of a little boy with blonde hair and big blue eyes, a smile as big as a world. He looked as happy as children can look when everyone loves them and they know it. "Cute little guy, right?"

"Very. How extensive is the damage?"

Paul put the picture away. "Don't look too bad so far. Some trouble with his kidneys, and some neurological trouble with his legs. He has to wear braces for now. But his mind's good. They checked that out. And the blue patch is down the back of his neck. His parents are looking into getting it removed."

People with money could do that kind of thing, hiding the visible evidence of the condition. It would be in his medical records, his school records, but nobody else would know a thing.

"You realize that the only difference between a mutoid and me is that I can hide being an empath," Alex said.

Paul jerked his head around quickly. Though he knew what Alex was and sometimes even called on his skills, he avoided talking about it openly.

Today Alex wanted to shock him a little. Now he'd shock him some more. "But Jaguar's more like a mutoid," he said. "She can't hide what she is. Her heritage, everything she is, gives her away."

Paul moved his beer glass around, frowned at Alex. "What's all this for?" he asked.

"I figured out a way to get there. But I'll need your help."

"You? Go to One? You won't even get off the shuttle before they turn you around."

"Not the way I have it planned."

"C'mon, Alex. You gave her back-up. Why do you have to be there? It's not like she can't take care of herself."

There it was. The resistance Alex anticipated. Paul was glad to send replaceable personnel into danger, but not his best supervisor. Not for any number of nephews or sisters. But Jaguar always said that Adepts were masters of manipulation, and she was right. Alex used his skills to best advantage.

"Then I won't go," he said evenly. "Jaguar can investigate on her own, and when the shit hits the fan you and I can watch from here."

Paul's face went tight. "Christ," he said. "You're a manipulative son of a bitch. Anyone ever tell you that?"

He shrugged. "Jaguar's mentioned it now and then."

"You don't have to look so goddamn proud of it. But it's not like—I mean, you haven't *seen* anything, have you?"

"You really want to know?"

"No. None of it. Just tell me what I gotta do."

Alex got comfortable, and proceeded to do so.

* * * *

Planetoid One

Jaguar kept her time with Francis simple, and adhered to her promise not to dig. After the guard dropped him off and left her alone with him they pulled their folding chairs to the table—the only furniture in the barren room—and used their two hours to put together a complicated puzzle.

Francis liked puzzles, the slow process of matching shape to shape soothing him, creating order in his disorganized nervous system. She had no trouble, and learned nothing worthwhile. She only noticed that Francis seemed twitchier than usual. He had a new tic in his face, and a tremor in his hand. She'd have to ask Adrian to find out what meds they had him on. Whatever they were using wasn't working.

After lunch in the cafeteria she went back to her room to find a packet of papers on her desk. It had a large A scrawled across the front, followed by the words, 'courtesy of R.'

Diane's permanent file, from Rachel, via Adrian. She grinned. Rachel wasn't playing around with any of this.

She sat and opened it, slogged through a lot of evaluations and information about her benefits package, and moved on to the records on Diane and the schizophrenic girl. Here she quickly found an item of interest.

Regina hadn't mentioned that the girl was schizophrenic because she was a mutoid, or that she'd died shortly after all the dust had blown away. Cause of death was exsanguination, suicidally created. She'd apparently slashed her wrists, though that wasn't stated directly.

The transcript of Susan Eideler's testimony on Diane's involvement with the girl was a lot more straightforward.

When asked what made her suspect Diane, Susan said, "Diane's gay. She won't admit it, but she is. And she showed special interest in the girl, so I was worried."

Asked how she knew Diane was gay, Susan answered, "Because she's had affairs with women since she's been here."

"Did she now?" Jaguar murmured, and thought about it. Diane had been engaged to a man, so bisexual would be more accurate than gay, maybe. But Susan—at what candy shop did she buy her treats, and what did it matter to her where Diane bought hers? Jaguar saw lots of fertile ground for questions here. She closed up the file and went to her next task, her interview with Susan.

They met in the same room where she spent time with Francis, because Regina thought she'd get better results if she was in a room without cameras.

"And who'll believe me if I don't have a record?" Jaguar asked pointedly.

Regina had opened her eyes wide. "I will," she said.

When Susan entered the room Jaguar thought maybe Regina was right. Susan's mood, easily read, was both truculent and confident, the confidence probably stemming from the fact that she'd been put in a room without surveillance. And Jaguar knew that overconfidence would get you every time. Armed with the material she'd gleaned from Diane's personnel file, when Susan was seated she dove right in.

"So. Were you pissed at Diane because you hate gays, or because she wouldn't have sex with you?" she asked.

Susan's jaw dropped, then she composed herself. "Listening to gossip?" she asked.

"Reading the facts you didn't want me find in Diane's personnel file. When you accused her of sleeping with a mutoid girl you testified she was gay, but in denial about it. While she may have liked women in that special way, I know she'd never abuse a mutoid. So was it homophobia, or homophilia that got you?"

Susan's hand, resting on the table, clenched and unclenched. "That's why I didn't want you digging around in Diane's life. You make it all seem so sordid."

"What do you call accusing her of raping a prisoner? Joy and light?"

"I—I didn't accuse her of rape. I had a suspicion and we're required to report," she said, and Jaguar, watching her face carefully, noted the lie.

Based on that, she made another judicious stab in the dark. "Where'd the suspicion come from?" she asked. "Because she didn't want to sleep with you anymore?"

Susan's hand made a fist and she moved it forward as she leaned in hard toward Jaguar. "Stay the hell out of my mind."

Jaguar laughed. "I was just reading your face. If I want what's in your mind, it'll go more like this."

She reached over and put a hand on Susan's wrist, held it there, kept her eyes in focus. Maybe Francis was off limits, but Susan wasn't.

Quickly and expertly she skimmed the surface of her thoughts, following the trail through the associations that inevitably led to a few brief and pertinent glimpses of what had happened between her and Diane. Then, to her surprise, something else occurred.

A series of images, disjointed, flashes of faces and scenes, the kind she associated with her capacity for clear-seeing.

Susan's hand reached out to another hand, small and well-kept, couldn't tell if it was male or female. Susan with a gloating smile. Then, the hand she'd touched working a small black box, a technology Jaguar didn't recognize. The same hand, at a keyboard, changing one number on a line of incomprehensible gibberish. A sense of satisfaction, felt by whoever owned this hand, showing on Susan's face.

Then Susan jerked away, pushed her chair back and stood.

"You can't do that here," she growled.

"So sorry," Jaguar said. "My mistake." She leaned back and deliberately relaxed. She hadn't asked to work her clear-seeing, and doing so left her jangled, wanting only to be quiet and study what she'd seen. But she had work to do here, and she'd seen something else, more immediately pertinent in Susan's thoughts.

"Does that mean I shouldn't mention what I learned? That you were indulging in the infraction of—what is the word? Fraternizing is entirely wrong, but sororitizing isn't a word as far as I know. Hmm. Having sex with Diane? Fucking your Teacher?"

"I wasn't her supervisor then," Susan spat back at her. "There's no code against what *we* were doing."

Hecate, Jaguar thought. Like she needed Alex dragged into it now. She ignored it and kept digging. "So you and Diane were having a fling. Did Ned know?"

Susan's face showed reluctance, then pride. "They broke it off. What happened with me made her realize she wasn't a good match with Ned."

"Really? But she didn't leave him until after the mutoid girl incident. Maybe that little debacle was your way of letting him know about you two? Very convenient, if you ask me."

"I did what I thought was right," Susan said firmly.

"Right for you. But she left you anyway. Because you reported her?"

Susan shifted uncomfortably. Jaguar caught her wrist again quickly, and when Susan pulled back, just as quickly released her. Easy to read what was in her. It was an open wound, still oozing. And what she saw in it surprised even her.

She blinked up at Susan. "Oh," she said. "Hell."

Susan's tightly held face worked hard against its own collapse. For the first time, Jaguar felt sorry for her. And for the first time, she thought she understood the tangle of emotions she'd somehow stumbled into with Diane, with Susan, with this case.

Whether it was true or not, Susan believed most firmly that Diane had been in love with someone else. In love with Jaguar.

She thought back to the time they'd shared, scanned her memories for anything indicating that kind of attraction. She came up blank. If it was there, she'd missed it. Probably Diane, strict about protocol, would go far to hide it, and Jaguar, not wired that way, wouldn't necessarily feel it. Or possibly Susan was jealous for no reason.

"Did she tell you it was me, or were you just being paranoid?" Jaguar asked.

Susan glared at her. "I'm not paranoid. She talked about it. About you."

"Diane was no gossip-monger," Jaguar said.

"It wasn't like that. I—I knew something was wrong, and I made her tell me. She felt like she owed me the truth. Then I found out what you were doing with the prisoners, what you really are, and I let her know."

Old pieces of dusty old puzzles fell into place, making sense at last. Diane was already struggling with her attraction to women, and then her attraction to her Teacher. Finally, she couldn't forgive herself for falling in love with an empath. That struck Jaguar as particularly sad.

"Just so you know, we never had sex," she said to Susan. "Nor did she ever ask me to. In fact, she must've gone to a lot of trouble to hide what she felt, because I didn't have a clue."

"But she wanted to," Susan blurted out. "That's all that mattered."

"Not after you snitched on me she didn't," Jaguar pointed out.

"Yes, she did. She just had one more reason to hate herself for it." Susan's voice was hard with long-nurtured, impotent rage. "But she did the right thing. She got rid of you. *She* had integrity," she said, as if Jaguar never had, and never would.

"Why're you pissed at me about it?" Jaguar demanded. "I didn't go after her."

Pain crossed Susan's face. No, Jaguar thought. She couldn't be angry at Diane. She loved her too much. There was too much at stake there. Diane's charismatic energy, her way of drawing people to her, of show-ing them their best selves, was too great a lure. And if she rejected you, did that mean you weren't the person her warmth reflected back to you? Did that part of you go away, too? For Susan, apparently it had.

"It doesn't matter," Susan said. "None of that matters. She's still dead, and Francis still killed her. None of this makes a dent in that."

"Sure it does. It gives two other people a motive for killing her. And it gives you a great big motive for wanting me here so you can kill me, too."

"That's—that's ridiculous," Susan said.

"Not at all. A woman scorned is still scorned, whether the scorner has a penis or not. And you're not someone who actually lets go of anger. You save it up, let it accrue interest."

"Are you actually trying to say I killed Diane?"

"I'm considering it as a possibility. There's still a chance the murder wasn't motivated by personal issues. Could be some system wide cor-ruption like smuggling or embezzling. For now, you just go on the list."

"There's no embezzling here," Susan said.

Jaguar noted her complacency when she said this, and that she said embezzling rather than smuggling. She also noted how very different it was from the anger she showed about her own motives.

"Not embezzlement, then," Jaguar said. "Smuggling?"

"Hmmph," Susan said. "You wish. Anything to make us look bad."

"Then murder," Jaguar said definitively.

"If you mean Francis killing Diane—"

"I mean, someone hoping to kill me."

At this, a flash of fear, quickly smothered. Enough for now, and all she was likely to get.

"That's even more ridiculous," Susan said quickly.

"All theories are ridiculous, until you find out one of them is right," Jaguar said. She stood. "You can go now. I've got what I came for."

Susan sat and gaped. Jaguar was about to tell her to get the hell out when she saw a shimmering of color and light just behind her. She stared at it as it shaped itself into two women. Mathias and Lopez.

"Jesus Christ," she groaned. "Not you two again."

Susan turned and looked where she was looking, then back. "What are you talking about?" she asked.

Jaguar shook her head, and the forms dissipated. "Nothing," she said. "Get out of here. I'm done with you."

"You're crazy," Susan said. "That's what you are. We should have you here, on medication."

"Keep dreaming," Jaguar said.

"I mean it," Susan continued. "People like you—you mess with minds and it does something to you. There's research on that. We've done research about it."

Jaguar thought if she stood there another second, she'd follow her impulse to clock Susan in the jaw. Instead, she took the high road.

"Fuck you," she said mildly. Then she turned on her heel and left the room.

CHAPTER 8

Adrian wasn't sure which annoyed him more; the fact that Rachel was a better hacker than he was, or the fact that she already had a girlfriend.

In two days he'd learned more from her than he had in all his years as a con man. It was a shame, in a way, that he wasn't going back to that business. He'd clean up big this time around. Well, he thought, maybe someday. For now he'd do as he was assigned, and take care of Jaguar.

His job of record—mostly inputting data and reconciling records from various departments—allowed him plenty of time for dipping into the personal emails of those on Alex's hot list for suspects. So far he'd found plenty of gossip about Jaguar, none of it complimentary.

Some of it rehashed her history, and some made comments on how tight her jeans were. There were also the usual comments about empaths, but then he found a story floating around about her talking to herself, or to imaginary friends, in the halls. From his experience with Jaguar, he knew that if she talked to someone, there was someone there, so he'd have to ask her about that. In the meantime, he moved on to email from production manager Derek Rhinehart.

Just as he accessed those files he saw his supervisor, Jamie Bender, approaching. He quickly closed up his search and went back to work.

She came up behind him and put a hand that was thick and encrusted with cheap rings on his shoulder. Her hair was way too blonde for reality, and she smelled of someone who drank too much wine and used too much perfume. Adrian resisted the urge to back away. Instead, he forced himself to smile at her, his best smile. The one that implied she was of interest to him in many ways.

"Hey, Jamie," he said. "How's it hanging?"

"Isn't that what I'm supposed to ask you?" she replied, letting her fingers work his shoulder.

"Ha," he said. "Careful, or they'll get you for harassment."

She laughed, but removed her hand. "Me? I'm like, miss innocence, considering."

"Considering what?"

"What else goes on around here."

"Oh? Please do tell."

She pursed her very red lips, her version of a seductive smile. "I shouldn't."

"But you will," he said. He'd quickly realized that gossip was the food of the people on Planetoid One. They loved nothing more than to eat it, or offer it up on a platter. The juicier it was, the more that confirmed your status here. Fresh gossip was power in this place.

"Oh, Adrian. You're so bad," Jamie said.

"But in a good way," he said. "Go ahead. I'm new here, and starved for some hot dish."

She shook her head, her carefully composed curls not moving an inch. "All my dish is pretty cold. You probably already know about the woman from Three who's looking into Diane Lasher's murder?"

"I heard about it, but nobody'll tell me the whole story. I'm guessing they don't know."

"Because they don't have access to all the information," Jamie said, bridling proudly. "What she's doing is secure. *Very* secure," she said.

"But you have access."

"Of course I do. That's my job," she preened. "She's not just investigating Francis Durero. She's also looking into what happened with Diane and that poor dead mutoid girl."

"See, I don't even know about a mutoid girl."

"Of course not. That's from the Infirmary, and they're always tough to get into. Now they're being extra careful because of the investigation. We're under orders to let that woman nowhere near them."

"Orders from who?"

Jamie waved a pudgy hand. "Higher ups."

"Suits," Adrian said, shaking his head. "So what happened to the girl?"

"Well, like I said, not everyone knows, but I have to spot check the surveillance cameras in the infirmary, and I happened to see it before it got erased."

"Keep going," Adrian said, maintaining patience as best he could.

Jamie leaned in and Adrian resisted the urge to back away. "There she was, just donating blood—there's a regular blood donor program here—and she rips out her IV, makes a big mess. She starts bleeding all over everything, tearing through the rooms. And the whole time she's screaming, 'Don't let them kill me. Don't let them. They eat us alive.' Stuff like that."

Adrian whistled, low and long. "That doesn't sound good."

Jamie shrugged. "She was schizo, so everyone figured her meds were off. But I'm not so sure. There was some stink about Diane—you know—abusing her. And then she ends up dead, and the surveillance tape just goes away. So you tell me."

Adrian nodded solemnly. "I see what you mean. And you don't want that Addams woman to know about it?"

"Absolutely not. Orders from Susan Eideler, and she's a bitch on wheels."

"I'll hold the fort. Thanks for the heads up." He allowed himself to touch Jamie's hand lightly, to indicate his continued interest. Then he moved on to something that interested him much more. Something that had to do with Infirmary records she might know about. Records he thought were trying to hide something.

"Hey—maybe you can help me, since you're all about Infirmary stuff. I'm trying to figure out these damn billing codes. What's 223? It's a death code, but it just says 'natural causes,' and I need something more specific for insurance records."

"Oh, God," Jamie said. "Death codes are so strange here. Everyone complains about them. You'll have to talk to someone in records. Go see Marie Rapport. She's Infirmary. Tell her I sent you."

"Thanks," Adrian said. "You're the best, Jamie."

"How would you know?"

Adrian pulled up his courage. "Maybe someday I'll find out," he said, hoping like hell he never had to make good on that.

* * * *

When he got to the Infirmary he was allowed into the clerical offices, just outside the wards. He found Marie Rapport easily, and decided she was a much better prospect than Jamie, in more ways than one.

Her figure was full of curves, her long blonde hair soft and inviting, her blue eyes sharp with intelligence. In very short order he made it clear that he admired all her assets in the most respectful way possible, and was given an access code otherwise unavailable to him through the very old trick of looking like he knew it already. Though he was digging with a spoon rather than a shovel, it was a place to start. And he figured if the world was a computer, Rachel could dig to hell and back with no more than a spoon.

With that out of the way, he decided to explore a few other avenues of interest. As Marie sat at her desk, he leaned against it comfortably and asked, "Hey—you know any way to earn some extra cash around here? The work's interesting and all, but they don't pay much.'

She smiled as if she approved of a man with ambition. "There's a few stores that hire part time, though most places just use mutoids," she rolled her eyes to indicate her opinion of that.

"You don't like them?"

"The dumb ones irritate me, and the smart ones scare me. They look at you like they can see through your clothes."

"Huh. Well, anyway, I was thinking of something a little more lucrative than retail." He leaned in close, confidentially. "I heard there's other jobs for the right people. The ones who can keep their mouths shut."

Marie's eyes narrowed. "If you've been listening to that gossip about Derek, you'd better stop," she said, sounding distinctly offended.

Adrian backed off, held out a conciliatory hand. "Derek? Who's that?" he asked.

"You know. Rhinehart. Production manager. All the talk that he's got the best housing and a place on the home planet in Monaco because he's—well, escorting Regina Hawthorne around."

"Governor Hawthorne?" Adrian asked, looking appropriately aghast. "But she's got thirty years on him."

"At least. And as if she would. She's the most single woman I ever met. Very independent. And he's a nice man. Quiet and courteous."

Adrian grinned. "Just the way you like them," he noted. "I'll keep that in mind. But I didn't mean that. I just heard sometimes the big guys want someone to run their errands for them. Private stuff. I'm good with private stuff."

"Oh," she said, unbending enough to smile. "That. I suppose we all have our secrets. Thank God."

He leaned in close again. "Absolutely," he said.

She didn't object. In fact, she rested her chin in her hand, her elbow on her desk, which brought her very pleasant face even closer. "Hard to keep them around here," she said.

"I'm getting that," he agreed.

She looked around. "It's being all closed in that does it," she said. "Sky island fever, they call it. Creates lots of gossip. And we can't even talk about the weather, since we don't have any, so people dig right in to the messy stuff."

"I'm good with messy, too," Adrian noted. "At least, I know how to clean it up."

"Huh," Marie said. "That's funny."

"You're not laughing."

"Funny, strange," she corrected.

"In what way?"

"That's one of the rumors going around—when Diane Lasher got herself killed, which I'm guessing you know about already. Some people said it was a Clean up job—by a professional. A Cleaner, you know? Because she knew something she shouldn't."

This surprised even Adrian. He thought fast. "Because of that mutoid girl who died?"

"You heard about that, too?"

"Yeah. Donating blood, and she goes nuts, rips out the IV and so on."

"That," Marie brushed it away. "I thought you meant about her and Diane having sex. Which is why people said it was a clean up job. You know. Sweep that right under the rug."

"Oh," he said, disappointed. Just more gossip. "That. Do you believe it?"

"Not at all," Marie said. "I just thought of it, when you said you clean up messes." She smiled at him, very friendly. "You're not like a mole or anything, are you? Here to spy on us?"

"What I'm spying for has nothing to do with work," he said. "Do you like to dance?"

As it turned out, she did, and Adrian began to think there might be more than one advantage to his new job.

* * * *

Planetoid Three

Adrian reported to Rachel as soon as he was free to do so, and she appreciated his capacity to hack human emotions, a skill as particular and rare as computer hacking. Using the access code he gave her, she worked her way into infirmary records, which turned out to be a maze of almost indecipherable data. A messy system, she thought, and tsk-tsked to herself about it.

Data on items as simple as death rates wasn't kept in any one place, but distributed in a scattered way, some of it recorded in cause of death, some in death dates, others in age or by the crime the prisoner was convicted of. To find the total you'd have to correlate each death individually with all the other factors they were filed under, then consolidate them. It would take days. She shook her head at it and moved on, seeking something that made sense.

A few hours later, when her neck was stiff and she was about to give up, she came across an obscure reference to something called the BD program, filed under Auxiliary Services.

"What the hell is BD?" she murmured, and pursued it. Another hour of trailing numbers, and she felt a strange chill go down her spine. She double-checked the numbers, and came to a conclusion that left her stunned.

BD stood for blood donation. And Planetoid One sold a lot of blood.

In fact, checking their numbers against those on Two and Three, it looked like they sold more than the other two Planetoids combined. She had no idea if that was meaningful or helpful, but it was strange, so she sent that, along with everything else, to Alex.

She took a break to stand and stretch, and thought seriously of calling it a day. She was already three hours into overtime, and getting hungry. But the death rate numbers niggled at her, disturbing her sense of order. She sat back down, thinking maybe she'd just diddle with them a little bit more. If she could create a program that would crunch the numbers into a few coherent stats, it would be time well spent.

An hour later she was well into starting that process when her telecom buzzed. She punched the receive button without looking.

"What?" she said, her focus on her program.

"Me, Rachel," a voice replied, and she looked to the telecom. Alex.

"Oh. Hi. Sorry. I was deep in."

Alex smiled. "No apology necessary. Find anything good?"

"Maybe. I won't know for a few hours. You need me for something else?"

"A few things."

"Start with thing one," she suggested.

"How's my paperwork going?"

"All pushed through," she said. "It'll be another day before we get the sign-off from One, though."

Another day. Give me patience, he thought, and give it to me now. Then, he moved on. "Okay. Thing two. Talk to me about blood donation on One."

"You read that already? You're fast. Like the report said, they sell a lot. In fact, they give the biggest sellers on the home planet a run for their money. Beats one of them by 5 percent."

"How in hell do they manage that?" Alex asked.

"Good question, and I can't answer it yet. It all goes through the infirmary, and their records are a mess. Meantime, Adrian's looking deeper into it. He says he smells a con."

"Anything more specific?"

"Not yet. Just that it has to do with their medical records."

"Not their production records?"

"He's following his nose, which says they're hiding too much on the medical side, and I'm inclined to agree. Lots of mandatory reporting data is obscured by other data, organized in a way that's unreadable."

"Nothing unusual about messy records in big systems like ours," Alex said.

"Trying to read their stuff makes ours look like See Jane Run. I'm going through death rates now, to see if I can come up with something that makes sense."

"Okay. Keep at it. And keep me posted."

"Will do," she said, and signed off.

She glanced up at the clock, thought she really should take a break and get something to eat. Then she shook her head. Jaguar wasn't getting any breaks. Neither was Alex.

The clock kept ticking, and she turned her face back to her work.

CHAPTER 9

Planetoid One

The Cleaner was satisfied with his work so far.

He'd used his Projection Amp successfully in the halls and the interview room, setting it precisely to the neural input of his subject so nobody else would see what she saw. That was tricky, something very few people knew how to do, and he felt a natural pride in it.

He'd chosen the images he projected carefully, based on her long history of protecting women. Seeing images of the women Francis killed would create a good amount of cognitive dissonance and emotional instability in her, putting her off her game. In most cases, if you did that right the subject would screw themselves.

He'd wanted to use Diane Lasher in the projected images as well, knowing her vexed history with his subject, but it wouldn't translate to his amp. He still wasn't sure why—maybe some corruption in the digital format. In the meantime what he had was good enough to make her look bad to a security guard, who would spread the word in reports and gossip. That was an important part of the discrediting process, and it was going well.

From all he knew of her, he also figured it would unbalance her in some important ways. In spite of her long career of dealing with hardcore criminals, her history showed she was the type to actually believe in ghosts and other imaginary friends.

By all reports she was smart as hell and shouldn't be buying into nonsense like that, which made part of him want to take her by the shoulders and shake her hard. She'd survived Manhattan during the Killing Times, just as he'd survived LA. Surely she knew better. There were no ghosts in Manhattan or LA.

In fact, more than once he wished to see them, a child thinking they might have the power to save him. Some nights he'd woken up crying for the ghost of his mother or father to come and help him, but they never showed. He couldn't imagine any ghosts had helped her.

Still, he wouldn't piss and moan about her beliefs, since they worked to his advantage. Instead, he took his initial success and started moving it into the public realm. The next time she saw ghosts, she'd have a much bigger audience to witness her insanity.

And he had other moves in the works. He'd found a way to encourage Francis out of his long vacation from killing, something which could easily leave her either further discredited, or dead. He also had an alternate back-up plan for dead. It wasn't as pretty as his A Plan, but it was effective. He'd made good choices, and was happy with them.

Initially he'd considered using her supervisor, who was also her lover according to gossip. Ultimately he decided against it. Dzarny was known to be damn protective of her, and not somebody to mess with. In general the Cleaner found there was nothing worse than a man with an obsession, so he left it alone. His technology was much more reliable than the unpredictable motion of the human heart. Using his tools, he felt the pleasure of control, the pleasure of his art. And the particular picture he'd paint for her should be a masterpiece.

* * * *

Jaguar made her way through a useless interview with the ME who performed Diane's autopsy, and another even more useless interview with the orderly who found her body. After, she had lunch with Regina, in her house, where the food was real, and very good.

As they ate, Jaguar thought about old times, days when she and Diane would sit at this table and argue amicably about the right policy for the Planetoids, about programming for prisoners, about everything. She was visited by a vivid memory of one lively discussion on the problems of testing runs when Diane's face lit up, she lifted her arms and waved her fork around. "Don't you just *love* this?" she demanded. "Don't you just love *us*?"

Regina's eyes shone at Diane, her protege, someone she was clearly grooming for a governor's position. Both of them turned to Jaguar, who showed her satisfaction by leaning back and smiling broadly.

Now, at the same table, both Regina and Jaguar were more subdued. There was a lot they couldn't talk about these days. Jaguar's objections to the programming had gone well beyond amicable discussion. And she still didn't feel safe talking about Alex.

Instead, they talked about problems with the ventilation system, the way gossip flourished here and how much harm it could do, some of the less touchy programming innovations, such as the psychodrama settings they were trying to build.

But as they made their way through soup and sandwiches Diane was an invisible presence, memory of her life and her death as palpable as the food. By the time they got to coffee, Jaguar gave up trying to avoid the topic.

She sighed, shook her head. "You must miss her," she said.

Regina knew who she meant. Her face grew wistful. "Very much," she said. "I hoped—well, she was like a daughter to me. I thought she'd go far. And she was always such a pleasure to have around."

"She was," Jaguar agreed. "Even after she got me booted, I knew that about her."

"I know how difficult it is for you to be here," Regina commented. "I see it in your eyes."

The corner of Jaguar's mouth lifted in a wry smile. "Trying to stop the execution of a man who's convicted of killing a good friend who tried to have me fired, while I deal with a bunch of people who hate me? Not too bad."

Regina laughed. "Tell you what. Get through your next meeting and then take the night off. Go dancing at the Terra. You can skip the grant-writing meeting this evening."

To Jaguar, that sounded almost like heaven. "You want to join me?" she asked.

"Absolutely not," Regina said. "You don't need me hanging around while you flirt, and I don't want to hang around and watch you."

"More information than you need?"

"Something like that. Have fun."

She planned on it. But first she had to get through an afternoon meeting, on the financial status of export programs.

After her leisurely lunch with Regina she was running late, and she wasn't sure how to get to the meeting room where it was held, so she stopped in the corridor and asked directions from a janitor—a mutoid who was emptying trash cans, and who dragged a limp leg as he walked.

He nodded at her question and moved his arm in a gesture that said 'follow me.' He walked ahead of her, silent. She followed, feeling like she'd entered a Hollywood film set, and was trailing Igor to the master's den.

When they got to the stairwell door that led to the computer rooms and the infirmary, she stopped him. "Hey—Are you sure this is right?"

He made a noise that might have been laughing, or allergies. He went through the door. She threw her hands up, then moved after him. Only when she pulled the door open did she realize what she'd just seen.

He didn't open the door. He walked through it.

She bit her lip to keep from cursing soundly, out loud. She entered the stairwell and looked down. There he was, just ahead of her, either a projection of her own aberrant mind or somebody's idea of a joke, gimping onward.

As she trailed after him she noted she felt no static, as she had with the images of Francis's victim. Memories of an assignment she'd had on

Planetoid Three's Virtual Reality site recurred to her. The energy of the VR had caused her psyche to spit out a retrojection of a holodemon, her own personal devil. But what part of her psyche would throw a mutoid at her? Maybe if she got a little closer, she could figure it out. She shook her head, and kept walking.

When the mutoid passed through the door at the bottom of the stairwell she sighed, then opened it and found herself once more facing a sign that said 'Infirmary'. This time the arrow pointed right. Apparently she'd been led to the same place, from the other side.

"Okay," she muttered. "I get it. There's something important in the Infirmary. Now can I go to my meeting?"

In answer the mutoid, who stood a few yards ahead, grinned and waved her to him.

She put her hands on her hips and addressed him.

"Who are you and what the hell do you want from me?" she asked. "Or what the hell are you, if that makes more sense."

He glanced over her shoulder, waved her forward more frantically.

She planted her feet where she was. "Not until you tell me who you are, and what you want," she insisted.

"For starters, I'd like to introduce myself," a voice said behind her.

She whirled to it, her hand raised in an attitude of attack. The speaker took a step back, raised both his arms.

"Whoa!" he said. "Didn't mean to offend."

She backed up, blinked up at him. He was a big man, broad of girth and shoulder, tall, with close-cropped hair and bright blue eyes. The kind of man who would puff up fast if he didn't watch what he ate, and the kind of man who probably wouldn't watch what he ate. Though he wore a blue suit and white shirt, somehow, she imagined he had tattoos.

"Sorry," she said. "I was looking for a room. I'm late for a meeting."

He gave a polite laugh. "Not a lot of meetings in the infirmary," he noted.

"Yeah. This man gave me directions."

"What man?" he asked. "The invisible one you were talking to?"

She looked back toward the infirmary. The hall was empty. "The one—well, he's gone now. I think maybe he didn't really know where he was going."

"Mutoid?" the man asked.

"Actually, yes."

"You really can't trust them. Where are you trying to get to?"

"Conference room C21—in the Business Hall?"

"Then you're in luck. I'm heading that way. Probably for the same meeting. Fiscal reports?"

"That'd be it," Jaguar said without enthusiasm.

"It'll be just as bad as you imagine," he confirmed. "Derek Rhinehart's running it. A nice man, but they don't make them any duller. You're Dr. Addams, aren't you? The Teacher from Three who's making everyone crazy?"

"My reputation precedes me," she noted.

"It certainly does. And you seem to be living up to it."

She raised an eyebrow at him. "I haven't blown up anything yet," she said.

"I was referring to a different part of your reputation. It's not all bad, you know." He looked her up and down, and she got it.

"Glad to hear it," she said mildly. "And you are?"

"Clyde Holmesby," he said, and stuck out a surprisingly small hand. "At your service."

He was, she thought, almost everything a PR man should be. Looked you right in the eye when he wasn't staring at your more private parts, exuded confidence, and had a smooth, deep speaking voice. His hand smelled vaguely of Old Spice, as if he'd used it in the past and it lingered around his person. Still, she suspected he had tattoos, and that wasn't what you'd expect from a PR guy. She wondered if he was an ex-prisoner, often the case on the Planetoids.

"I've heard your name," she said. "Regina told me you were on the home planet."

"I was. I'm back now. Glad to be back, too. I've got a ton of work to do, with our new Buy a Bear Christmas program. But I'm sure you'll hear all about that at a different meeting."

"Right," Jaguar said. She still had to interview both this man and Derek Rhinehart, though she doubted she'd get anything useful from either. If they were in on something, they'd lie, and she had no way to make them tell the truth. If not, they'd have nothing to tell her.

She sighed. "Shall we go ahead to our fate?"

"Right this way," he said, and waved her on.

They walked, making small talk. Since they couldn't talk about the weather, because there wasn't any, Clyde rambled on about which bits of bubble dome machinery weren't working.

He started with the new ventilation system, which was incredibly cost-effective, but didn't mesh well with the older systems it fed. Since it went in they'd had all kinds of problems with temperature regulation, with lighting. He talked about it at some length, apparently confusing Jaguar for someone who gave a rat's ass, then concluding with the obvious.

"Y'know," he said, "we can build a planetoid. You'd think we could get the lights to work, right? I mean, am I right?"

That carried them into the conference room, where others were already seated around a large oval table while Derek set up his presentation at the head of the room. Clyde brought her around and introduced her to everyone there, ending with Derek. Taking hold of his dishrag hand and shaking it, looking at his bland face and listening to his toneless voice, Jaguar had a sinking feeling about both the interview with him and the upcoming meeting.

"I trust you find your residence is comfortable, and the staff is giving you all you need to complete your job?" he asked politely.

"It's all fine," she said. "Everyone's been very cooperative so far."

"I'm glad," he said. "I, of course, will be available for interview at your convenience."

Jaguar wondered if he was partially deaf, or perhaps tone deaf, his voice was so aggressively monotone. "I appreciate that," she said.

"Well, I liked Diane a great deal. We worked closely together in production programs, and I'm hoping someone will get to the bottom of this."

"Don't you think Francis did it?" she asked, surprised.

"Frankly, no," he said, looking defiant.

"Now, Derek," Clyde chimed in, with the air of a man who was humoring an obsession. "You know Francis is riddled with problems."

"I still don't think he did it," Derek said firmly. "He was very fond of her, and he'd been doing quite well in the work programs. There was no reason for him to—to go off the deep end."

This was apparently the strongest phrase he had in his store. After declaring it, he expressed his deep dismay by shaking his head slowly back and forth and tsk-ing gently.

"Really," Clyde said. "If not Francis, then who?"

Derek slewed his eyes around. "You know my thoughts on the matter."

"Ned? You still think Ned? That weenie?" Clyde laughed heartily, but looked a little nervous. Ned was in his office, one of his workers. "Anyway," he added, "you should save your thoughts for the official interview. Right now, I hear you have something happier going on. Aren't you escorting our buyer from the home planet around this week? Carrie Jones?"

"I am," he said, then sighed with resignation. "She wants to go dancing."

"Nothing wrong with that. She's a pretty woman."

Derek looked mildly shocked. "I don't dance."

"Well, I do. I'll go with you. And maybe we can convince Dr. Addams to join us. I'm guessing you're quite a dancer."

"I hope they have the air conditioning working," Derek said dismally. He turned to Jaguar. "I sweat a great deal."

She was saved from the need to create a response by Clyde, who touched her arm. "Let's find our seats, shall we?"

He led her around the table, but the chair he stopped her at was already taken. A woman with a high forehead and long black hair sat in it. She smiled broadly, revealing a mouth that needed a few more teeth. Jaguar noted the blue patch on the side of her neck, the tag on the sleeve of her white shirt that identified her as a prisoner. She wondered if attendance at meetings was part of her punishment.

"Who let you in?" she asked amicably.

Overhead, the lights flickered indecisively and someone at the table said, "Oh, God. Not that again."

The woman in Jaguar's seat chortled and Jaguar shrugged. "You stay put. I'll find another chair."

"What?" Clyde asked.

She turned to him, saw his confused aspect. "It's not a problem," she said. "She can sit there."

He frowned at her. She turned back to the seat, gesturing to it by way of explanation. It was empty. She lifted her head, saw that others in the room were staring at her.

"Never mind," she said, and took the seat.

Clyde scratched at his head and looked like asking a few more questions, but Derek called them to order. Clyde sat, pulled a pitcher of water to them and poured some into the empty glass at her place. "Wish I could offer you something stronger," he murmured as Derek cleared his throat and began to talk.

Jaguar didn't bother listening, but instead spent time trying to figure out what the hell was going on. The problem was that she needed more information. Needed to get closer for a longer time with whatever was popping up all around her like prairie dogs out of holes. At least the holodemon had the decency to introduce himself, to spend time with her.

When figuring shit out failed her, she amused herself by dipping briefly into the minds of the others gathered around the table. She knew she could do so without anyone suspecting her. She was good at that, and they'd all be thinking about anything except what was going on in the room, their thoughts loose and perhaps helpful to her.

She got nothing, except a rude comment about the relationship between the size of Clyde's hand and his more private appendages. The woman who thought it had a bitter look. Apparently she'd been led to expect bigger things from him.

Dipping into Clyde's mind was trickier because he was paying attention to her, and therefore might connect the feeling of intrusion, however slight, directly with her. She decided to forego the opportunity. To keep from yawning, she reached for her water glass.

As she did, she noticed a slight tremor in the table. She stopped her hand from reaching, pressed it down on the sleek surface instead. Definitely vibrating. She looked around. No one else seemed to notice. Probably, she thought, some of the machinery that runs the place, humming under the floor. Something they're all used to, which seemed unusual only to her. She reached for the glass of water again.

It moved, sliding about an inch away.

She caught a gasp before it escaped, cast a glance around. Again, no one had noticed. But the room was getting colder, and they did notice that. One of the Supervisors pulled her suitjacket closer. "There goes the air-conditioning again," she grumbled.

The lightbulbs flickered briefly, went out and returned. Someone down the table from Jaguar made a tsk sound. Derek looked up, waited a moment, then continued talking.

Flickering lights. Bad temperature regulation. These were the complaints associated with the new ventilation system. But Jaguar knew of a different explanation. One that would also account for the very ephemeral people who kept leading her to the same place. She decided to put it to the test.

As Derek droned inexorably on she reached for the water glass again, and again it shifted just out of her grasp. She could have seen it as the strange motion that sometimes occurs over a thin film of water on a slippery surface, but just then Derek reached down to pick up his laser pen and it skittered away from him. He hesitated, reached for it again. This time it skittered all the way down the table, stopping directly in front of her, focusing its beam directly at her heart.

Everyone turned her way. She sensed a growing energy, something building toward crisis.

She smiled. "Quite a tilt in this room," she noted, and slid the laser pen back to the Derek.

As it moved across the table each glass of water followed, gliding smoothly behind. They met in a huddle in the center of the table, a strangely formed inanimate pack of creatures. Jaguar blinked. The room grew colder.

"Is someone playing a joke?" Clyde asked.

"More weird than funny if you ask me," someone replied..

Jaguar ignored them. Something was building. Something. It tingled in her skin, at the back of her neck, in the coldness of the air. It was imminent. It was—

"Look out," she snapped, and pushed herself away from the table, got her head down on her lap, covered it with her arms.

As she did every object on the table went into motion, shooting across the room into walls, flying up to the ceiling and crashing back down, spinning in mid air in front of them. Glasses shattered and water sprayed over the table. Jaguar peeked out from her protected position and saw people grabbing for notebooks, getting under the table, simply standing and staring. Someone was screaming. Someone seemed to be praying.

A hand brushed against her shoulder, and a voice, female and familiar, spoke within her.

You have to save us.

"A little late for that, isn't it?" she answered.

In response, a glass smacked her hard on the back of the head. "That," she said petulantly and loudly, "is quite enough."

And it stopped.

All objects found a resting place and rested. Everything settled down where it had been, and the volatile energy she'd felt dispersed. Warmth returned to the room.

She uncovered her head and sat up. Everyone stared at her.

"Well," she said. "Derek—you were saying?"

CHAPTER 10

Afternoon moved into evening and a variety of experts entered the conference room, trying to figure out what the hell happened. Regina had been called and would be there as soon as she disentangled herself from a more pressing prisoner health issue. Susan showed up almost immediately, though Jaguar didn't know who called her or what she had to do with any of it.

And of course, everyone else remained, nervous and inclined not to look at her. Derek stared at his laser pen sternly, as if it deserved a reprimand. Clyde moved between solicitous concern for her and a clear desire to detach himself from anything to do with this.

Jaguar sat in the leather swivel chair at the head of the table, her long legs stretched out and crossed at the ankles, her head propped up by her hands behind it, her eyes closed. An expert with a hand-held scanner stood at her side, asking questions.

"Are you carrying any unauthorized electronic, protonic, or laser devices?" he asked.

"Nope," she replied.

"Are you carrying any authorized—

"—No," she cut in.

"Have you—

"No," she said. "No, no, no, no, no. Anything else?"

The expert clucked his tongue at her. "Dr. Addams, when you do that, it creates a striatia in pitch and timbre, dragging the stressor readings into a chaotic zone."

"That'd be your problem," she responded.

She sensed someone else walking toward her, and from the feel of the energy—striated with anger, maybe—she guessed it was Susan.

"It'll be your problem when you're arrested," Susan said.

Jaguar answered without moving or opening her eyes. "For what? Broken glasses? Ruffled feathers? None of which, by the way, is my doing."

"This was a deliberate attempt to interfere with the functioning of a Planetoid prison facility. That's a felony."

This was the second time Susan had mentioned the possibility of capturing her as a prisoner. At least, Jaguar thought, she dreamed big. "That's extreme even for you, Susan."

"What you did is extreme," Susan rasped back.

Irritated, Jaguar sat up and opened her eyes. "I didn't *do* anything," she said. "This was either an expertly crafted piece of techno-fun, or a telekinetic joke, and I'm not a techie or a Telekine. Ask Regina. Ask the damn Pentagon, for fuck's sake. It's in the very thick file they have on me."

"Nobody else could or would do such a thing," Susan said.

"Sure they could."

"Who?" Susan demanded.

"Any Telekine worth their salt. And they didn't have to be in the room."

"That's convenient."

The hell with it, Jaguar thought. Nobody here would ever believe anything she said. She leaned back. Closed her eyes again. "Then maybe you have mice," she muttered.

Susan didn't respond, and Jaguar was aware of another presence approaching, then standing behind her. She felt a hand on her shoulder. She opened her eyes again, twisted her neck, and saw Regina.

"Will you tell them I'm not a Telekine?" she said.

Regina showed a much different face than she had at lunch, her lips pinched and lines showing around them. She spoke crisply. "I can't, Jaguar. Your testing run was never completed, if you remember. A technology meltdown. Three of them, in fact."

Once again she'd done it to herself, Jaguar thought. She'd blown out the testing technology to avoid being identified as an empath so they could hire her. Now it made her a suspect. And Regina seemed to be taking that seriously.

"You think I did this?" Jaguar demanded.

"I think," Regina said, "it raises some questions. For instance, is it possible you have psi capacities you can't control under stress? Maybe causing events you don't intend?"

Regina might think she was offering an easy out, but that accusation was actually worse than deliberate mischief, discrediting her ability to manage her arts. She answered accordingly.

"Sure," she said. "Otherwise, what's the fun in having them?"

"Jaguar, it's a serious question, with serious consequences riding on your answer. I'm told you seemed to know what was coming. And it stopped when you said stop. So I'll ask again—Is it possible you have psi capacities you can't control?"

Jaguar swiveled her chair to look at Regina fully. "No," she said, cool now.

"Are you sure?"

Jaguar scanned the faces in the room. She turned to the resident expert, let her tidal gaze rest on him and plucked a small but troubling thought about his internet activity from the deeper recesses of his mind. *Naughty naughty*, she whispered inside him. His face flushed deep red and he turned away. She moved on to Derek Rhinehart, who was worried she'd discover his tattoo, which said 'mother' and was in a rather odd location.

I'll never tell, she whispered into him, and he pressed a hand to his temple.

She moved away from him, and turned her gaze directly at Regina, who took a small step back, began to lift a hand as if to ward her off, then quickly subdued the gesture.

Jaguar allowed herself a smile. "I'm quite sure," she said.

A moment passed while the others in the room shifted uncomfortably and Susan looked daggers at her. Good, she thought. Let them feel what the empathic arts could do. For all their fear and ridicule, they didn't have a clue.

When Regina spoke, she had no more questions about control.

"Do you have any alternate explanation for what happened here?" she asked.

"Did any of your people test positive for telekinesis? That's one option."

"I'll check into it," Regina said. "Any other ideas?"

"Like I told Susan, a technogeek prankster. Maybe one who wants to make me look bad, since we might as well admit I'm not Miss Popularity here. Or maybe," she added, "you've got ghosts."

At this, Clyde let out a small and nervous chuckle.

"Jaguar, really," Regina said, but she was also smiling ever so slightly.

"I'm just saying. What happened is textbook poltergeist. The room went cold, electricity fluctuated, objects moved randomly. So—ghosts."

"You can't really mean that."

"It's all I've got," Jaguar said. "Either that, or someone who wants to make you believe you have ghosts. And I don't know enough about technology to tell you how they'd do that, in case you were about to ask. Regina, believe me, as I sat here listening to Derek slowly regurgitate every insipid financial fact I've never wanted to learn, my thoughts weren't any deeper than wondering if I brought a good pair of dancing shoes with me. If you remember, I'm supposed to go dancing tonight."

Regina looked at her hard and Jaguar let her. Taking her own personal survey, as she should. It was her turf. After a moment, her head moved a fraction of an inch in a nod. Jaguar relaxed. Regina just said she was in the clear, and so she would be.

"Let's leave the room to the experts," she said. "Probably it'll turn out to be a meaningless joke. And you'll get your dancing, Dr. Addams. You've earned it."

CHAPTER 11

Jaguar was glad enough to get herself inside the Terra Lounge, where she could blow off some steam, and report the day's events to Adrian.

Her first move was to head to the bar and order a tequila, with lime and salt. While she waited for it, she looked around. They had a DJ tonight and the bar was crowded, the dance floor seething with people. Among them she spotted Susan, doing a bad imitation of fast dancing with Ned Tackerson. She turned her face away, hoping they wouldn't spot her. She didn't need any more crap in her day.

When her drink arrived she readied the salt and lime in her hand, and did the right thing with the shot. She closed her eyes and savored the tingle and warmth as it entered her system.

"Good?" someone shouted at her over the music.

She turned, and saw Clyde standing behind her, a beer in hand. At a table not too far away she saw Derek, looking morose as he sat with a very attractive dark haired woman who was working to catch the eye of an equally attractive man nearby. "Hell," she said softly.

"What?" Clyde boomed. "I didn't quite catch that."

"Hello," she shouted back. "You abandoned Derek?"

Clyde laughed. "It'll do him good. I'll rescue him in a while."

He was in dressed down mode, wearing t-shirt and jeans, looking like he was trying to be hip and failing miserably. He was born to wear suits, which hid his paunch and lent him the trappings of importance.

"I'm glad you came out," he said. "Can I get you another drink? After today, you must need it."

Before she could answer he signaled the bartender, who brought her a second round. She let it sit, not sure she was quite ready for it, and not sure she wanted to accept a drink from Clyde. He was the type who'd make something of that.

She turned back to him, and he opened his mouth to speak just as the DJ put the next selection on. An old tune called Jailhouse Rock. She imagined they heard that a lot here.

"Dance?" Clyde shouted at her. "Leave your drink. The bartender'll watch it."

The bartender nodded, and Clyde got behind her, put a hand on her back and moved her toward the dance floor.

To her surprise, he wasn't a bad dancer. At least he knew how to manage a reasonable jitterbug. But his hands had a tendency to go places she didn't like, and she was glad the song ended before she felt obliged to whack him on the side of the head. The next song was Rank Rock, something from Springer Todd's group, Rumors of Pigs, and she wouldn't have minded staying on the dance floor for it. But Clyde shook his head and led her off the dance floor, his hand at her back again.

"I'm a jitterbug man," he said in her ear. "Can't do this new stuff."

She was contemplating telling him to remove his fucking hand from her person when she spotted Adrian, heading toward the bar, looking around for her. She lifted a hand, caught his attention, and he waved to her.

"Friend of yours?" Clyde asked, not sounded happy about it.

"From the home planet," she said. "I asked him to meet me here. Thanks for the dance."

She picked up her tequila from the bar and made her way toward Adrian. He met her halfway, saw the look on her face and waited.

She put a hand on his shoulder, spoke close to his ear. "Save my life again," she said.

He grinned. "How?" he asked.

"That man—the burly one—make him believe I've got more important things to do than dance with him."

"Sure thing," Adrian said. He put a hand to her hair, smoothed it back from her face. "Will that do?"

"Subtle and effective," she said. She lifted her tequila in salute, got ready to throw it down without salt or lime. She was totally unprepared for what happened next.

Without warning, without anything she could see or hear, something or someone bumped into her hard enough to knock her off balance. Her drink went flying, the contents spilling onto her shirt, the glass bouncing across the floor as she fell into Adrian, who caught her and held her until she righted herself.

"What the hell was that?" he asked.

Jaguar pulled away from him, looked around. "Someone bumped into me."

"Who?"

"I don't know. I was busy trying not to fall. Didn't you see?"

"I saw you throw your drink away. How much've you had, anyway?"

"That would've been my second. I'm nowhere near drunk enough."

They both looked around, but all they saw was a waitress stooping to retrieve the fallen glass. When Jaguar looked back to Adrian he was chewing on his lip, thinking hard.

"What?" she asked.

"Nothing. Just—I didn't know there was such a thing as pink tequila."

Pink? That made no sense. Adrian pointed at her shirt and she looked down at it. The stain the tequila made was a definite pink. Hot pink, in fact, all over a white silk shirt.

"Rat fuck," she said. "I liked this shirt." It was a simple button down, but tailored to suit her, and it looked great with her tight black leggings, her stiletto heeled boots. She scrubbed at it with her hand and only made it worse. Adrian caught hold of her hand and stopped it.

"I think you're missing the point," he said.

"That it's pink? Probably the lighting."

"Maybe," Adrian said.

The music moved into something hot and fast. "Let's dance," she suggested. "I've had a helluva day. We'll figure out the rest when the DJ goes home."

* * * *

Jaguar danced hard, for a good long time. She noticed that both Clyde and Derek didn't stick around too long after Adrian showed up, though the buyer Derek was escorting stayed to play with the very attractive man, whose eye she eventually caught.

At one point Susan saw her, glowered briefly, then ignored her completely, for which Jaguar was grateful. She wanted nothing more complicated than moving fast to loud music. She and Adrian spent the next few hours doing just that, and then Adrian called it a night. He had to get up early, he said. After all, he was a working man now.

They left the blasting sound of the Terra Lounge and walked down the quiet hallways, their ears still buzzing. As they approached her corridor, Jaguar turned her mind back to business.

"Adrian, you really didn't see anyone bump into me?" she asked.

"Not a soul or a body. Anyway, if someone did, I'd expect you to pull your knife on them."

"I can't," she said. "They took it."

"Does Rachel know?"

"I haven't been able to tell her or Alex."

"Don't you two—you know—talk?"

"Not here. The bubble domes interfere."

"Huh," he said. "For once, I have the advantage over you." He turned on his earpiece, which he'd switched off for the dancing. "Go ahead. Say it again. She's listening."

"She'll enjoy hearing about the flying glasses, too," Jaguar said.

Adrian eyed her. "Is that true? I heard some kind of gossip about an incident at a meeting, but I thought it was bullshit."

"All true," she said, and explained what happened. "And there's something Alex should know," she added. "Something I didn't mention. At the end, I had empathic contact. A voice saying 'you have to save us.'"

Adrian frowned at that. "Save us? What's that mean?"

"I don't have a damn clue," she said. "I'm just reporting. But it was empathic, so it was in the vicinity."

Adrian rolled his eyes, touched his earpiece. "You got that?" he asked quietly, and listened, nodded. "Yeah. There's more." He filled Rachel in on the rest, and then turned back to Jaguar.

"About that pink tequila," he said. "That still worries me."

"Maybe it's just what tequila does to silk," she said.

"And maybe not. I should get it checked out."

"How?"

"I've buddied up with someone in the lab. She'll take care of it for me."

"Ha," Jaguar said. "You work fast."

"I always did," he said demurely.

"In certain realms. How about the infirmary—you find anything there?"

"Rachel says their records are a mess, but she's digging. And I smell something not right. You know about the mutoid girl who died?"

"I do. That was in Diane's file."

"How about all the blood?"

"Pardon me?"

"The blood donation program, which is huge here. We're looking into it. That, and the death rates."

"What about the death rates?"

"It's kinda weird. Usually those stats are just laid out, with cause of death, all the pertinent information—just a simple table. Here, it's all buried. Wait a second—" He paused, listened to whatever was being said in his ear. Then, to Jaguar. "Okay, Rachel says she's got a program running to figure it out but so far all she's getting are crazy numbers."

"How crazy?" she asked.

He listened, nodded. "Like over fifteen percent annual."

"Is that a lot?" Jaguar asked. She didn't keep track of stats.

"Yeah," Adrian said. "A lot of a lot."

She ruffled her hair. "Well, keep digging. See what turns up."

They stopped in front of her door, and at this point Adrian turned his earpiece off again.

He looked at her directly, no bullshit about his interest this time. "You want company?" he asked.

"Sorry. No joy for you."

He sighed. "Is it Alex?"

"How'd you guess?"

"I saw it coming miles away. From somewhere near Leadville, Colorado, in fact."

She smiled at his reference to their past, when he'd been her prisoner and ended up helping her save Alex from a group of animated dead men in Leadville. "Then you saw it before I did," she admitted.

"I think lots of people saw it before you did. So you're not even, like, playing around a little?"

"Not happening, Adrian," she said.

He eyed her. "That's new," he noted. "He must be special."

Her expression was as complex as good coffee, and just as warm. "He took my knife in his chest to save my life," she said. "Special enough for you?"

He gave a whistle, soft and low. "I can't compete with that." Then, he smiled. "I always suspected you were a romantic. Good to know I was right. But I'll need your shirt anyway. I'm getting that pink shit tested."

He held a hand out for it. She grinned back at him. "Close your eyes," she said.

He raised an eyebrow at her. "That serious?"

"Yeah," she said. "Do it."

He did so.

She took off her shirt, put it in his hand, then kissed him on the cheek. "Here's to old times," she whispered to him.

Adrian smoothed the shirt. He heard the sound of her door opening and closing. He opened his eyes and saw she was gone. "Yeah," he said. "Old times."

As he walked away he paid no attention whatsoever to the surveillance cameras, or to the man who stood in shadow, a small recording device held in his hand.

CHAPTER 12

In the last hours that could be called night on Planetoid One, The Cleaner sat in his room, stared down at his recorder and frowned. He was reviewing the information he'd retrieved from the meeting he witnessed between Dr. Addams and her friend, and he didn't like it.

The equipment, more sensitive than his hearing, had picked up enough of their conversation to tell him she knew too much, and this man was helping her find out more. And he'd taken her shirt, which, if tested, would show something he didn't want made visible.

Somehow she'd managed to get back-up, and they were drawing too close to the truth. He ran a hand over his face. He'd had a rough day, and he wasn't used to that. His jobs always went smoothly, always stayed within his consummate control.

This was shaping up differently. First, that meeting, which was more than he'd bargained for. Some of the events were his creation. The moving glasses. The laser pen. The flickering lights. But he'd programmed an ethereal outline of one of Francis's victims, and it never appeared, though something did, at the wrong time and in the wrong place, because she talked to it. He didn't know what it was because he couldn't see it, which was also all wrong. And he'd programmed only one glass dumping water onto her. The rest—the cold in the room, all that glorious mess—wasn't part of the program. Something must be wrong with his equipment.

He didn't have time to check it before going to the Terra Lounge, where he had to make sure her drink was taken care of. He'd worried about the color, but he knew it wouldn't be visible in the dark glasses the Terra Lounge used, not something she'd notice as she slugged it down. It certainly wasn't supposed to end up on her shirt. And why did that happen?

It looked as if someone had knocked her hard, but he couldn't see anyone. That had to mean another equipment failure. Or, more accurately, equipment that worked too well. Equipment that created ghostly illusions beyond his control.

As a result he was still awake, checking his recorders and his amp, reconfiguring his formulas from previous EMF and HE readings, recalibrating everything and deciding what to do next.

He hypothesized that the problem was in the thinking computer chip he used. If it wasn't perfectly calibrated, it could extrapolate beyond his commands. He hated thinking computers for that reason, but the regular ones couldn't deal with the complexity he required.

That was the trouble with technology. As soon as you got it to do what you needed, it could also get ahead of you. Even more frightening, it might be smarter than he was. In the meeting it created events that were much more effective than his plan to discredit her. On the other hand, what happened at the Terra Lounge was much less effective, so why would the damn chip create that? Did it know something he didn't? He hoped not.

When another hour of searching showed him nothing to confirm or deny his hypothesis, he gave it up. He had to move on.

He put the amp down and thought. He could report this to the client, but he'd found it was a bad idea to let them in on glitches in assignments. They got frantic, wanted to back out, or came up with stupid ideas they'd insist he tried.

His other option was to say nothing and speed up his program. He had two contingency plans in place, either of which could cut the discrediting process short and send her quickly to dead. His client might not be completely pleased, but they'd be less pleased if Dr. Addams figured too much shit out.

Another moment of thought and he decided. He wouldn't report it. The last thing he needed right now was a nervous client. Instead, he'd use his first contingency plan. It was the simplest, one he could put into motion from his own room, using a remote he'd already installed. It wasn't particularly elegant, but it would get the job done, and sometimes that was the best you could hope for.

He got his notepad, accessed the right file and set it into motion. Immediately, he felt relief.

By tomorrow this time, this job would be history. Even if she was a cat, she had only nine lives, and she must have dumped at least eight of them by now.

Planetoid Three

Rachel went home for supper, then returned to her office to check her program one more time. She wanted to get that information to Adrian as quickly as possible, and while she was there she could do a little research about the pink tequila, which had her worried.

The halls were quiet, softly lit. Her mind was on her work as she opened the door and turned on the light, so it took her a moment to realize someone was already there.

Sitting at her desk, staring at her, was a large man, his white hair streaked with black, and his pale blue eyes stark as lightning against the dark blue patch that ran across his face. A mutoid. A big one. She let out a small scream.

She was about to scream again, even louder, when the man held up a hand. "Rachel, it's me. Alex," he said.

She pressed a hand to her heart. He stood and took her elbow, helped her to her own seat. "Okay?" he asked.

"Fine," she said. "Just fine. Sort of."

"Sorry," he said. "I didn't realize my disguise was that effective."

"It'll work," she admitted, and fanned herself a little, catching her breath. Then she scanned him. "It's the eyes, really. Like wolf eyes."

"Vilkacis," he said.

"What?"

"Lithuanian werewolf. That's why I picked them."

"You would. Aren't you supposed to be on a shuttle?"

"I've got about forty-five minutes, and I wanted the latest report before I left."

"Oh. How'd you know I'd be here?"

He held a hand palm up. "Rachel, what am I?"

"That. Right. Good thing you are, too. You'll want this info before you leave. It's pretty . . ." Rachel paused, sought the right word. "Wild."

"So am I, right now. Give it to me," Alex said.

Rachel did. She told him first about Jaguar's knife being taken away, and he thought about whether or not he could get another one to her. The scanners wouldn't pick it up, but he was pretty sure they'd do a strip search on him. She'd have to do without. And knowing she lacked that defense made him even more anxious to get to her. What Rachel said next didn't help any.

Adrian had reported that office gossip was all about Jaguar, saying she was crazy, talking to invisible people in the halls and in meetings. Then, the incident at the Terra Lounge and his worries about what was actually in her drink and what made her toss it, which was also invisible.

"Shit," Alex said. "Someone's messing with her. Big time."

"You don't know the half of it," Rachel said. "All hell broke loose at a meeting, with flying water glasses and flickering lights and so on." She gave it to him, and he listened, from beginning to end.

"She had empathic contact?" he asked when she was done.

"That's what she said. The rest of it—the grapevine's convinced she did it, and she's bonkers, but she said it was either a Telekine or ghosts."

He ran a hand over his face. "Ghosts?" he asked.

"Ghosts," Rachel confirmed. "Or a Telekine."

Alex thought it through. Everything he'd heard so far would effectively discredit any opinion she had about Francis or, if something ugly showed up in the tequila, get her well out of the way. In its own way, it was not a bad solution, if you wanted Francis dead. If you wanted her out of the way. But who was behind it? Maybe, he thought, knowing what happened would give him an idea of who could make it happen.

"Run through it again," he said. "Give me the sequence of events."

Rachel did so, and Alex thought through ways to make that particular sequence of events occur. Most of them had nothing to do with ghosts, which didn't mean it wasn't ghosts. A good Telekine could do it in his sleep, though he didn't relish the idea of going up against one of those again. Messy, he thought. A messy situation altogether.

"Do me a favor," he said. "Two favors, actually. Start a search for drugs or toxins that turn alcohol pink."

"Already searching. I came back to check on it," she said. "And Adrian's having the shirt tested. What else?"

He thought about what he knew from Adept space. Thought about his options. Then he looked to the clocks on her wall, which showed both Planetoid and home planet time. Still early on the East Coast.

"I have to make a call," he said. "When it's done, you may have another task to complete."

Rachel relinquished her seat to him and Alex punched in numbers on her telecom. The viewscreen showed the logo for the Defense Department, and then an officially attractive female appeared on screen, her voice courteous and smooth.

"Special Ops," she said. "How may I direct your call?"

"Get me General Durk," Alex said.

The voice and face remained smooth. "He's in a meeting. May I take a message?"

"Only if you take it to him right now. Tell him to get out of his meeting and come talk to me. It's Supervisor Alex Dzarny. Planetoid Three."

"Sir, I doubt—"

"—I doubt he'll thank you if he misses me," Alex cut in. "Just let him know who it is."

The face disappeared, but in short order it was replaced by General Durk himself. He took in Alex's changed aspect wihtout comment, his thick, square face expressing no emotion, his wooden hand tapping slowly against the desk. "Supervisor," he said, then waited.

"General," Alex replied. "I need some information from you."

"Go," he said.

"Former Navy SEAL Operator Scott White. Tell me what he did for you."

The wooden hand stopped tapping, something Alex recognized as a sign of surprise. He hadn't expected that question. Not at all. "You don't know?" he asked, staying bland.

"I have general information. I need corroboration. And specifics."

The general's hand went tap, tap tap. "That's classified," he said.

"So am I," Alex replied.

"Why do you need to know?"

"I'm considering having him back up Dr. Addams on an assignment of considerable risk to her life. I want to know if he'll cover her ass."

The General's mouth twitched an eighth of an inch, which Alex took to be his way of grinning. "It's an ass worth covering," he noted.

"It is. So will he?"

"Yes," he said. "Without a doubt."

Alex studied his face, replayed his words and their tone to himself. He meant it. "What was his job with you?"

"Data collection and analysis, primarily on superluminary transfer of cognition, and post-mortem energies."

The military continued to investigate psi capacities, but they never talked about it except in the most complex of euphemisms. Alex took a moment to translate. Scott was working with telepathy, something he already knew. But he was also a ghost hunter, collecting information on post-mortem energy, doing whatever Psi Ops did with that information. That was news to him. Pertinent news.

He felt a tingling in his hand, the Adept energy at work. Jaguar might have ghosts, either manufactured or real. Scott knew about ghosts. "Perfect," he murmured.

"I'm glad you think so," Durk said drily. "Is that all?"

"Not quite," Alex said. "If I send him and it turns out he's on some game of yours, I'll hunt you down and kill you. You know that, right?"

"If you think you can," Durk said.

Alex smiled. "With my training and my obsession? What do you think?"

He lifted his wooden hand, let it drop back to the desk. "Anything is possible," he said. Then, "Scott is exceptionally skilled and we were sorry to lose him, but he had a preference for the SEALS. When he was honorably discharged to pursue a civilian career I asked him to return to my office on a consultant basis. He declined. Politely."

"He's very polite," Alex noted.

"He is. And if anything untoward occurs it won't be through him."

Something tingling on the edge of those words, Alex thought. Not through Scott. Durk knew something, and was inviting Alex to play.

"Who will it be through?" he asked.

"I was speaking hypothetically. Dr. Addams draws attention to herself."

Alex sighed. Dealing with Durk could be incredibly tedious. "Keep hypothesizing," Alex suggested. "With examples."

Durk tapped some more, made a decision and spoke. "A hypothetical example might be another party on One, who makes it more urgent to cover her ass."

Alex had a moment of anger. Durk did know something, and he'd known for a while.

"You could've called," he said, trying to sound cool.

"I wasn't worried about her."

"And now you are? Never mind. Is it anybody you might hypothetically know?"

"The most likely candidate is someone who contracts with both military and private sector, in a variety of tasks. Collection. Clowning. Cleaning. In this instance, I'd theorize his assignment is Cleaning."

Alex felt a chill move up his spine. He knew all the terms. Clowns created distractions, deflecting crimes in progress. Collectors stole whatever they were asked to steal—data, items of value, sometimes people. And Cleaners straightened out messy situations—usually, by killing the person who made the mess. This was not just an attempt to discredit her. It was an attempt to kill her.

"Is he one of yours?" Alex asked.

"We were speaking hypothetically. However, if you gather any information to indicate an affiliation with my organization, I'd prefer having it delivered directly to me."

"I'll do what I can," Alex said, "But if Dr. Addams is involved all bets are off."

"I'm aware of that," Durk said, and shrugged it off. He didn't waste time on elements outside his control.

"If you had a hypothetical name for the Cleaner," Alex noted, "I might be able to manage it better. And I'd owe you one."

The general considered, made some executive decision within the depths of his brain, and spoke. "You already owe me," he said. "And I will cash in my chips."

He disappeared from the screen. Alex let out a long breath, then turned to Rachel. "Get Scott on One," he said. "Now."

Rachel blinked at him. "Scott White? Sir and ma'am Scott?"

"That's the one. Wake him up. Bring him up to speed and get him there. If possible, I'd like him completely open."

"What? No job?"

"Nothing he has to report to or on except Jaguar. He'll be her personal bodyguard, which she sorely needs." Alex thought some more. "He'll need a room, I suppose. And a cover. Can you take care of that? Tonight? We don't have time to get Paul's approval, so you'll be on you're own."

"Nobody there knows him?"

"He came straight from training to Three."

"No problem, then," she said. "Nothing to it."

Alex, feeling how imperative it was for him to be on Planetoid One, stood to leave. He moved to the door, but then his innate courtesy nudged him the ribs. He stopped, took a moment to study Rachel, who was already bent over her notepad, working at the tasks he'd given her. He could count on her to find a way, through whatever legal or extra-legal means were available.

"Rachel, you never ask what'll happen if you get caught doing this kind of thing," he said.

She turned her wide brown eyes up to him. "It doesn't matter, does it? I mean, as long as I can keep you and Jaguar safe."

He moved back to her, put a hand on her shoulder, by way of blessing, of gratitude. "We'd be dead without you, Rachel," he said quietly. "Long since dead."

Then he left his office quickly, before he saw her press a hand against her heart, just for a second. She blinked back an unexpected tear, and bent her back to her work.

CHAPTER 13

The hands at Jaguar's throat were large and strong as they squeezed her pharynx shut. She knew better than to pull at them. Instead she looked up into the eyes of her attacker. Francis, his hands at her throat. And over his shoulder she saw Diane, watching her with careful eyes.

Alex moved in behind Diane, a head taller than her, his wolf eyes intense with fear.

Wolf eyes. Light blue. She wondered about that. Alex's eyes were dark as night.

"Hide," he commanded. "Now."

Jaguar woke with a gasp, saw her own hand reaching out, grabbing for something or someone. For Alex, because he was there, right in front of her. When her hand stayed empty she stopped, got still. In a moment, full consciousness returned.

"*Rat* fuck," she said with feeling.

Just a dream, but a strong one. It had the feel of empathic space, the tingle of Alex's arts in it. She wondered if she was somehow picking up on his Adept dreams. She hoped not. It wasn't much fun. Though she supposed it was even worse if the dream was from her own art of clear-seeing. That would make it more immediate, and not something she'd penciled in for the day.

She ran a hand through her hair, pushed herself up. Her clock said 7 am. Early, but after a night of dancing, she was hungry. She wanted toast.

She's stocked in bread and cheese and tea for her own room so she could eat here, without any other human presence. The thought seemed wonderfully decadent to her right now, a guilty pleasure. She got out of bed, found her bread and cut a few slices, brought it to the toaster oven. As her hand reached out to open it, her intercom crackled into life.

She turned to it. Static was replaced by a low voice, a strange voice.

"Don't touch it," the voice said imperiously.

She looked at her hand, at the toaster oven, back at the intercom. "Who's there?" she asked.

Static returned, and then a whispering as of many voices. It dissipated, and was replaced by the first voice she'd heard. "Don't touch it," the voice repeated.

As it spoke, she realized what made it strange. It was too slow, like a recording played at the wrong speed.

"Is this a joke?" she asked.

Again that whispering, as of many people, and the first voice returned, even slower now.

"If you touch it, you'll die," it said.

The intercom crackled, and was silent.

Jaguar put the bread down and stared at the toaster oven. She lifted a hand toward it, not to touch, but to perceive what energy it was putting out. She sensed rather than heard a humming, and felt a charge way too strong for a toaster oven. The current was running too high. There was a short in the system. If she'd touched it, she wouldn't have felt a thing for a long time. Maybe not ever again.

She lowered her hand, walked over to the intercom and studied it. She didn't feel the static she'd felt around the images of the women Francis killed. If this was a trick, it was a different kind. She made sure the charge around the intercom was running at normal, then pressed the button that put her through to security. Nothing happened. She pressed again and a voice responded, sounding a little distracted.

"Security," it said.

No drop in pitch, no static. Just a clipped male voice, slightly irritated. She dipped into his mind long enough to learn he was watching an interesting net show that could loosely be construed as a sexual harassment program, if you took out the word harassment.

"Good porn?" she asked.

"What?"

"Never mind. I don't give a rat's ass what you do in your cubby hole. This is Dr. Addams. Did you just call me?"

"No, miss," the voice responded, sounding guilty. "Do you need assistance, miss?"

She rolled her eyes. "It's Dr. Addams. And no, I don't need your assistance. But something's wrong with my toaster oven. Who do I talk to about that?"

"Maintenance, mi—Dr. Addams. Extension 5562."

"Thanks," she said, and ended the communication. She went to her telecom and punched in the extension for Maintenance, told them she had a problem in her room.

"What kind of problem?" a desultory male voice asked.

"My toaster oven's not working, and I want toast."

"Yeah. I'll send someone with a new one," the voice said.

She made herself coffee and sat brooding with it. There was a lot to brood about, but none of it got her much of anywhere. When she heard a knock on her door, she was glad enough to stop. She went to it and admitted a burly man with a lot of hair and very large hands.

"There's a short in my toaster oven," she said.

"Okay," he said. He moved to it, reached a hand out. She grabbed his wrist. Her hand didn't reach all the way around.

"Don't touch it," she said. "It's live."

He pulled away. "If it was live, it'd be humming," he said.

"It is. Can't you hear it?"

His face expressed something rude about female hysteria. "I don't hear a damn thing," he said.

"Then humor me. Don't you have gloves? Insulated gloves?"

He gave her a scornful glance. "Lady," he said, "it's a toaster," and he put his hand on it.

For a brief moment he lit up like a Christmas tree. Then he dropped.

"Mister," she said, "you're toast."

* * * *

The toaster oven had shot its wad and was quite dead, but the security guards who took it away used gloves when they removed it. She saluted it as it passed. A vigorous if small appliance.

Regina showed up just as the paramedics gave up on resuscitation efforts and pulled a sheet over the maintenance man's face. Her own normally calm face was tense and pale as she watched them take him away. She put a hand on Jaguar's arm. "Are you all right?"

Jaguar nodded at her door as it closed behind the stretcher. "Better than he is," she said. Then she shook her head. "I told him to use gloves. He wouldn't listen."

"Surely it can't be—a toaster oven killed him?"

"Not a bad way to get rid of someone, if you think about it," Jaguar noted. "Looks like an accident, and easy enough to set up without leaving any trace behind. A sliced wire, or even a remote change in the charge'd do it."

Regina's hand tightened on her arm. "Are you saying this wasn't an accident? Why would anyone want to kill that man?"

"I don't think they did. I think they wanted to kill me."

"But—a deliberate attempt on your life?"

"Alex warned you it might happen, didn't he?"

Regina frowned at Jaguar, frowned down at the floor. She took her hand off Jaguar's arm and put it to her forehead, sat herself down on the small chair near the desk. "This is awful," she said quietly.

Jaguar looked at her ashen face and moved toward the intercom. "I'm getting the medics back," she said.

Regina raised a hand. "No. Don't. I'm—I'll be fine. I just need a minute."

"Lower your head," Jaguar suggested. "Get the blood back in it." Regina complied. Jaguar sat on her bed and waited.

In short time she raised herself up, and her cheeks showed spots of color again. "Sorry," she said. "It was the shock of seeing that poor man."

"Shock's a good word for it," Jaguar noted.

Regina blinked at her, then giggled. "Jaguar, you really are quite evil. Making jokes at a time like this."

"You look like you need it. You're sure you're okay? I don't have anything restorative to offer beyond water, but I could see about getting brandy or something."

Regina waved it away. "Really. I'm fine. Just—concerned. And incredibly relieved you weren't hurt, and feeling guilty that I'm relieved about you and not as sad as I should be about that poor man."

"Complicated," Jaguar noted.

"Indeed. I'll feel even more guilty if it turns out to be deliberate. But, of course, it could have been *just* an accident."

She looked to Jaguar for confirmation. Jaguar gave her a cool grin. "Sure. If you prefer."

Regina frowned, shook her head. "I don't understand," she said

"Lately it seems Planetoid One operates on preference rather than truth. You'd prefer to blame the flying water glasses on me. You'd prefer to believe Francis killed Diane. You'd prefer not to see that someone's trying like hell to get rid of me, in a variety of ways."

Regina took this in, and offered a sympathetic glance. "You're—angry," she said.

"You bet," Jaguar agreed. "You're supposed to have my back."

"I do," Regina assured her.

"Yeah? Well, I just had the pleasure of watching a man get fried by a small appliance that would've killed me first if I touched it, and I still haven't had my toast. Granted, he was a chauvinistic idiot who couldn't get his head out of his ass long enough to realize you don't need a penis to understand electricity, but I don't think he deserved to die for that. Do you?"

Regina's next words were careful. "I understand how upset you are, but I'm not sure you're the right person to judge this situation without prejudice."

"I was the only one here," Jaguar replied.

"Yes, well, that's the problem, isn't it? You're too involved, emotionally. Given the reports I've had on you, that much is clear."

Jaguar drew herself up tall, crossed her arms at her chest. "What reports?"

Regina let out a long breath. "A security guard said you were—well, talking to yourself in the halls. Clyde mentioned something similar. A mutoid in the hall, and someone in your chair?"

That. Of course. "How damn convenient," she said. "Anything else?"

Regina took a breath, and when she spoke she sounded reluctant. "I didn't mention this before because, well, I know how Susan is about you. But she said during your interview with her you started talking to people who weren't—weren't there."

"Yeah," Jaguar said truculently. "Besides that."

"Jaguar, that's quite enough, isn't it? I mean, really. Given your reputation, here and elsewhere. Susan's already talking about empaths who lose their minds, get—get—"

"Shadowed," Jaguar said. "The term is shadowed, and I'm not. I know how to work my arts."

Regina shook her head. "I've always supported you in what you do, who you are, even if I don't necessarily understand it myself. But you can't blame me for worrying, after all I've been hearing."

Of course not, Jaguar thought. Put it all together and she looked like a crazy woman. Even the woman who always took care of her thought that, and since Regina wasn't an empath, she'd never fully accept the kind of reality Jaguar had to deal with. How could she? And how could Jaguar let her know it, when she was adamant about refusing empathic contact, about not delving into that world herself?

Suddenly she felt trapped, and had to still a rising sense of panic. Someone trying to kill her was nothing new. A deliberate attempt to ruin her reputation, especially with people whose good opinion mattered to her, using methods she couldn't figure out—that was terrifying.

"I'm not shadowed," Jaguar repeated firmly, "And I'm not hallucinating, if that's what you think."

"Then what is it? More ghosts?"

"Regina, it could be lots of things—technology to create holofigures, someone trying to make me look bad, someone who really wants me to go away. Isn't it your job to figure that out? It's your Planetoid."

Regina let out a long breath. "Jaguar, honestly, my first guess is that you're angry about being here. That you're under pressure you don't deserve, and it's—it's affecting you, as it naturally would. But I assure you, if someone here was trying to hurt you, I'd know it."

"Would you? Well, right now I prefer my anger to your assurance." She went to her door, opened it. "Do you mind? I'd like to be alone."

Regina stood and moved toward the door. Once there, she stopped, turned back to Jaguar. Her face was full of conflict, full of pain that almost made Jaguar regret the harshness of her stance. "I'll look into this, I promise," she said. "If there's any chance it was meant to harm you, I'll find out and do what's necessary. And I'll gladly post guards at your door, if you like."

"No thanks," Jaguar said. "I'm better off on my own."

Regina held up a helpless hand, let it drop again. "Is there *anything* I can do for you?"

There it was. An opening, and she took it. "Sure. Send me back to Planetoid Three, where I belong."

Regina's lips went thin. "I can't do that. Not yet."

Jaguar's hands curled into fists at her side. When she felt them doing so, she deliberately uncurled them. "Why not?" she asked.

That was the important question. Regina, Uber-governor of Planetoid One, could do just about anything she wanted. Maybe she'd been sincere about wanting Jaguar here to keep Francis alive when she thought there was no risk in doing so. But by now she knew better, and she could send her home, if she chose. So why wouldn't she? If she cared about Jaguar's well-being, why would she keep her here?

Regina opened her mouth, said nothing, closed it again. Apparently her own agenda, whatever it was, was more important to her than Jaguar's life. Yet another betrayal, brought to her courtesy of Planetoid One. Her art of clear-seeing swirled around her, signaling danger, and the possibility of pain.

"That's too bad," Jaguar said quietly.

Regina turned and left the room. Jaguar closed the door behind her.

CHAPTER 14

When Alex arrived on Planetoid One he was greeted by persistently cheerful team members, who took him by the arm and led him forward. As they walked the halls from the shuttleport to the exam rooms he'd be in for a while, those who passed by glanced at him and away, their averted eyes indicating a politely hidden revulsion. He wondered if mutoids and others who grew up with that particular look grew numb to it, didn't notice the way it seeped into them and became self-disparagement.

He was spared it soon enough. The team members scuttled him quickly into the infirmary, where he was probed medically, blood and skin cells taken from him, all his orifices examined as thoroughly as possible.

Though he was only in the outer areas he observed what he could, opening himself empathically to what moved through this space. He felt a surging of energies, and not all of them were from patients or the people who worked here. Some had a distinct heaviness he associated with his mercifully brief time stuck in a room full of dead men. He took in all he could, reserving it for later reflection.

After the infirmary he was taken through a series of psych evaluations that lasted the rest of the day, then led down a hall to his cell, where he'd have a week of lockdown residence as his adjustment to his new situation was observed. This section of the bubble dome was a secured series of halls, each hall with its own secure door, behind which were single rooms, also locked. Everything was painted in beige or a soft green, colors meant to inspire calm.

Only the newest prisoners and those with records of violence returned here at night, though during the day most of them took part in various work programs. He would have janitorial duty, starting tomorrow. Rachel had arranged for Adrian to control his schedule, coordinating it around Jaguar's, putting him as near to her as possible at all times.

While he was walked toward his cell he saw a familiar face—a strong young man with bright blue eyes. He wore a security guard's uniform. Scott, already here. Alex paused to thank any available deity for sending him someone like Rachel, a true miracle worker.

Then he made it a point to stare deliberately into Scott's face. That young man looked at him, then quickly away, as everyone else did. No flicker of his eyes betrayed that he knew him, though Rachel had given him a photo showing him what he'd look like. Then, another pleasant surprise. Scott's voice, speaking within him.

Good evening, sir.

Alex replied. *Really, you can call me Alex.*

Yes, sir.

Alex allowed himself to smile. Mutoids often smiled for reasons no one could determine. Scott kept walking, not looking back. Good man, Alex thought.

Then he was put in his lockdown cell, the door with its double locks and laser fencing closed behind him.

This, he thought, would be the worst. Waiting through one more night, when he was so close but still incapable of acting in any way. No empathic signals would get through the laser fencing to either Scott or Jaguar. As he lay sleepless on his cot, his only thought was that nothing should happen. This night, he repeated over and over, let nothing happen this night.

Some time in the middle of the night his door opened, and a security guard poked his head in. To his relief, it was Scott, who was letting him know he had the means to get into his cell.

Alex spoke, subvocally.

Where is she? he asked.

In her room for the night, sir, came the reply.

You're staying nearby?

Right outside her door, all night, he said. *That's the assignment.*

Thank you, Alex said.

"You need anything?" Scott asked him out loud.

He shook his head. The door clanged shut.

Alex rolled over on his hard bed and tried for sleep. He thought he'd need it, and he trusted the solid and immovable stance of this former Navy SEAL, guarding what was precious through the night.

CHAPTER 15

The next morning, after another interview and a few more personnel routines to get through, Alex was released from his cell for work duty. He plied his mop up and down a hall near Jaguar's room. As he worked, he sent his thoughts out to her.

He found her quickly, already in the interview room with Francis, doing her time with him for the day. He'd studied maps of this building before he arrived and knew she wasn't very far away. Two corridors, a left turn, and two doors down. He could get to her quickly if necessary, a thought that gave him great relief.

The message he sent her was simple.

Jaguar, I'm here.

Her thoughts returned to him, with some surprise.

Alex? You got here?

Yes. In your corridor. You're with Francis? All is well?

He felt her immense satisfaction even before she answered. *It is now. I can finally get some work done.*

What followed was the turning of her thoughts back to her job. He saw an image: Jaguar, leaning close to Francis, who clutched a small stuffed bear. She'd waited for Alex to arrive before she tried empathic contact, but since he was here, she'd go ahead. The tingling in his spine told him this wasn't actually a good thing.

A security guard walked by him, slowing her steps. He worked his mop and hummed. The guard moved on.

Jaguar?

Alex, hush. There's something....

Something. Crows walking on his grave. On hers. He stilled his thoughts and used a small trick he'd learned in the streets of Manhattan, effectively wiping out his presence to the consciousness of those around him. This made him, for all intents and purposes, temporarily invisible. He dropped his mop and moved toward the interview room. Maintaining invisibility and contacting someone empathically at the same time was like juggling laser swords, but he tried it.

Jaguar? Okay?

No response. She was intent on something. There—he felt her concentration, along with another energy. Something in the room with her. Something like what he'd felt moving in the air at the infirmary yesterday.

Suddenly, he had the sensation of being dropped into emptiness. His Adept vision, unfolding just one small step ahead of actual events. Her hands were about to struggle against other hands. There would soon be a violent cessation of breath, a drop into an abyss.

Jaguar—back off.

Her response, occurring in time that was yet to be, was not something he wanted to hear.

Alex, find me, she said.

A few seconds between vision and event was all he he had. He broke into a run, not caring anymore if he was seen. Let anyone who dared try and stop him.

* * * *

When Jaguar entered the interview room the sight of Francis waiting for her, clutching his bear, did nothing to improve her outlook. She'd brought another puzzle, but she really didn't feel like doing that today. Especially when she saw the look of both hope and desperation on Francis's face, and that small bear, with its great green eyes.

She blinked. Green eyes?

The bear's eyes were black. At least, they were before. Disconnected knowledge began to connect itself into a coherent whole. What she'd learned in endless meetings about the export programs. Something about what Diane Lasher knew that got her killed.

But not by Francis.

"Did Derek give you a new bear?" she asked, sitting down across from him.

"My bear," Francis said, wrapping his hand around it.

"I know," she said reassuringly. "Can I see it?"

"No."

That was clear and definite. Okay, but she needed to see.

"Does Derek give you new bears all the time? And you hold onto them for him? Is that what he does, because he likes you?"

"I get the special bears," Francis affirmed.

"How often does he give you bears, Francis? Once a month?"

No answer to this, and then she was interrupted by contact from Alex. He was here. Somehow, he'd managed it. She was surprised, though she knew he was persistent as a truffle hunting pig. Reliable as death.

Her first response was a great sense of relief. She'd been frustrated in this task from the start, but now she might be able to get somewhere. He'd told her not to try empathic contact until he got here, and here he was. She reached over and touched Francis's hand softly.

"Francis," she said, "look at me."

He did so, his face open and without burden of fear. She moved into him quickly, looking beyond his wounded face, reaching for what lay within his soul. That's where his brother would be, either as a true ephemeral or a shadow of old emotions. At least she'd find out which one.

As soon as she touched his center the room went cold, and she heard a sound like a sudden intake of breath. She halted her exploration, lifted her head to see what had entered the room.

Directly behind Francis she saw two women, translucent and shimmering. Mathias and Lopez.

"Not you two again," she complained. "What now?"

But they didn't answer. Instead, they sizzled into nothingness, as if a hand had wiped them clean from a board, only to be replaced by something bright, something like light superimposed against air. Jaguar saw no face, no human form, but she felt a familiar energy, full of light and enthusiasm.

"Diane?" she whispered.

You have to save us. Save me, she said urgently, speaking within her, her words a clamoring of fear and pain.

The words she'd heard in the meeting room. And her first response was caustic.

"Like you saved me?" she asked. "I don't know if I can get dead people fired."

The response was laughter, bright and swift. A response only Diane would make. If it was technotricks, they were done by someone who knew her. Or, she supposed it could be her own memories, spitting out residual sensory impression, remembrance of her time here brought to life by the confluence of heavy energy in the bubble dome. That, combined with her own projection of what she thought Diane needed; to be saved from her own prejudice.

She let the feel of the energy permeate her, trying to figure it out. As she did so, the voice whispered into her again, even more urgently.

Back off, she said. *Lowdosing.*

Back off from what? Empathic contact? Even dead, Diane hated empaths? "Oh, for fuck's sake," she said. "Give it a break."

Immediately she felt the table shoved suddenly forward. She whirled back to Francis, saw he was on his feet, his face changed.

"Don't touch him," he roared, his voice, not really his voice, full of fear and fury.

She stood, knocking her chair over as Francis lunged forward quickly, reached to her and grabbed her wrist, swung her around the table toward him. He was strong, easily catching her at her throat, lifting her and pressing her against the wall.

She tried to kick at him but found no purchase. She brought her hands up to clap him hard on the ears but he stopped them with his free hand and held her by the wrists. Strong. He was strong and fast.

She didn't panic. She had other moves to make. Keep his fingers off her carotid. Work him empathically. She pressed her thoughts against his, and all she felt was his rage. Rage at death that came too quickly. Rage at the woman who caused it. It was large and unmalleable, a force of nature rather than a decision, a hurricane of emotion.

Inside her, inside Francis, she heard a whispering of Diane's voice.

Damon, don't. She's here to help.

It did no good. She couldn't breathe, air cut off and the room getting smaller, disappearing into a circle of darkness that rimmed her vision like the closing pupil of a cat's eye. She thought of the dream she'd had, Alex's voice telling her what to do. Hide, he said. The Adept told her to hide.

Now she knew what he meant. She had one more move to make, and she made it. Before vision dispersed completely, she breathed a thought into the air, sending it out to him.

Alex, she said. *Find me.*

* * * *

By the time Alex got to the interview room what he'd seen in Adept space had just occurred. He threw the door open and stumbled in, saw Francis holding Jaguar by the throat, pressed into the wall.

"Put her down," he said sharply.

Francis turned, looked at him dumbly.

No time to argue. Seconds counted. Alex opened empathic contact and moved to him, pushed a hand hard against his face and made one demand only. *Let her go. Let her go.*

He might obey, or he might attack. Either way, he'd drop her.

Francis grunted, and let go. Jaguar's limp body slid to the floor. Alex shoved him away like a misplaced piece of furniture and knelt down to her, touched her face.

No breath. She wasn't breathing.

His hands were shaking, unready to feel what he felt. He forced himself into calmness. Hadn't he seen this, with crows walking over his grave, her grave? Hadn't he known since the first moment he saw her sitting across the desk from him, her face a study in mystery and truth? This is what they had together. This risk. This possibility. Always.

Quiet, he told himself. You saw this. It's why you're here. Do the work.

He felt at her neck and found it whole. Felt at her throat for a broken windpipe. All was smooth and connected as it should be. He put his hand behind her neck, bent over her and breathed into her mouth. She didn't respond.

Breathe, Jaguar. Breathe.

"I'm sorry," Francis said dolefully. "I didn't mean to."

He ignored Francis, breathed into her.

Breathe. Just breathe.

"I didn't want to," Francis continued. "He was scared of her. My brother. He was scared. She's one of them."

"Quiet," Alex said, terse and tight, "Be quiet."

He heard Francis sigh deeply and move away. A chair scraped against the floor as he pulled it out and sat in it. Alex bent over Jaguar and breathed into her. Her lips were warm. Still warm. How many lifetimes had passed since he walked into the room?

Breathe, Jaguar. Drink this air, my breath, anything, Jaguar, breathe, dammit, breathe.

What did she need? Kiss of Life? No. That wouldn't work here. If he had to, he'd do a Death Walk. Go in and bring her back. Bring her back or go with her. Find her, she'd said. Find her. The memory of what he'd seen in Adept space moved within him, and he took it in.

A blink of time. A slice of understanding. He knew what she'd done, why he had to be here for her.

She'd used an empathic move to go into hiding, crawling into the darkest space available to empaths only, a mockery of death to keep death at bay. It would take another empath to retrieve her, but she knew he was on the way. If they were robbed of flesh and hope and time, still he would find her.

He pressed his palm against her warm face, seeking her thoughts. And there she was, in a murky place between living and dying, not certain which way to move.

God fucking dammit, Jaguar. I told you to wait. Can't you fucking listen to me for once?

A pause. A turning.

I did wait.

Her tone was petulant. He didn't know whether to yell at her or laugh. Instead he spoke into her clearly, quickly.

Breathe, Jaguar. You have to breathe.

Then, her ragged intake of air, action performed at his command. Her arms flailing as she jerked upright, fell back, jerked up again, her eyes open and searching, breathing as if she just learned how. And in all the universe, she would follow his light, familiar and strange as her own.

"Here," he said, catching her hand and pulling her close, holding her against his chest. "I'm here, Jaguar. You're okay."

He wrapped his arms around her, pressed his mouth against her hair, luxuriating in her movements, beating heart, breathing lungs. Alive. Alive.

* * * *

They sat for some time before she groaned and moved in his arms. "That was rough," she said.

"Rough," Alex agreed. "Very."

She rested her face against his chest. "Is this where you say I told you so?"

He touched the red mark at her throat. "Maybe later," he said.

She ran a hand through her hair, then lifted her head to offer a weak grin. It disappeared as she observed his sky pale eyes, his hair, the dark blue patch of skin. "Oh," she said. "Oh. You're…"

"A mutoid," he finished for her. "That's how I got here."

She reached up and touched his hair. "Bleaching is hell on your hair, you know that?"

"Rachel already mentioned it."

"I'll let you borrow my conditioner." She sent her glance around the room. "We can't stay here," she said. She tried to stand and failed. He caught her arm and pulled her back down.

"You're not okay yet," he said. "Sit still. Tell me what happened."

She breathed in deeply, breathed out again. "Damon. Francis still carries him. A true ephemeral. The meds just buried him deeper."

"And you had to dig," Alex noted grimly.

"Just a little," she noted. "But I did wait for you."

He uttered some choice words and she offered a grin in response. "It would've been fine, but I was distracted."

"By what?"

"Ghosts."

That, he thought, wasn't something he heard every day. "Ghosts? Plural?"

"Well, some of them may be, and others probably aren't. But one was Diane."

Diane. He thought of Rachel's report, the woman she'd seen, sort of. "How do you mean that? Sensory impressions? Residual energies? Retrojection or memory?"

"I'm pretty sure it's her," Jaguar said. "If she'd hang around a little longer I'd be certain, but she won't. None of them will."

He sighed. None of them. "How much time do we have to talk about this?" he asked.

She glanced at the clock. "In about five minutes the guard's supposed to come and take Francis away. He won't get near the room before then. They leave me strictly alone in here."

"Go figure," he said drily. Then, "We'll discuss the ghosts later. Tell me what happened with Francis."

"All of it?" she asked.

"Full report," he said, knowing how lucidly and efficiently she could do so.

She gave the whole incident to him, quickly and concisely, and when she was done, Alex considered. Pieces of the puzzle were falling into place, and the picture they created wasn't pretty. There were still a few crucial elements missing, however.

"The bear was different this time?"

"Yes. A new bear. Different color eyes. Maybe they're using them somehow—for some kind of transport."

"Maybe. And the word you heard—lowdosing?"

"I'm not sure what that meant, unless. . . ." She stopped, frowned.

"Unless," Alex filled in, "Francis's meds have recently been lowered."

"Yeah," she agreed. "Unless that."

They both knew what that meant. If meds kept Damon suppressed, then lowering the dosage would allow him free play. And it was possible someone had deliberately done so, hoping he'd kill Jaguar, who was so obviously an empath. If that was the case, what she'd seen of Diane was real. A real warning, from an old friend.

But the other words she said—the same as what Jaguar heard in the meeting room, before all hell broke loose. Save us. Save me. He didn't have a clue what that was about, nor did he have time to pursue it.

"I'll get word to Adrian to check his blood levels for meds," he said. "In the meantime, no more digging. You got that?"

"Maybe since I know what to expect—"

"—No. He's not your prisoner, Jaguar."

"If we were on Three—"

"—I wouldn't assign him to you." He put two hands on her face, bringing her gaze to his. "Dr. Addams, you've had a busy morning practicing your resurrection skills so I'll cut you some slack. But you know Francis killed seven women and no men, and odds are high someone here is trying hard to kill you. So later on, when you get your brain back, you can think about why it makes sense for you to steer clear right now."

She twisted her lips around some, offered a shrug as grudging consent. "Adrian told you about the tequila?" she asked.

"He did," Alex confirmed. "That, and the flying water glasses at your meeting."

"But not about the toaster," she added cryptically.

"The what?"

"It's a long story," she said. "And it's been a really long day."

"Go back to your room," he suggested. "Take the afternoon off."

She shook her head. "I've got a meeting, and then I have to interview Ned Tackerson."

"Right," Alex said. He looked around, concerned about time, and intrusion. "When and where can we talk in private? You've got a lot more to tell me."

She frowned, chewed on her lip. "There's my room. With security cameras. In fact, this is the only room without them."

"Of course it is," he said.

"But I can take care of the cameras. Can you get to my room later?"

"I'm in first week lock-down. No exit unless someone lets me out."

She raised an eyebrow at him. "It's a lock, Alex. Break it."

She was better with a lock than he was, and he was more than willing to admit that. However, she had her own deficits. "You can't be invisible, can you?" he reminded her. "Besides, it's a combination lock. Digital and steel bolt, with laser fencing. Even you can't get through that."

"Steel bolt? Jesus. Are you here as a serial killer?"

"Multiple counts of exposure. And no commentary on that. We don't have time. Scott can get me out, but it's risky so I'd rather reserve it for emergencies. Is there any other way?"

"Scott?" she asked.

"Your bodyguard. Rachel arranged it. He just got here."

"Well, then. More back up. Where do you work tomorrow?"

"Mopping. Your corridor. Ten to one."

"I'll find you."

"Okay," He started to push himself to standing, but her hand on his face stopped him.

"Wait," she insisted. He did.

"I knew you'd show up," she said, and something in her voice compelled him to lean down and kiss her. He drew her close, felt her body responding, felt his own doing the same. Not now, he told himself. Not just yet.

With great effort of will he pulled away and stood, gave her a good long look. There was more on her mind than recently surviving strangulation. For her, that was almost normal. She was hanging on to something that went deeper, and swirled with greater complexity.

"What is it, Jaguar?" he asked.

"I'll tell you when we have time. Meantime, I'm incredibly glad to see you," she answered.

He reached down, ran a finger against her cheek. "Ditto, Dr. Addams," he said.

And he was out the door.

Then, quickly, he was back in her corridor, back to his mop. Shortly after that, the guard went into the interview room and took Francis away.

Jaguar followed close behind, passing Alex as she went on her way, not acknowledging him except to brush her hand casually against the handle of his mop as she passed.

CHAPTER 16

The Cleaner bent over his recorder, staring at the code that scrolled across the screen. Something was wrong. Every 13 lines, the number 13 would turn up.

Everything else was scanning, the numbers showing that the recorder was working properly, and then 13. Randomly, inexplicably, making no sense to his practiced eye, which could translate code into event in an instant. After 13, the damn thing went back to scanning as it should.

He turned it off. "Hell," he muttered. "Bloody bloody hell."

That's what his life felt like right now.

His equipment was letting him down, and even worse, she was still alive. His plan with the toaster oven was perfectly reliable, and somehow she'd escaped it. And he'd backed it up with another plan, making sure that damn mutoid was primed to choke her. Not taking any chances, he'd even distracted her with more ghostly images, then poked Francis good with signals from his projection amp to push his neurology over the edge. In spite of all that, she'd shown up at her next meeting looking like nothing unusual had disturbed her day.

She should have been twice dead. How many lives did the fucking cat have?

He drew in breath, calmed himself. Anger wouldn't help him any, and he hadn't failed. Not yet. This was a setback, nothing more.

He'd placed a data recorder in Francis's bear and he'd get that back, see if it had anything useful to tell him. As for her, he had a few other contingency plans. He favored the one that used her belief in ghosts to push her over the edge because it left the least corollary evidence, but it would take a little time because he had to set his equipment precisely, which was a joke right now. He'd set it precisely already, and it responded randomly. A part of him wondered if she knew about him, and was using her own psi capacities to interfere with what he did.

As he thought this, somewhere in the back of his mind, he heard General Durk's raspy old voice, and it was laughing at him.

He wouldn't listen. He just wouldn't. She didn't know. She couldn't. He bent over his equipment, and went back to work.

* * * *

By noon Alex was in the bathrooms, spraying disinfectant around the urinals. He wasn't at it long before Scott walked in, glanced at him, and moved to a stall.

In a moment, Alex heard his voice, subvocal.

Need anything, sir?

I need you to stop calling me sir, Alex replied. Then, after some thought. *There's a few things. Ready?*

Go, sir.

Alex told him quickly and succinctly. Scott should be prepared to get him out of his cell as needed. He had to get some instructions to Adrian about testing Francis's blood. And he had to keep good watch on Dr. Addams. There'd been three attempts on her life, and they could expect more. Finally, he reported what Durk said about the Cleaner, and asked him to be on the lookout.

When he was done, Scott responded simply, *Yes sir. I'll handle it. Anything else?*

I think that's enough.

Scott exited the stall and moved to the sink to wash his hands. Alex gave him the equivalent of a telepathic tap on the shoulder. *Scott?*

Something else?

Just be careful. And thanks.

Alex watched him walk away. Not once had he given any indication with his eyes or his body language that he knew Alex. He was well-trained, and very good at his job.

Alex had been a supervisor for many years, and he knew the secret to good management was to get the best people you could, tell them what had to happen, and let them figure out the details. If you got the first bit done right, you were golden. Now, though they were all dancing on the edge of disaster, at least he knew he couldn't ask for a better team.

He put his head down and went back to sanitizing urinals.

* * * *

Scott went on his way, and as he walked he thought of his current tasks. The locks on Alex's cell weren't a problem. Rachel, who thought of everything, got him on the Planetoid with papers that gave him a uniform, a master key, a room to crash in, and a food card for the cafeteria. Then she'd scrubbed him clean from the system, which meant he was essentially a ghost, able to go where he wanted and do what he needed. Rachel, he'd decided, was good to have around.

Now he had to let Adrian know what Alex wanted, which was no problem at all thanks to her. When he strolled into the computer room the occupants of various cubicles glanced at him, took in his uniform and looked away. Security guards were always around, and people always paid more attention to uniforms than faces.

He found Adrian at his cubby, working his computer. He approached, stopped at his desk. "Adrian?" he asked.

Adrian looked up at him, smiled. Rachel had directed him to a surveillance photo of Scott, so he knew who he was, why he was here. Then, quickly, he remembered he was supposed to be talking to a security guard and made his face serious. "Everything okay, officer?" he asked.

Scott nodded. "I found something that might be yours." He handed him a piece of paper, and Adrian looked it over. The instructions on it were clear. He was to have Francis's blood tested for meds levels. Pronto.

He stared at it, thinking of how he might accomplish this. First, he had to let Rachel in on it. "It's a blood test request for Francis Durero," he said out loud. "But I don't have the requisition number for that prisoner." He handed the paper back to Scott. "Must not be mine," he said.

"Any idea who it might belong to? Can't have this kind of thing just floating around."

"No," Adrian said. "Sorry."

"Okay," Scott said. "Thanks." He was about to leave, but Adrian stopped him, a thought occurring to him. "Officer," he said, "since you're here, I have a question for you."

Scott stopped, waited.

Adrian considered his words. One of the biggest problems with this assignment was the difficulty of communicating. He had his earpiece for Rachel, who was a kind of goddess of information, everything flowing through her. But getting that information to Jaguar was tricky, given all the surveillance. Since he wasn't an empath he had to find other means to talk to her.

"Here's the thing," he said. "There's all these rumors that someone's spiking drinks at the Terra Lounge. That some asshole thinks it's funny to drop bad shit into people's drinks. You know anything about it?"

Scott kept his face blank, as a good security guard should. "What kind of sh—substance?" he asked.

"They're saying it's Praxoline which, you know, is pretty bad."

Scott did know. Alex told him about the attempt to spike Jaguar's drink, and knew this was his way of reporting what it was spiked with. And he wasn't happy to hear this news.

Praxoline was a hallucinogenic, used mostly by military for interrogation purposes. It got people to spill their guts, but left them without much guts left. People who took it often ended up permanently insane, or dead by suicide. Even the military had stopped using it, since it didn't allow for much in the way of follow-up.

"I know," Scott said. "Can you tell me where you heard this rumor?"

"Some woman I met at the Terra Lounge. Name of Rachel."

"I'll pass that on, see if anyone else heard about it," he said. "But I wouldn't worry too much. There's no reports of anyone taking Praxoline, and it would be pretty obvious if someone had."

"Okay," Adrian said. "Thanks. That makes me feel better. A guy likes to have his drink when he goes out without worrying about it, right?"

"Absolutely," Scott said, and meandered on.

As he went, he thought about what Alex told him—a Cleaner, going after Jaguar. Now this. Praxoline. A military drug. His work on the Planetoids was almost as tricky as being a SEAL. He smiled, glad he'd asked to work with Supervisor Dzarny. Everything he'd heard about him and Dr. Addams was turning out to be true.

But right now he knew his next task. He had to find a quiet space where he could communicate telepathically with Dr. Addams, and let her know what he'd learned.

* * * *

When Scott was gone, Adrian spent some time pretending to work while Rachel, who heard his conversation with Scott, talked to him about what should happen next.

"You need a blood test for Francis?" she asked.

"Right," he said quietly. "But I don't have—"

"His medical ID. It's 5776423. If you can—"

"—Yeah, I can," Adrian said.

He'd take the number to Marie, tell her he'd lost the file and needed to complete the standard random testing required by their insurer. He'd ask her to rush it through to save his ass. If she balked, he'd suggest she bring it to his room after dinner, an offer he knew would interest her.

"Good man," Rachel said, and was silent.

Adrian sighed. Marie was fine, but he'd seen seen photos of Rachel. Very pretty, and the second smartest woman he'd ever met. "Good woman," he muttered. "And a damn shame."

"That's not what my girlfriend says," Rachel's voice said softly in his ear.

Adrian, flustered, started to stutter out an apology. Then he gave it up, and laughed.

"Get out of my head," he said, smiling. "You're worse than Jaguar."

"Who do you think taught me?" she replied.

Adrian, still smiling, got together his files and made his way to the infirmary offices.

* * * *

Jaguar went back to her room to change into a tight pair of jeans and her second scariest pair of boots, hoping to create an effect for her interview with Ned, which was to take place in the cafeteria. Clyde had suggested that, saying Ned would be more comfortable if the meeting was informal.

"He's a little ornery about it all, so go slow with him," Clyde had suggested. "I'll come over and bring you some dessert after a while. Make sure it's going okay."

"That's really not necessary," she told him. The last thing she needed was Clyde hanging around.

"Maybe not," he said, "but it'll be my pleasure."

That, she thought, was exactly what she was afraid of. But short of sticking a fork in his face, she didn't think she could do much to stop him.

As she was changing she was surprised to feel telepathic contact.

Ma'am? a cool voice asked politely.

Scott, she said. *How are you?*

Fine, Ma'am. Supervisor Dzarny asked me to let you know something.

Go ahead, she said.

He filled her in on the news about the Praxoline, let her know that blood testing for Francis was in the works.

Thanks, she said. *Anything else?*

Not right now. I'll be available as you need me. Any time at all.

Don't you need to sleep now and then?

She felt his amusement. *During Hell Week we get about three hours,* he said.

She grinned. *Welcome back to Hell Week, Scott.*

Yes, ma'am, he replied. And then he was gone.

She made her way to the cafeteria.

When she got there she stopped and surveyed the room. Right away she saw Alex, busy wiping at tables in a slow and clumsy way. A new experience, she thought, to feel so well guarded in the middle of Hell Week. She asked herself how she liked it, and answered herself that she liked it a lot.

After she gave Alex a nod to acknowledge his presence she saw Clyde, who was seated at a table, a tray of food in front of him. She lifted a hand, caught his eye, and he waved in return.

She made her way toward him, and as she did, she saw Ned reach him first, his body tense, his face tight. She couldn't hear, but she could guess what Clyde said to him as he stood, put a hand on his shoulder, talked close to his ear. Ned nodded, looked up and saw her. She found a table away from the crowd, sat at it, and gestured for him to come over. He straightened himself, put on the look of a man walking toward the gallows, and approached.

"Hello," he said when he got to her.

"Ned," she replied. "Have a seat."

He did so, folding his hands on the table and staring at her hard.

She scanned him. He had very Nordic good looks. Light blonde hair, blue eyes, finely chiseled face. Diane's defection to another camp must have been a blow to his ego. She gave him a smile, prepared to exercise tact in dealing with his wounds. Before she could do so, he spoke.

"You should know I'm only doing this as a favor to Clyde," he said. "Durero killed Diane, and he should be executed. You're just a trouble-maker, and I don't like troublemakers."

So much, she thought, for tact.

"Nice to meet you, too," she said, "I understand Diane Lasher left you for another woman. Was it something you said?"

He flared his nostrils at her. "I don't have to discuss my personal life with you."

"Yeah you do, when your personal life gives you a damn good motive for murder. Better than anything Durero's got."

"Our decision to split was mutual," he said. "And we stayed friends. Anyone'll tell you that. Making me out as her killer is just one of your fantasies, like the imaginary people you talk to. That's the problem with your kind. You believe your own fantasies."

Her kind. Troublemakers. Empaths. It was too much. She brought her fiery eyes to lock with his, saw his eyes widen in surprise at her sudden stab into his thoughts. She felt nothing more interesting than ego and pride, so when he started to squirm she released him, pulled back and spoke out loud.

"Look," she said, "I got my ass dragged here because your former squeeze was strangled by person or persons unknown. Now I've got to hang out with a possessed man who hates women and a bunch of rat fuck pencil pushers like yourself who hate empaths, and that's not my favorite fantasy. So if you strangled Diane in a fit of jealousy because she preferred the company of women to the minute pleasures of your bed, I'll find out. That's what *my* kind does."

Ned's face turned a variety of colors as he stood and pushed a finger in her face. "It's women like you that make men want to kill someone," he said. He left, shoving roughly past Alex, who wiped a table nearby.

Clyde, who was approaching her with a plate of cake in each hand, also looked surprised. "What happened?" he asked as he handed a plate to her.

"Not much. And not much fun," Jaguar replied.

"Didn't go well?" he asked sympathetically. "I'm sorry. I knew he had a chip on his shoulder about it, but I thought he might pull it up, be professional." He pushed cake at her. "Have some of this. It'll make you feel better."

Jaguar stared at the plate. In her peripheral vision she observed Alex, moving closer.

"Thanks, but I'm not really hungry," she said.

He reached for her fork and cut off a chunk, brought it up toward her mouth. "Chocolate and raspberry," he said, tempting her.

Then, somehow, Alex was next to them, and somehow, his whole pail of dirty water slipped from his grasp, sloshing over Clyde's legs and splashing up onto his lap.

"Hey," Clyde yelped, jumping up, the fork clattering to the floor. "Damn mutoids. Can't you watch what you're doing?" he growled, swiping at himself.

Jaguar bit back a smile. "I think," she said, "he was."

CHAPTER 17

The next morning Alex was running a mop down the hall near Jaguar's room when he heard the click of heels moving toward him. He kept mopping.

The clicking passed, stopped, then started again, back in his direction.

He kept mopping, not looking at her as she drew near.

"Are you new here?" she asked.

He raised a gleaming grin to her. "Pretty lady," he rasped. "You're a pretty lady."

That's what people expected of mutoids. That they would be strange, intrusive, slimy. Especially if their conviction was for exposure. He raised a hand to her face and touched it.

"You shouldn't let them do that, Dr. Addams," a new voice said. Alex startled, dropped his hand, resumed mopping guiltily.

"Hello, Karen," Jaguar said to this woman, another Teacher. "I was asking if he could help me move the desk in my room. I can't manage it alone."

"We could get one of the regular janitors to do that," Karen said.

"Suit yourself," Jaguar said. "I didn't want to bother them, but if you insist."

"Oh hell," Karen said. "Go ahead. It doesn't matter."

Jaguar waited for her to go away, then turned back and crooked a finger at Alex. "Come with the pretty lady," she said. "I've got work for you."

He dropped his mop and scuttled down the hall after her. When they entered her room, she made a small gesture, cautioning him to quiet. "The desk is there," she said, pointing, "and I want it over there. You take that side, I'll grab the other."

They shifted it, and as they did so, Jaguar lifted her eyes, indicating the pinhole where the surveillance camera kept watch. She spoke to him, subvocally.

When we're done, go to the door and start to open it, then stop.

He did so, watching her as he waited. She held a hand up to the camera, concentrating.

Alex had seen her knock out technology before, creating a temporary ring of interference, or blocking the source for transmission. She said it was a simple energy shift, but it was an unnamed art, peculiar to her.

She brought her hand down and saluted the device. "Take a rest," she said to it. Then, to Alex. "Okay. We're alone."

She moved to the bed and sat. He went and stood next to her, looking down, lifting a hand to touch her face. She leaned into it, then pulled back. They had work to do. She surveyed him.

"You look more like a werewolf than a mutoid," she said "Kind of sexy."

"I'll take that," he said. "How are you?"

She shrugged. "When I'm not waiting for someone to kill me, I'm bored," she said. "I've been to more meetings in a week than I expected to attend in the entire course of my natural life. Has anyone," she asked, "ever actually died of boredom?"

"Yes," Alex said. "If they get lulled into complacency. And how was Francis today?"

"No trouble. I brought puzzles. He likes puzzles." Jaguar slid from sitting to reclining, stretching out on her side and leaning her head on her hand. "It was fun watching you dump water on Clyde," she noted.

"Even more fun to do it." He sat on the bed next to her, making an effort to keep from reclining next to her. "Did Scott get you the word about the Praxoline?"

"He did. He's a pretty good telepath."

"Yes. And Adrian, a pretty good hacker, found out Planetoid one used to manufacture Praxoline—part of a military contract. Regina eventually put a stop to it."

"You think that's relevant? The military part, I mean."

"Not this time. I'll explain in a minute. First, tell me, did you buy the drink yourself?"

"Clyde paid for it, but he never touched it. I left it on the bar while I had a dance with him."

"Notice anyone lurking nearby?"

"Ned and Susan were there. And Derek Rhinehart, in morose attendance on a woman. That, and a few hundred other people."

"That's too bad. I was hoping to narrow the field. Jaguar, it looks like you have a Cleaner after you."

"Hell," she said. "Really?"

"Really," he affirmed, and told her about his conversation with General Durk. She took it in, mulled it.

"Cleaner's are pricey. Somebody means business."

"Somebody also knows only a pro could take you out," he said.

"Flattery, Alex?"

"Truth, Jaguar."

"Hmmph. Does Durk know who the client is?"

"He gave out no names, of client or Cleaner. But he did say if we caught the bastard we should deliver him back to the military, so I'm guessing it's someone he knows. I also had the impression it was someone he didn't like much."

"Great. So now what? Do I stop eating? Stop drinking?"

"There's public drinking fountains. They can't drug those. And I can have Scott get food for you."

"I have to say, I'm kind of enjoying having minions."

"Most queenly creatures do. Now tell me what you didn't say yesterday," he requested.

She didn't ask what he meant. She understood. Still, she paused, ducked her head down, then brought it up again. "I'll tell you about Susan first," she said, and proceeded to do so, filling him in on the affair with Diane, the report she made about the mutoid girl. Alex knew part of that story from Rachel, though the complications of the various love interests was news.

"I'm sorry you got caught in the middle of that," he said when she was done. "It had nothing to do with you, really."

"It still doesn't, but here I am. And it gives Susan a good, strong motive. If she killed Diane, maybe there's no systemic problems after all. Maybe it's purely personal."

Alex shook his head, surprised to hear her say this. She knew better. "A Supervisor's salary wouldn't pay for a Cleaner, so even if she's our killer, there's something else going on."

"That," Jaguar said, rolling onto her back and resting an arm across her eyes. Something she didn't want to talk about. Something she hadn't told him yesterday.

He went subvocal. *Tell me, Jaguar.*

She let out a long breath, and he felt her move into his thoughts. She used no words, but showed him what happened with the toaster oven and her subsequent conversation with Regina, who would not send her home. When she was done she receded from contact.

He gave her a minute, looked down at the bruises on her throat, touched them lightly. "Still hurt?"

"Just about everything here still hurts," she said.

"Especially Regina," he said.

She shifted, but didn't emerge from under her arm. "It's not certain she's involved. She might be using me to uncover the crap, too obsessed with her programs to give a damn about my health and well-being. That's not much better for me, but it lets her off the hook for being an idiot."

"It's possible. But she goes on the short list. You know that, don't you?"

"That's why I told you. And we still have zip for evidence."

Again he gave her a moment. Too much betrayal in this place. Far too many ghosts, of various kinds. And it wasn't that long ago she'd dealt with her most important ghost, a Greenkeeper who almost killed them both. Maybe it was her year to deal with all that and move on. He certainly hoped so.

"Let's look at what we do have. Lay it all out," he suggested.

She lowered her arm, stared at the ceiling and thought about it. Back to business. Back to the job at hand.

"Okay," she agreed. "We've got something hidden in the infirmary, and a very very large blood selling program. We've got stuffed bears leaving here on a regular basis, going out into the world. We've got a tangled up love affair, a hired killer on board, possibly connected to the military, Regina hiding something, and weird events that might or might not be ghostly. What's all that add up to?"

"The problem is," Alex said, "There's too many moving parts. We should eliminate one or two, and see what's left. Let's defer the ghosts for now."

"Wish I could," Jaguar muttered. Then, she frowned. "Ghosts," she said.

By now, Alex knew the look of Jaguar with an idea. "What?" he asked.

She offered a non sequitur. "Alex, what's the death rate on Planetoid Three?"

"100 percent. Same as everywhere else."

"I mean for prisoners. During their time with us."

"That. Around two percent, annually. Why do you ask?

"Because that's the sort of thing you know without looking it up."

"I mean, why do you want to know?"

She looked up at him. "Because it's more like fifteen percent here. That's what Rachel told Adrian, who told me."

"Annually?"

"Yes. It's been rising steadily in the last few years, according to Rachel."

"Oh," Alex said. "That's—really bad. What the hell made you think of it now?"

"You said ghosts, I thought of dead people. Of eliminating the ghosts."

Alex spent a moment admiring the strange motion of her mind. Then, his own strange motion began, putting together one and two and three. "Do you have any experience with ephemerals? I mean, the real deal," he asked.

"Tons. They were everywhere in Manhattan, during the Killing Times."

Yes, he thought. They would be. "You never mentioned."

"It never came up." She shrugged. "My grandmother was good with dead people. She taught me a thing or two."

"Right. So you can tell the difference between the real thing and residuals, or something manufactured?"

"Always could before this," she said. "Here—there's lots of interference."

"It's also gotten trickier lately," he said. "New technology."

There was lots of controversy about ghost hunters who used equipment that seemed to be recording information, then turned out to be manufacturing apparitions, ghostly events. Projection amplifiers, they were called, and they'd knocked more than one ghost hunting TV show off the air. They were incredibly effective, creating not just visuals, but also the feeling of impending doom, the heaviness of the dead.

"I know. Makes me question everything. Especially since I usually feel the presence rather than see them, and I'm getting both now."

"Maybe all the laser fields and energy systems here make them visible more readily," Alex suggested.

"I considered that. Or they could be holofigures, or retrojections, or incipient insanity. And some of them—the women Francis killed—definitely feel like technotricks. Lots of static, no weight, if you know what I mean. Then there's Diane, who feels real, but doesn't hang around long enough for me to tell for sure. And there's Damon, definitely a true ephemeral. Alex, if I'm not already bonkers, I will be soon if I can't figure this out."

"But you're not yet bonkers enough to try contact with Damon again," Alex reminded her.

"He's the only one I know is real, and if I contact him again he can tell me about the others."

"I'm guessing he'd rather kill you than talk to you."

"You got an alternative for getting me out of here? Like, maybe the Rapture will begin? Or we'll be hit by an asteroid. Any of those sound pretty good right now."

He reached down and put a hand on her arm, stroked it lightly. "Here's another idea. I'll work with Damon. Tomorrow, when you do your time with Francis."

She eyed him suspiciously. "In what way?"

"Just like you," he said. "Find out what he knows and get him to move on. If we can get him out of Francis we can at least take one person off your growing list of potential assassins."

"You've done that before? Purged an ephemeral?"

"Sure," Alex replied. "More than once."

"You never mentioned."

"It never came up."

She processed this. Moving an ephemeral out of someone was a particular skill, and she had no idea he could do that. She gave a slow smile. "Nice to know we've still got a few things to learn about each other," she said.

He ran a finger across her face. "Quite a few things," he told her.

Catlike, she moved into his touch, enjoying it. "Show me one," she said.

He leaned over her and grabbed her hands, kissed them and held them above her head, then pressed them down as he lowered himself over her.

She relaxed into pleasure until she caught sight of her clock, which made her groan, and not in a good way. "Hell. I've got a meeting."

"Skip it," he suggested, releasing one arm and running his fingers lightly along the side of it. "Stay here and learn something new."

Her slow eyes took him in, watching him watch her. "We'd have to be quiet," she said.

He brushed a hand across her forehead.

So be quiet.

He put his mouth against hers and kissed her. She wrapped her hands around the back of his neck and pulled him close.

This was madness, he knew. And he didn't care. She moved within the beating of his heart, and he had no room to do anything but live the madness, the most joyful madness of their souls.

They made love in stillness, captured by the sensation of floating in a silent place, where only touch and vision remained. They were disembodied by it, yet full of nothing but physical, animal pleasure, humans without words. A shining new pleasure to learn.

* * * *

When he was rearranging himself before leaving the room, he turned to her as she finished dressing, then ran a hand through her hair.

"Tomorrow," he said.

"Tomorrow," she agreed, "and tomorrow and tomorrow."

He grinned. "I am a supremely fortunate man," he said.

He moved to the door and she went with him. When he opened it, he was still looking at her, with an expression that was not in character for a mutoid.

And on the other side of the door, Susan Eideler stood gaping at them both.

"What the hell is this?" she hissed.

Alex didn't have to stretch to look shocked, dismayed, confused. He ducked his head down and brought his arms up, cowering as if Susan might hit him.

Jaguar put a hand on his shoulder.

"He was helping me move things around," Jaguar said. "Karen okayed it."

Susan pushed him aside and came into Jaguar's room.

"What was he moving?" She asked, looking at the rumpled bedcovers. "The bedsprings?"

Jaguar pulled herself into full form and pointed a finger at her. "Get out," she said. "Now."

Susan's hand clenched into a fist, which she began to raise, but Jaguar had her by the wrist and was twisting before she could complete the gesture. Then Susan was on her knees, Jaguar holding hard.

"Violence," she said, quoting a training brochure, "is not an acceptable solution to problems on Planetoid One." She moved her eyes just enough to tell Alex to leave, and he did so, sidling out the door and quickly getting out of sight. Jaguar could manage this with no problem.

She gave him a moment, then released her hold on Susan, who scrambled to her feet and cast a glance full of daggers.

"You think you can get away with anything, don't you?" she said. "But everything you did is on tape. All of it."

"So's the bad punch you threw at me," Jaguar noted.

Susan flicked a glance around, nervous. Then she regained her composure and moved out the door, turning for a parting shot before she left. "I've never met anyone as low as you," she said with dignified venom. "You're nothing but a cheap slut."

"Trust me," Jaguar said. "I'm not cheap."

Susan shut the door hard behind her, and Jaguar closed her eyes, leaning her face into her hands.

* * * *

During the remainder of the day, through the convoluted system of information loading that now existed on this assignment, the bucket was passed from Rachel to Adrian, from Adrian to Scott, and Scott to Jaguar.

Under Rachel's direction Adrian had gotten the information he needed about Francis, whose med levels were much lower than they should have been. Someone had decreased his dosage considerably.

Very few people had the authority to do so. His doctor, Regina, Susan. Of course, someone else might have changed his prescription without authority. It was, both Adrian and Scott thought, the kind of thing a Cleaner could probably figure out.

Rachel, who immediately connected this kind of finagling to the infirmary, went back to that source and started rooting around for anything suspicious associated with what they already knew about that place, or the blood donation program.

What she found was an anomaly she didn't quite understand, so she passed it by Adrian, in a conversation held when he was in his room alone, and free to talk. Getting him in that position was increasingly difficult, as he continued to cultivate the relationships he needed for his own human hacking programs.

"I'm looking at the distribution routes for the blood supplies," she said. "They don't make any sense."

"How so?" he asked. "And make it quick. Marie'll be here any minute."

"You've got an impressive recovery rate," Rachel noted. "But we won't get into that now. So they've got two large buyers, which makes sense. Red Cross and Flying Angels. Two biggest blood providers on the home planet, one civilian and one military. After that, it's a a few hospitals, which also makes sense, but then there's a bunch of really small brokers, not associated with hospitals or—or anything I can tell, for that matter."

"Name some for me," Adrian said.

"There's Tin Soldiers, in Bolivia. Frankfurt Family Ties. Crimson Tide in the US—kinda gruesome if you ask me—Bandoliers in Mexico. I don't even know what the hell they are. I can't find them anywhere."

The wheels in Adrian's brain turned this over for a few seconds, but they didn't need any longer than that. He recognized at least one name on the list from his own days as a con man. If she kept reading, he figured he'd know more. "They're smurfing," he said.

"Um—what?"

"Smurfing. It's from an old TV show. These little blue people who lived in large groups. Then it came to mean anyone having a large group made up of lots of small pieces to keep an operation going. Usually an illegal one. Bankers making lots of small financial transactions in a way that avoids a record. Drug dealers who purchase small and legal amounts of drugs from stores, then put them together for illegal production of another drug."

"I get that," Rachel said. "But how does it apply here?"

"They've got a huge supply of blood, and they're distributing it in small pieces to lots of places. One of them—the Bandoliers—is a front I used to do a little work. They sell a fountain of youth vitamin at exorbitant prices. If anyone tested it, they'd find out the main ingredient is citrozine, which doesn't keep you young, but sure makes you feel like you are. I'm surprised they haven't been caught yet, but there it is. Everyone's busy."

"Holy shit," Rachel said. "They make citrozine on One."

"There you go," Adrian said. "Now you know how they're transporting it. In the blood supply."

On her end of the line, Rachel felt a tingle of satisfaction. They'd found the key. The how and what and why. Now all they had to do was find the who. And the how and what and why limited that field of play appreciably.

"How do we prove this?" she asked.

"Best way is to get the blood they've doctored, but I'm not sure how to do that yet. The smurfing part'll be hidden in with the clean exports, which is why they're taking so much blood. Hiding a tree in a forest."

"And I suppose why they're death rates are so high. They're sucking their mutoids dry."

"Yeah," Adrian said. "Fucking vampires. Listen, start digging into finances for the principals. Follow the blood money."

"I will. Make sure Jaguar knows," she said.

"You bet. I'm—oh, hell."

As she listened, Rachel heard his door open, heard a female voice speaking, then Adrian speaking back. After that, he turned the earpiece off and was gone.

She was left on her end, hoping he'd be quick in his amorous endeavors, and find Jaguar very soon after.

CHAPTER 18

After Alex left, Jaguar looked at her schedule and saw yet another meeting she was supposed to attend. She arranged herself accordingly and was walking down the hall, on her way to it, when she saw Clyde walking toward her. He happened to be carrying a small stuffed bear.

She thought of what Alex said—that they had to eliminate the unimportant variables. And she thought of what a bad mood she was in, and how many reasons she had for that.

Some ways down the hall she saw Alex with his mop.

I'm going to Clyde, she told him. *Eliminating a variable.*

What? he asked, and she felt his consternation, but she had no time to explain. Clyde was upon her.

She walked up to him, put her hand out toward the bear.

"I'll take that," she said.

He had been grinning, ready to flirt, but his forehead knit in confusion. "Take what?" he asked.

"The bear," she said. "You're bringing it to Francis, or one of the other mutoids, aren't you? One of the special bears? Maybe filled with citrozine to smuggle out?"

He blinked hard. "Are you crazy?" he asked, and to Jaguar's eyes, it looked like he meant it. But she was in too deep to stop now.

"Maybe," she said. "If so, you can prove it by giving me the damn bear."

When he continued to hold on to it, Jaguar knew that if it didn't have citrozine in it, it still had something. She reached out and grabbed it. He hung on. She tugged harder. He tugged back.

They began grappling in earnest, Jaguar cursing fluently under her breath. Alex moved closer, thinking it was okay for a mutoid to be interested in this kind of play.

"Give it to me, dammit," Jaguar growled at him.

Clyde said nothing, but Alex saw him let go with one hand and raise that hand toward her throat. "Not this time," he muttered, and moved in.

But Jaguar, in the absence of distraction by ghosts,was much too quick for him. She found her footing and in a neat move kicked Clyde's legs out from under him.

He landed on his back on the hall floor but continued to hang on to the bear. Jaguar put the heel of her boot to his face. "Give," she said. When he didn't she brought her heel down, pressing it lightly into the corner of her eye.

Simultaneously she gave the bear a fierce tug. Clyde still didn't release and it came apart, stuffing flying out. With it went a small black square of plastic that had a tiny center of glowing red. It skittered across the floor and Clyde rolled, reached for it. Alex stepped forward, put his foot on it and stood there, looking blank, as a mutoid would.

Just in time, he thought, because at that moment two security guards and Regina Hawthorne showed up. "Stop this," Regina said crisply. "Both of you, in my office. Now."

Jaguar moved away, looking pissed, and Clyde stood quickly, looking nervous. A piece of the teddy bear hung from Clyde's hand. Another piece from Jaguar's.

Alex couldn't help himself. He threw his head back and laughed.

* * * *

In Regina's office, Jaguar stood with her arms crossed at her chest while Clyde waved his arms, claiming not to know a damn thing about any of it.

"Derek asked me to give Francis a new bear," he said, "Told me the old one was getting ratty. So I did that, and I was bringing the old one back to dump it and she attacked me. I mean, I know this is all important for justice and so on, but Regina, really. She went after me. For a damn teddy bear."

Regina turned cool eyes to Jaguar. "Explain, please," she requested.

"I thought he was hiding something in it. It's the one Francis had, and it wasn't ratty. Looked suspicious to me."

"Citrozine," Clyde said. "She said it had citrozine in it."

Regina eyed her, then held a hand out to both of them. "Give it to me," she said, and took the remnants of the teddy bear they both held. She pulled both apart further, looking carefully through the stuffing, sniffing at it, then dumping it onto her desk and poking at it more.

When she was done she lifted her head to Jaguar. "I'll have it tested, but as far as I can tell it's just stuffing," she said. "Nothing more."

"Guess I was wrong," Jaguar said. She'd seen Scott walk to Alex and pull him back as she was being led away, saw the quick motion of Alex's hand, passing something to him. Whatever was in the bear was already being taken care of. She could afford to let it go.

Regina's mouth opened, then closed again, pretty tightly. She worked her way carefully into her usual calm demeanor. "Next time you have a suspicion, I'd appreciate it if you'd tell me first," she said. Then, to Clyde, "You can go now."

"I want it on record," Clyde insisted. "I got the bear from Derek and delivered it. Took this one away. That's all."

"It's on record," Regina said.

He looked like he wanted to say more, but then shrugged, turned, shuffled away. Jaguar moved to follow, but Regina stopped her. "Not you," she said. "We're not done yet."

Jaguar sighed, turned back. "What's up?" she asked brightly.

"Don't," Regina said, "just don't try your everything's cool act with me. Did you seriously think we're smuggling citrozine hidden in the—the *teddy* bears we export?

"I was considering it," Jaguar said. "I'm not anymore."

"But Jaguar—why would you think that?"

"A hunch," she said.

"Where did the hunch come from?"

"A meeting I went to, where they talked about your citrozine production. And noticing that Francis had a new bear. Can I go now?"

"No. There's something else."

"Go ahead," Jaguar invited, thinking she knew what it was. Susan, reporting she'd had a mutoid in her room. But that wasn't it at all.

"Surveillance recordings showed you taking off your shirt in the halls, giving it to a man," Regina said.

At this, Jaguar grinned. "What of it?" she asked.

"That's not done here, Jaguar. We keep those—those interactions more private."

"Sure," Jaguar said. "No problem. Is that all?"

"Not quite. Susan was in earlier, with some wild story about you having a mutoid in your room."

Of course, Jaguar thought. This was how Regina did things. Put you off guard with the lesser problem first, and when you were relaxed, brought out the big guns. "And?" she asked.

Regina looked shocked. "Jaguar, you don't mean to tell me—"

"—I don't *mean* to tell you anything, Regina. I told Susan he was helping me move some furniture in my room, which Karen okayed. If she didn't believe me, that'd be her problem. And why the hell does everyone have so much interest in my sex life, for fuck's sake?"

At this, Regina relaxed into a smile. "Jealous, maybe," she suggested. "You look like you have too much fun. When you're not attacking employees."

Jaguar ran a hand through her hair, let out breath. "Tell Susan—never mind. There's no point. *Now* are we done?"

"We are, unless you have something to tell me about your progress in this God awful investigation. Have you gotten anywhere? Between attacking employees and having fun, that is."

"Maybe," she said. "Ned Tackerson also had personal motive, and opportunity to kill Diane. For that matter, so did Susan, who was in love with her. Did you know that?"

"I didn't. That's not pretty," Regina said.

"Not at all. But it's a goldmine for a good lawyer. Either of them should give you enough reasonable doubt to keep Francis alive."

Regina thought. "I'd rather not use that kind of thing if I don't have to. So sordid."

"You want me to create a non-sordid murder for you? Jesus, Regina."

"I—I suppose I hoped there'd be some outsider, someone not so involved here."

"Like a maintenance man, already conveniently dead? You want me to put it on him?"

"Isn't it possible? Not him, specifically, but someone like him. A failed rape attempt, but a total stranger, maybe?"

Jaguar threw her hands up in the air, groaned with feeling.

"Give it a few more days," Regina said. "We don't know that either Susan or Ned were involved, and I'd hate to drag their reputations through the muck to—to—"

"To save a mutoid," Jaguar finished for her.

"I didn't say that."

"You didn't have to."

"You have no idea what I'm thinking," Regina said, her voice now sharp with anger.

"That's right," Jaguar said, just as sharply. "And isn't it about damn time you told me?"

"Maybe you should tell me what you're imagining, first," Regina replied.

Jaguar felt inclined to continue the process of eliminating what messy bits she could, so she talked, and talked honest. "I'm imagining Diane knew something illegal was going on here, and that's what got her killed."

A crease formed in Regina's forehead. "Something—illegal?" she asked.

"Like smuggling," Jaguar said. "Which is why I went for the bear. And I imagine you suspect something, too. At least, that's what I've seen in my brief dips into your personal space."

Regina didn't blanche, but she did look angry. "I know practice is different on Three, but you're not allowed to do that here," she said.

Jaguar laughed. "What'll you do? Fire me?"

"Jaguar—"

"Really, Regina. You brought me here to investigate. Did you *imagine* I'd sit on my thumbs and whistle until you let me go?"

At this, Regina sighed. "No. Of course not. I know you better. Only, I hoped to have a little more control over the process."

"Get in line," Jaguar suggested. "Listen, why don't you just tell me what you know? It'll make everyone's life ever so much easier."

Regina licked at her lips, ran a finger across the surface of her desk. When she spoke her words were careful. "Jaguar, I'm in a difficult position. If—a big if—there's something going on here beyond Diane's death, it would need to be handled in a way that wouldn't harm the system. Carefully. Judiciously."

As Jaguar stared at Regina and wondered at the infinite capacity of bureaucratic suits to deny reality, she saw a slow, dense light form behind her. It was full of enthusiasm, and it was not willing to let any of them take the easy way out.

Save us, it whispered into her. *Save me.*

She didn't respond. The last thing she needed was more confirmation of her insanity. Instead, she leaned over, put her hands on Regina's desk.

"If you want judicious, you should've called a judge," she said. "But you didn't. You called me. That means you get the truth. And the truth is I didn't come here to ease your conscience by establishing reasonable doubt for Francis. I came here because he didn't kill Diane, and I intend to find out who did. How's our mutual respect agreement hold up under that?"

Jaguar watched the light behind Regina dissipate, watched her mentor's face closely, and in the briefest widening of her eyes, a certain tightness across the bones of her cheeks, she read one thing clearly. Regina was afraid. Deeply afraid, in a very personal way.

But this shifted quickly. Regina pressed her lips together, brought her eyebrows down. Determination. Not, Jaguar thought, a sequence of emotions she wanted to read in that face. Guilty or innocent, she was hiding something, and intended to keep on doing so.

When Regina spoke, she was composed. "I'm sure it'll hold up just fine," she said, offering her most soothing smile. "All the way through to the end."

To the end, Jaguar thought. And she had a feeling they weren't far from that. She took her hands off the desk. Straightened her back.

"Okay," she said. "Then we'll proceed."

"Of course we will," Regina said, sounding more like her usual self now. "And it will be fine, Jaguar. Just *fine*. You'll see. This, too, will pass."

****

Planetoid Three

As Jaguar was leaving Regina's office, Rachel was still in hers, consolidating all her hard work on the death rates, making sure she had a clear record of what she'd found in case it was needed. When that was done, she went through her mental file of other tasks, and thought of something she'd started some time ago, which she'd dropped to pursue the infirmary records.

Before he left, Alex had asked her to dig a little deeper into Regina Hawthorne's past, and she'd started some programs to do just that, but she hadn't checked back on them to see if anything turned up. She decided to do that before she went home.

What she found was mostly what she already knew. Regina was devoted to her job, had won a variety of awards for it, including the Women's Professional League Humanitarian Award, a pretty big honor.

Her personal history during her tenure was unremarkable, including no lovers, no scandals, nothing more scintillating than a love of contra dancing, which she occasionally pursued on the home planet.

Rachel was about to close the file when she saw the small red light blinking next to the part of the program that scanned for anything in Regina's life previous to her Planetoid work. She'd created that light to notify her only when a subject had somehow interacted with the legal system. She went to that section of her report, and opened it.

For a few moments she was silent, a little stunned, just reading. Then she sat up hard, pressed a hand to her ear to make sure her earpiece was working.

"Adrian," she said, a little louder than usual. She hoped he had his earpiece on, and didn't much care if he was in a bad moment to receive information.

"Not now," a voice whispered back, sotto voce.

"Right now," she insisted. "Whatever you're doing, figure out a way to stop and listen. There's something you have to let Jaguar and Alex know."

She heard a distinct sigh, a confusion of voices, one of them female. Then feet walking across a room, a door opening and closing, water running.

"I got a bathroom break. Make it quick," Adrian hissed at her.

She did so, and when she was done she heard him whistle soft and low. "Okay," he said. "I get it."

"Good," she said. "Make sure it gets where it needs to go."

CHAPTER 19

Jaguar had all night and much of the morning to process the conversation with Regina, and it got her nowhere pleasant, and nowhere closer to anything like evidence. But no strange ghosts or psuedo-ghosts plagued her throughout this time, so her only problem was her own thoughts, which were bad enough.

By mid-morning, when she was scheduled for her daily interview with Francis, they hadn't gotten any better. Then, she felt the nudge of telepathic contact from Scott, which made them even worse.

Ma'am? he asked.

Right here, she replied. *You got something?*

A few things. From Rachel and Adrian.

Go, she said, and he did.

The blood donations—Adrian thinks they're used to smuggle citrozine out. That's why they take so much.

Jaguar took this in, let it roll around a little. Not the bears. The blood. It made sense. And it was just the kind of scam Adrian would recognize. *Tell him good work,* she said. *Him and Rachel both.*

I will. There's more. About Governor Hawthorne.

Jaguar found herself going tense and forced herself to relax. *Tell me,* she said.

Rachel found an old record, from when she was pretty young. She was married, had a baby. A little boy born with a defect. Her husband—he killed the baby, then himself.

Jaguar closed her eyes. Rachel, who knew their job was to find a prisoner's fears, thought this was relevant. So did Jaguar. The information wanted to coalesce into an ugly shape, but she wouldn't let it. Not yet. It still didn't constitute evidence, much less proof. There were still too many variables to account for.

Ma'am? Scott asked.

Okay, she said. *Anything else?*

Just that she had the news stories of it expunged. Managed to do it with all except the one Rachel found.

Yeah, Jaguar said. *Rachel's good.*

Scott paused. *Do you need me?*

Just—hang out near the interview room. She filled him in on the plan for the day.

On my way, he said, and ended the contact.

Jaguar sighed, and made her way toward the rest of what looked like a difficult day.

* * * *

The conversation with Scott made her late for her time with Francis, and when she got to the room he was already inside, seated at his table, the guard standing impatiently by the door.

"Sorry," she said to him. "I had a few things to take care of. I'll want an extra fifteen with him, to make up for it."

"Sure," he said without feeling. Guards and prisoners, she thought. Both dulled expression and probably feeling in the face of their situation.

He walked away, leaving her alone. She entered the room and saw Francis sitting with his bear, humming to himself softly, staring at the juncture between wall and ceiling.

He often fixated on a small object in the room. A place where the white ceiling paint bled into the green wall. A screw in a light fixture that stuck out. She looked where he was looking. A piece of dust stuck to the corner, dead hair and skin gathering in a loose clump to find its way up to this place. Ghosts of cells from the people who used this room. More ghosts.

She sat down across from him. "Hi Francis," she said.

He blinked, eyed her a little suspiciously. Probably, she thought, he felt her tension. The door opened behind her, but she didn't turn to it. She knew who it was. Footsteps moved toward her, and she felt a hand on her shoulder.

Alex. He massaged her shoulder briefly, felt the tension in her and sent her his own sense of assurance. He bent and kissed the top of her head.

"My turn," he said. She stood and he took her chair.

"I'll stay in contact with you," she said.

"I know."

He sounded calm. Looked calm. Nothing at all of tension in him. She continued to hover behind him.

"I heard from Scott," she told him. "You?"

He nodded. "We'll talk about that later," he said. "Work to do first."

She continued to stand where she was. He twisted around and looked at her. "Stand well back, Jaguar," he said. "I've got this."

She made a noise, but moved back toward the wall, giving herself a good visual vantage point. Alex turned back to Francis, not wasting time.

"Francis," he said, "I'm here to talk to your brother."

Francis's eyes went wide with fear and he shook his head.

"It's okay," Alex said. "I know what I'm doing."

Jaguar recognized that tone of voice, that particular way he had of making people believe him. It had worked on her, too, and for good reason. He never spoke anything except the truth as he knew it. Not for the first time, she realized he was totally trustworthy. Not for the first time, she realized what a rare trait that was.

Francis sensed this as well, and nodded. Alex put his hands to the broad, dark face, focused, and spoke. "Francis Durero," he said, "See who you are. Be what you see."

From her position, Jaguar established empathic contact with Alex rather than Francis, listening rather than participating. If he needed her she'd be there. Until then, she was a silent presence, just observing.

The first thing she saw was Alex's quick dip through Francis's surface thoughts. The first thing she felt was the care he took in soothing any fears he found there. He moved carefully through Francis's daily concerns—what would they serve him for dinner, would he be allowed to draw today, why did his sneakers pinch. Small elements of physical and emotional comfort made up his daily round. With all due care, Alex continued to deeper realms—touching on old fears gently and, Jaguar realized, lovingly. He was, she had to admit, very good.

She didn't often get the chance to witness him at work in this way, and though she knew he was capable of intense personal love, she hadn't experienced how that energy worked in him when it met less personal demands. She found herself breathing in deeply, taking in the strength of it as if she was drinking an elixir, pure water poured down her throat in the desert.

She touched his thoughts briefly. *Alex*, she said. *I didn't know*.

She felt his smile. *Yes, you did,* he replied. *Now let me work*.

He turned back to his task, moving through the darkness of the murders Francis had committed, not judging them, not commenting on them, just witnessing the act. And in fact there was no emotion attached to any of them. His hands clutched the throats, but he wasn't there. In each instance, the hands were under other control.

He didn't do it, Jaguar thought. Not really. In each case, Damon had taken over, asked him to step aside, and he trusted his brother without question, without doubt. Nor did he have the cognitive capacity to explain what happened beyond what he'd said repeatedly at his trial. His brother told him to.

The entire Justice system chalked that up to him being a mutoid. Nobody once asked if he might be carrying a ghost. No surprise there. The dead couldn't be held accountable in a court of law. Complicated, she thought. Even Planetoid Three, for all its innovation, didn't allow ghosts as prisoners.

She heard Alex sigh as he recognized the same truth. No need for him to linger here. There was no fear to explore. He moved on. In a maneuver accomplished even more smoothly, he bypassed any other consideration and went directly into the heart of what controlled Francis's killing hands.

Here, at the center of things, Jaguar had often found old traumas or mangled misconceptions long held secret and dear. None of that was in Francis. What lived at his core was something else altogether. Something that smelled familiar to her, because it had tried to kill her, too.

Damon. For real. Not a shadow memory. A true ephemeral.

Though she knew this was the case, Jaguar felt a shiver move up her spine. It was plausible, but rare. Much more common to find shadow memory, the excrescence of guilt or shame. Very few people had the experience of touching what they'd found. It was big. A big feeling.

She adjusted herself to this reality, and was simultaneously aware of a complete absence of fear or tension in Alex. He'd expected this, and knew how to meet it.

I'm speaking to your brother, Francis, he said. *You can rest. I'll take care of everything.*

Francis, trusting, sighed himself into quiet. Alex gathered his energy to a fine point and moved on, moved in.

Jaguar felt the boiling rage and pain that continued to make its home here. Then, startling her, a booming voice filled the room, disembodied, emanating from Francis, but not of him.

I didn't kill her, it roared.

Alex continued calm and sure, speaking directly to Damon. *Diane? I know you didn't. So who did?*

Jaguar felt Damon's surprise. He hadn't expected to be believed. She sensed him probing at Alex's words, sounding them for truth. Then, his response, agitated but less filled with fury.

The people. They wanted her dead.

Anyone in particular?

The people.

Alex sighed. *Okay, Damon. We can take care of that. But you have to leave your brother now. You know that.*

A surge of anger, a surge of fear. The booming voice again.

No. Empaths here.

At this, Alex laughed, shocking both Damon and Jaguar with the sound. *Damon, the only people here who want your brother alive are both empaths,* he said. He tossed a nod at Jaguar. *Me and her. The rest of them hate empaths as much as you do. And they want to see Francis fry.*

She felt Damon's confusion, a moment of cognitive dissonance as he tried to take this in. Since his death he'd seen empaths as the enemy. Now he had to try and learn something new. But in Jaguar's world view, death didn't stop learning. In fact, it made it simpler. Truth was easier to discern without the trappings of worldly concerns.

Damon focused his energy focus on Alex, taking in who and what he was, sniffing the honesty in him. But Alex was a man. To him, that made a difference. He turned his attention to her, probing and angry. She stood her ground. Alex continued talking.

That's right. She's an empath. Risking her life to keep Francis alive.

Alex showed him the attempts on her life, the pain she felt at being here. As Damon took it in, he hesitated, worked to reconcile this with what he'd believed in life. His cognitive dissonance resolved itself into one simple word.

Why? he asked.

Because that's who she is. What she does.

Jaguar felt him mulling this. One moment, one action, had created an entire world for him, and now he had to face other possibilities. They rumbled within him like thunder, waiting to break into storm, and then they went still.

Alex perceived the shift, and kept moving forward. *You're doing your brother harm by staying with him,* he pointed out.

He showed him the review committee on Francis's execution, showed him all he knew of the danger Francis was in. Showed him also that if he'd killed Jaguar, Francis would already be in the execution chamber. Damon responded with more anger, and Jaguar tensed, but Alex dealt with it quickly and deftly.

Go ahead and call me a liar, he said. And Damon, reading the truth, could not.

A sense of his concern, his ephemeral hand reaching out, touching Francis. Big brother to little brother. *Can't leave him here alone.*

And Alex's response: *He's not alone. We're here.*

Damon's attention focused on her once again. *Her?*

Yes. Her.

Jaguar felt him probing her one more time, moving through her thoughts and emotions, sounding them against the possibility of lies, the improbability of truth. She stayed still and let it happen. When it was done, she felt both his remorse and his relief. He wanted to move on. Had wanted to for some time. But he had one more concern.

Where do I go? he asked.

Alex gave this some thought. *The families of the women you killed. Go see them. See if you can do anything for them. Maybe after that, you'll see a light. Follow it.*

She felt Damon's disturbance, but not at what Alex said. Something else troubling him.

Can't go, he said. *Trapped. All of us.*

At this, Jaguar felt a tingle. Thought of what Diane said. Save us. Save me. She felt Alex's hesitation. This was something he hadn't anticipated either.

What's trapping you? he asked.

The people.

Not very helpful, but apparently he didn't know anything else. Alex bypassed it. *Just leave Francis,* he said. *We'll take care of the rest.*

Alex looked back to Jaguar, and she felt Damon looking with him. Not for the first time, she admired Alex's sense of timing. The Adept, manipulating events to the end he picked out of the many possibilities available. And it worked.

Damon, recognizing her intent, recognizing what his brother needed beyond his own fear, relinquished his long-held post.

Jaguar felt his slow withdrawal from the body he'd occupied since his death. Felt his relief at doing so. All he'd done of murder was in defense of his brother. And though he couldn't give back the lives he'd stolen, he could leave that now, because someone else was shouldering his burdens in a new way. She wondered if all the women he'd killed would be alive right now if someone had seen this long ago and done something about it. If Francis lived in a world that acknowledged the importance of the spirit realm and responded accordingly.

Sorrow passed through her at the thought. She breathed in deeply and released breath slowly. Nothing to be done about it now. At least they'd gotten this done, and that was no small feat.

Damon's energy left the room, going to wherever he would linger until he could pass into what her people called the Pool of Souls, what others called simply the light. The air in the room grew less dense, easier to breathe. Soon after, Alex dropped his hands from Francis's face and bowed his head, looking down at the table.

Jaguar stood where she was, letting him return to himself. She knew how hard it was to do what he'd just done, how much it took out of him. The energy of ephemerals had a charge like no other, a reminder of mortality combined with the scent of infinity.

She considered the strength of his hands, lethal weapons that could be more gentle than the breath of air against a leaf. Considered the line of his jaw as it worked itself back to something like normalcy. She considered how they'd found each other, and what it meant to her that they'd done so. They both walked through darkness few people were willing to face, toward a light few people ever got to experience. They were blessed by that. Truly blessed.

She moved from her distant stance, walked to him and put a hand on his shoulder.

"Okay?" she asked.

He turned to her. Smiled. "Fine," he said. "It went well."

"I know," she said.

They both looked to Francis, who stared blankly ahead.

"You think he'll be all right?" Jaguar asked.

"We'll see in a minute," Alex said. "Listen, just so you know, the item I retrieved from Clyde's bear—Scott says it's a data recorder. For post-mortem energies. Army style."

"Hell," Jaguar said. "He said Derek gave him the bear."

"So we're about where we were, which is nowhere," Alex commented.

"No," Jaguar said. "We learned a thing or two here."

She turned her attention back to Francis, and in a minute he blinked at them, blinked around the room. He lifted his large hands and stared at them, then let them drop to the table. Once again, he looked to Alex.

"I'm—alone," he said.

"Yes," Alex agreed.

Francis stared for another second and another. Then he put his head down on the table and wept, sobbing without restraint.

Alex stood and moved to him, put a hand on his back. Jaguar came around the other side and did the same. They comforted him as best they could while he sobbed out his grief.

Jaguar wondered what Regina would say if she could see this scene, neither cold nor cynical. She thought of something a Mohawk man once told her, the story of his people, which said long ago a man known as the Peacemaker had faced his enemy, and instead of killing him, had combed the snakes from his hair, smoothed his twisted back, healed him and welcomed him as a leader of their people. That, she supposed, was what they did at their best. Combed the snakes from the hair of killers. Healed them. Made them into someone new.

Alex, she said, subvocally.

Yes, Jaguar? She used no words, but instead let him feel all she was feeling, let him know exactly what she thought of him, what his presence in her life meant to him. How it was terrifying to have found a man like him. Terrifying, to love so deeply. Miraculous and terrifying.

In response she felt the warmth in him, its source a blazing fire that would never die.

Then, a soft knock on the door, followed by Scott, looking in.

"Sir?" he asked. "The Guard's headed your way."

Jaguar nodded at Alex, who left swiftly and silently. Jaguar continued to stand with a hand on Francis's back, comforting him as best she could.

CHAPTER 20

Jaguar went through the rest of her day with a sense of peace she hadn't known since she'd arrived. They still couldn't name Diane's killer or show evidence for citrozine smuggling, but they'd gotten this far and she began to believe they'd get the rest of the way. And at least they knew one thing for certain.

There were ghosts. Not just memories. Not just technotricks. At least, not all of it. Damon was real. That meant her instincts had been accurate. Once again, she could trust herself to read her world. She needed that more than anything else here.

She continued to float on a cloud of calm born of this knowledge and, she realized, born of what she'd witnessed Alex do. Even during an excruciatingly boring meeting on Best Teacher Practices, she remained cupped within that feeling, all parts of her continuing to smile. The only thing lacking was someone to share her good will with, and she wished heartily that she could speak with Rachel, the one person who would understand besides Alex.

Then she had a placid dinner at the cafeteria, from a tray Scott delivered to her personally by the simple expedient of taking his own and putting it in front of her. As she ate, she saw Alex lingering in the hall, wiping at windows. Her day was complete. She went back to her room and laid down, falling into an easy sleep.

She would have slept all night, another first since her arrival, but she was woken just two hours later by her intercom crackling into life.

The sound reached through her dreams and she opened her eyes, staring into darkness.

"The interview room," a voice said, slow and muddy and filled with urgency.

Female voice. Familiar voice. Familiar energy, composed mostly of light.

"Diane," she whispered.

"Interview room," the voice said again, and then the intercom went still.

Jaguar hesitated. The last set of instructions she got from the intercom saved her life, so she should trust it, but maybe the Cleaner who wanted to kill her already knew about that and was using it to his advantage. It could just as easily be a trap.

"Diane, can't you get a little closer and show me it's you?" she queried impatiently.

No answer was forthcoming. She tossed possibilities around, sat up and rubbed at her face. What she'd give for a shot of tequila and a fast shuttle back to Planetoid Three. But that was even less likely than answers. She called it.

"Okay," she said. "On my way to you."

For now, she'd assume it was real. She might as well. If it was a trick, it still could lead her to what she needed to know. And what was the worst that could happen? Someone would try to kill her. She was getting used to that.

She rose, put on jeans and a t-shirt, and left her room. As she walked down the corridors she took a moment to try empathic contact with Alex, but all she found was static. He was in his cell. She couldn't get to him.

She glanced around, saw Scott walking slightly behind and to her left. Navy SEAL, who never slept. Right now she was glad of it. She spoke to him telepathically.

I'm going to the interview room. Following a ghost. I think. Or a killer.

Yes, ma'am. With you.

There was neither fear nor surprise in his response. Of course, as a SEAL, killers wouldn't trouble him at all. And since Durk trained him, he'd know a thing or two about ghosts, real or not. They continued walking, Scott trailing her. She worked to keep herself steady, not sure what she'd meet next. When she entered the interview room Scott waited a moment and then came in quietly and stood just behind her, staying near the door. Jaguar blinked around. Saw that she wasn't alone.

"Holy crap," she heard Scott say reverently, the first time he'd broken silence on the job.

"Holy everything," she murmured back. Then she gathered herself in and focused on what she faced.

The room was full of brightness and shadow, a teeming of threads both dark and light that cohered to resemble human forms, then dispersed into amorphous, shifting formlessness. A crowd of energy swirled the room, clustering to each other and away, drawing warmth from the space, raising the hairs on her arms.

Ghosts. Lots of ghosts. And as far as she could tell, they were all very real. She turned to Scott, seeking confirmation.

Technology? she asked him subvocally.

She felt him pulling himself back to discipline, considering. Then, his response.

None I know of, he said, trying to sound calm, trying to sound like a SEAL. *Projection amps don't do . . . this.*

She nodded. Projection amps only created what those who'd never met a ghost expected—a full but wavering image of a known person. But her experience was that unless you had her grandmother's skills, ghosts appeared as blocks of shadow or piercings of light, or some mix of the two. You'd perceive them in flashes that were more images in the mind, a sense of presence rather than an imprint on the eye. Just like what she had here.

And projection amps couldn't manufacture the particular way ghosts occupied space, the touch of forever they brought with them. The energy of the dead was a washing of eternity into the shallow pool of the mortal realm, a shot of perspective on your very small place in the universe.

The wavering forms she'd seen of Mathias and Lopez were filled with static, a technical attempt to mimic the kind of physical sensation ghosts created. But what she felt now wasn't generic static. It was much more particular, and much more insistent on itself. Dead or alive, these were people, each one of their shifting forms containing all the force and fullness of their lives.

Get ready for something strange, she warned Scott. Then she scanned the room, seeking and finding the light she knew as Diane.

"Hey there," she said out loud. "Long time no see."

She felt Diane stirring, amused. *We need your help,* she said.

"Yeah," Jaguar replied. "Ironic, if you ask me."

Jaguar felt Diane's wry assent, and her hesitation in proceeding. She understood what she was asking, and who she was asking it of.

Jaguar waved it away. Their past wasn't important. Not right now. "Tell me how," she said.

At this, Diane's gratitude, deep and piercing. *To know how, you have to know who. Ready?*

Jaguar braced herself. This, she thought, was not going to be pleasant. All they had to tell her would be given as direct images and feelings merging with her own thoughts, her own feelings. But it was the job, and the job was all that mattered.

"Go," she said.

With that, the sizzling cold energy of the spirit world drew in on her. The air chilled rapidly. If the lights were on, they'd be flickering. She licked at her lips, which were dry. She lifted her arms in a welcoming gesture, opened herself to what they had to share.

She felt them as a wave of energy pushing through her skin, her veins. Eternity swam up her spine. She was one of them now, experiencing what they'd experienced. She no longer owned herself.

What came next happened fast. Something hit her from behind, stunned her with an easy punch to the side of the neck, and there was a knee in her back, hands at her throat, getting tighter. Air left her body and she had the sensation of drowning, of guttering breath. Diane's death, becoming hers.

But these hands didn't belong to Francis. They were smaller, not as strong but more deft, more practiced. And they smelled of something sharp and sweet. A scent she knew. Cologne. Old Spice.

She lifted her own hands to her throat, tugged at what wasn't there. "I know," she gasped. "I know him."

The chokehold released her and she breathed again. Then, distantly, she heard Scott's worried voice.

"Ma'am, do you need help?"

She turned and saw him. He seemed very far away, well beyond her reach, but he was poised to grab her, to attack a ghost if he could, to do his job and protect her. She gave a curt shake of her head, gestured him to stay still.

"I've got this," she said, her voice thick and slow. "No worries." She turned back to her job. "Okay," she said to Diane. "What's next?"

A new sensation flooded her.

She was being drained. Drained of life, of energy, of blood, of anything that kept you alive.

She felt this once, twice, three times. As each ghost moved into her she felt it again, and again. All life drained from them. The blood donation program, killing them.

She tried to speak, tried to tell them she knew this already. But her voice was weak, only a whisper of sound.

"Who?" she breathed out softly. "Show me who."

Are you sure? Diane asked. *You're ready?*

She took in breath. Steeled herself. She wasn't, but she needed this information. More important to know than to protect herself.

Yes, she replied.

Her vision clouded and returned. Her consciousness was dim and far away. She was lying in a hospital bed, and something hurt, something stuck in her arm. She looked at it, saw the arm belonged to a young woman, dark haired, terrified and angry. There was a tube in her arm. It hurt.

She roared out sound, ripped out the tube, stood and ran screaming through the room.

They're killing us, killing us, killing us.

Blood everywhere. Screaming, and then hands that held her down, stuck a needle in her. She looked up, saw a woman bending over her, face calm and smooth, eyes kind. Jaguar looked into them and felt old sorrow course through her, new sorrow born out of it.

"No," she said. "Not you."

"Don't worry," the woman replied. "This, too, will pass."

Consciousness left her body. She floated up and up, watching the scene below with detachment. She would leave this place, fly up and away from here.

She felt the motion of it, joyful and free, a song that sang itself into light. She moved through a dark space, anticipating light beyond it, but something went wrong. Something grabbed her and pulled her back down and down, back to the place she'd just left. Pushing her back to where she did not want to be.

She was a ghost with other ghosts, flying amid a frantic circling energy, all of them battering against impermeable walls. No way out. No way out. Confinement within the torture chamber, held by those who killed her. She made a fist, punched it against air, gasped for breath and flailed for release, release, release.

Beyond her panic she saw hands, pressing buttons on a small black box with lights that flashed green, yellow, or red. Felt the satisfaction at information received and recorded. Felt the battering hands of the dead, wanting only to leave this place that had tormented and killed them. The combination of hot rage and cold detachment split her, a painful disjunction she felt in her flesh and bones. It would destroy her. Destroy her soul.

Then, the sensation of a hand on her shoulder.

Quiet, a voice said. Diane's voice. *Quiet. It's not you. You're here.*

Jaguar went still, felt the ghosts leave her, felt herself standing once again inside her own flesh, alone. She looked down at her feet, which still held her upright. Looked around and saw she was still in the interview room. She flexed her hands, remembering them. And she understood.

The new ventilation system, which recycled everything, was recycling the ghosts, keeping their energy trapped here. And someone wanted that to happen. Someone was using that, using the ghosts, for research, for their own benefit. Horrible. Horrible.

"I know how," she said dully. "I know why. And I know who."

She sensed Diane's sigh, which held the same sorrow as hers. Felt the pressure of a consoling hand on her shoulder. *Awful, isn't it?*

"Fucking awful," Jaguar agreed.

But you can save us, Diane said.

Save them. Save the woman who hated her for an empath. Save Damon, the killer. And none of that mattered.

"Tell me," Jaguar said.

She'd do anything to end their torture, which rang against her own fears like a bell. Those who had called her into this room felt that. The crowded populace of the dead entered her one more time, and she listened to what they had to say.

* * * *

Scott stood near the door, one eye on the possibility of intrusion, one eye watching Jaguar. He'd kept himself open to her telepathically, seeing what she saw, hearing what she heard. Because she was an empath, he also felt some of what she felt, and he shuddered at it.

It wasn't just the pain the ghosts brought, it was their very different form, the energy that existed outside of matter, straddling the borders between dream and waking. It brought with it premonitions of mortality, a taste of what all humans shared and hardly any wanted to make friends with. The smell of something like gunpowder was in the room, and everything was cold, heavy with sorrow and dread. It felt like every death he'd ever seen, all at once.

Part of him wanted to leave, go get Alex and hand this over to him. He had to press his feet into the floor to keep them still, press his hands against his thighs to keep from grabbing the door and wrenching it open. But barring her specific instructions he couldn't leave. Doing so would just be an excuse to get the hell out of here, and he had another order: Protect her. Serve her needs. And it was the pride of all SEALS that they'd never left a teammate behind, no matter what.

He stood his ground, waiting further instructions. He was hyperaware of his surroundings in a way he remembered from his time on active combat duty in the northern reaches of Russia, during the Chinese-Russian conflict. Every one of his senses hummed.

Then, in his peripheral vision, just outside the window at the top of the door, he saw motion, human motion, something outside the room. He cast a glance at it, saw it recede. He braced himself to attack if the form got closer, and saw it was hunkered down in a doorway across the hall, face bent over something. Scott peered through the darkness, seeking something he could identify, but it was impossible even for his exceptionally good night vision.

He filed it, kept it in his thoughts, kept his peripheral vision aware of it, and turned his primary attention back to Jaguar.

One by one he witnessed the ghostly figures, dark and light, flowing into her, each one permeating her with their lives and their deaths. He sensed their wounds, the genetic scars they bore, the violence that brought them here and the violation that killed them. And they poured all that into her, asked her to take it all in, each wound felt in particular, an entire life of pain carried through from flesh to spirit to her.

Her hands made small motions, fingers curling and uncurling. Her face tensed and then relaxed, showed sorrow and fear in turn, but she stayed rooted, glued to whatever happened within her.

He watched with increasing uncertainty and respect. She said she had it, but how could she? With all his training, all his combat duty, he wouldn't have been willing to try this. Still, he stayed where he was, waiting for what seemed an eternity until they wafted away like mist in the wind, taking their scent and their pain and their continuing death with them.

As they left, one brushed against him, like walking into a cobweb in a cool cellar. He startled at the touch.

Get Alex, a voice whispered into him. Female. Insistent. Then it was gone.

He shook himself hard. Looked back to Jaguar.

She lifted her face and smiled at him wanly. "Okay," she said. "That's done."

She took one step toward him, and collapsed in a heap at his feet.

* * * *

In the hall across from the interview room, the Cleaner worked his toys. This, he thought, should do it. He'd calibrated everything exactly, so that right now some pretty frightening images of the two women Francis killed were showing Jaguar their deaths, and connecting them to the neural pathways that would make those deaths feel like her own in a very real way.

That alone was enough to kill most people. The mind believed what it imagined even more than it believed external reality. That was where all the old urban legends about dying in your dreams really killing you came from. And since she was an empath, she'd feel it even more. But she was also special, well-trained in staving off death. He worked on the assumption that it would only weaken her, and so he followed it with a heavy dose of EMF to overload her neural response system. Then he hit her with a blast of HEF static, programmed to interrupt her particular synaptic circuits and send her into seizure.

Though she'd been a pain in the ass so far, nobody could get out of what he'd planned for her tonight. Still, he was tense as he waited to see what would happen next.

When the door to the interview room opened and he saw the young man who'd gone in with her carrying her unconscious form he felt both satisfaction and relief. Now he only had to send one more wave of EMF to fry her neurons beyond repair.

He worked quickly, opening his amp to take out the old batteries and put in a new set. He'd need fresh energy for the final blast. But when he opened the battery slot, he stopped cold.

There were no batteries in the amp. None at all.

He stared at it blankly. How could that be? It read normal for all functions throughout, and it was lighting the whole time, all green, and that couldn't happen without batteries. And she was unconscious, which meant something happened to her. He stared at the small round metal discs in his hand, back at the inside of his amp, his brain working hard to reconcile the anomaly. As he did so, he felt a rush of cold.

He looked up and found himself staring into the wispy outline of a face. A mutoid face, male, the blue birthmark covering chin and cheek. Laughing at him.

His hand began to shake and the batteries clattered to the floor. He was cold with terror, with whatever was sucking heat from the air around him.

With great effort he pushed himself to standing, made his legs work, and ran as fast as he could, away from whatever he was seeing, away from the laughter he heard all around him, away from everything he never wanted to know.

CHAPTER 21

Alex was awake, aware with a certainty beyond any doubt that he'd be needed. He sat on his bed, fully dressed, waiting for what might happen next.

Then he heard the knock on his door, followed by Scott's voice speaking softly. "Sir? I'm opening the door."

By the time he did so Alex was on his feet, ready to go.

"Where is she?" he asked, already moving out of his cell and down the corridor.

"I put her in her room, sir. She's not conscious," Scott said as he followed close behind.

Alex pointed himself toward her room and strode ahead. "But she's breathing," he said as he walked, a statement rather than a question. If she wasn't, he'd know.

Scott trotted to keep up with him. "I checked her vitals and they're all steady. She—she passed out. I think it was the ghosts. There were—well, there were ghosts."

"Plural?" Alex asked.

"Lots of plural," Scott said definitively.

"Tell me," Alex said, and Scott did, filling him in briefly on what had happened. When he was done, Alex considered.

"What you saw—they weren't holofigures or some other technology? Maybe ramped up electromagnetic field?"

"No, sir. I'm familiar with all that. These were—different. They were—people. One of them communicated with me." He shivered lightly. "It—she told me to get you. I saw her. Not with my eyes. In my mind. A woman with blonde hair."

Diane, Alex thought. "Okay," he said. "Good enough."

"I would've intervened but Dr. Addams said she had it." Scott continued. He'd been speaking formally, just reporting, but suddenly he broke rank, threw his hands up in the air. "I've never seen anything like it. They seemed to—to enter her. Sir, how could she let them?"

Alex surveyed him. He looked less like a Navy SEAL than a young man who'd seen ghosts, plural. He told Scott the same thing he'd recently said to a dead man.

"That's who she is," he said. "What she does."

"Yes, but—all that?"

"All that, and more," he agreed.

"And you're—with her, sir?"

"I am," he said. There was no point in lying to this young man, who probably figured it out long since.

Scott shook his head. "You're a braver man than I am," he said.

"Let's say a luckier one," Alex amended.

Then they were at her room. Before they entered Alex stopped. The security camera. He couldn't take it out the way Jaguar could, but he could block his and Scott's visibility briefly. After that, he'd need help.

"There's a security camera," he told Scott. "Center of the ceiling. As soon as you open the door, jump up on her desk and cover it."

Scott did so. When he was in place Alex went to the bed and sat next to Jaguar.

"She's really pale," Scott said from his position.

"Energy drain," Alex commented. "One of the signs of real ghosts, plural, in case you didn't know."

He checked her heart, her pulse, her breathing. Just as Scott said, all were well within normal range. He felt for her thoughts, found nothing dangerous or deadly. She was just literally exhausted of energy, the ghosts using hers to get their job done. He knew how to help with that.

He bent down and offered her his energy in the empathic Kiss of Life. Under his mouth her lips were cool and dry, but she shifted, sighed, and color returned to her face.

"Sir, should I leave?" Scott asked politely.

Alex grinned. "It's not what you think," he said. He twisted around to look at the young man, who had surely seen enough for one day. But he must be interested in the empathic arts or he wouldn't have worked with Durk. Wouldn't have applied to work specifically with Alex Dzarny and Jaguar Addams on Planetoid Three. "You ever read fairy tales? Sleeping Beauty? The old stories got it right. It's an energy transfer. The ghosts use whatever energy they can find to get their message across. They used hers. I just gave her a little boost from mine."

"Oh," he said. "Then she's okay?"

"I can't even begin to tell you how much better she is than okay," Alex murmured, brushing a hand against her face, kissing her lightly one more time, for good measure.

And just like a fairy tale character, she opened her eyes. Blinked at him. "Hi there," she said. "Unexpectedly busy night."

"Very. How do you feel?"

She pushed up on her elbows. "Like I drank a pint of tequila very fast. More importantly, how do I look?"

"Like a million of the best."

"That's good to know." She ran a hand through her hair. "I haven't done that much work with dead people since Manhattan. It's kind of tiring," she admitted.

"Is it now? You up for a small task?"

"What?"

He nodded toward Scott and the security camera. "Put that thing out of commission so he can get down off your desk."

"That," she said. "No problem."

She was a little wobbly as she stood, but Alex steadied her and she raised a hand toward the camera, focused briefly. "Okay," she said after a moment, lowering her hand and rubbing it against her leg.

Scott climbed down from the desk. Jaguar moved back to the bed and got horizontal again. Alex went and sat by her side, covered her hand with his.

"Thanks, Scott. You can go now," Alex said to him. "In fact, take the night off. Get some sleep. I'll cover for you."

"Sir, there's something you should know. A man was in the hall, watching us. He was working something. I think—maybe a projection amp."

Alex knew what that was. The latest way to create the impression of ghosts. "I thought you said they were real ghosts."

"They were," Scott said. "Whatever he was doing, it wasn't creating what—what happened. But I'm guessing he might be your Cleaner."

Alex grunted. Of course he was. "Anyone you know?"

"I couldn't get a clear view of him," Scott said, sounding angry at himself. "I didn't want to lose contact with Dr. Addams."

"I know who he is," Jaguar said.

Both men looked to her. "The ghosts showed me. It's Clyde. He killed Diane," she said, and her face went grim with anger. "I could rip his heart out through his lungs with my fingers and dance in his blood."

Alex, who knew she actually could do that, agreed. "Make it a Flamenco," he suggested.

Then Scott cleared his throat. "You want me to go get him, ma'am?" he asked, his voice a little rough.

She tilted her head at him, saw the bulldog determination in his face. She imagined him tapping Clyde on the shoulder, asking him politely to turn around, sir, then punching him out.

She smiled. "Maybe later. When we have enough evidence to bury him. Then you can have the first hit. But I get to eat his liver."

"Yes, ma'am," he said, with feeling.

She tossed a nod toward the door. "Get out of here. Like Alex said, get some sleep."

He moved to the door. Before he opened it, Jaguar spoke again.

"Hey," she said. "Scott."

He stopped, turned back to her.

"My thanks, too," she said. "Thanks for not interfering, and thanks for staying."

"Just doing my job, ma—I mean, Dr. Addams."

She laughed. "Progress," she said. "I'll have you calling me Jaguar yet."

He grinned and left the room. Jaguar turned her attention back to Alex.

"You want to tell me what else happened, ma'am—I mean, Dr. Addams?" he asked.

She turned to him, but she wasn't laughing. "The ghosts," she said. "They're being held here."

He paused, waiting for the cognitive dissonance to settle. "Held?" he asked.

"The new vent system recycles energy. Whenever they try to leave it throws them back here and they're trapped."

"Technology snafu?" he asked.

"No," she said. "I mean, yes, it was at first, but now it's being used intentionally. To keep them here and study them, like lab rats."

He shuddered lightly. Really? Hanging on to ghosts? What, he wondered, would they do for their next act? Club baby harp seals? Kick puppies? But it explained so much of what had happened to Jaguar.

"Show me," he said. "Everything you learned."

She raised a hand to his face and did so. She gave him everything she'd seen and felt; Diane's death, with Clyde's hands around her throat, the mutoids drained of life, their spirits unable to leave. And she showed him the mutoid girl, ripping out her IV and screaming, screaming. Then, abruptly, she pulled her hand away.

Alex looked down at her, surprised. She was holding back, and they weren't supposed to do that anymore. "What?" he asked.

"Gimme a minute," she requested.

At that, he understood. What they'd suspected. What she didn't want to be true. She was still trying to deal with what it meant to her. He took her hand, brought it to his mouth and kissed the back of it, then held it close in both of his. Her hands were like her, long and lean. Elegant hands, that did good work.

"Regina?" he asked.

She nodded, but stayed silent.

"No surprise, really. There was always only one person who could do this, Jaguar. We've both known that for a while now."

She shifted, bristled mildly. "It's not that simple. I owe her, Alex. Big time."

"As what? Mentor, role model, mother, friend?"

She turned her lucid eyes to his and he saw the dance of oceans in them. "More than that. She sent me to you," she said.

That was unexpected. Not something he'd considered. His hold on her hand tightened. "If you think I wouldn't have gotten you on Three without her, I'll have to reevaluate your accuracy rate," he said. "I knew exactly where you were, Jaguar. Exactly what you were doing. And I already had plans to have you transferred to my zone. Regina's part in it was just—expedient."

A smile came and went. "Oh, really? What if I didn't want to go?"

"I had a few ways to sweeten the deal. You would've said yes."

"I've always admired your confidence," she admitted.

He kissed her hand one more time, then returned it to her. "Good. Just so you know you don't owe her us," he said. "Not in any way. Don't let it interfere with what's next."

She considered her hand, flexed it, lowered it to her side. "There still could be other explanations," she said stubbornly. "But if she's involved there's trouble ahead. She's got lots of clout, in lots of places."

"Does that matter?"

"Not to me. I just thought it should be said."

"Because?"

"Because the ghosts asked me to do something that might make it worse."

"What?"

"Shut down one of the vents, so they can leave." She explained, and once she'd walked him through it he realized how much sense it made.

Engineers didn't consider the overlap between human energy and the energy of technology. Long ago, there was shock when radiation was shown to cause cancer. Later, there was more shock when microwaves were shown to cause depressive disjunction syndrome. Now a ventilation system was being used to hold the dead in thrall. He supposed he shouldn't be surprised at all. It was a lesson that had to be learned over and over.

"Did they happen to show you how?" he asked.

"They did. I'll only have to open one vent, pull a few wires, so maybe it won't be too bad, but I don't know for sure. It might get messy."

"Good," he said. He was angry, too. Angry at the system he worked in being used, angry at all the attempts to get rid of Jaguar just so it could keep on being used. Angry at those who would use her, use the mutoids, use ghosts to fulfill their own particular agenda.

Jaguar shifted, sat up and leaned against the wall behind the bed. "Okay," she said, "so you're pissed. But what if I do it? Then what? We can't very well go back to Paul and say a dead woman made me. Oh, and by the way, some ghosts told me who the murderer is. Told me all about the scheme here."

She was right. They had everything they needed and nothing the system would accept. And if she did this, she'd be the one in the hot seat, responsible for vandalizing a federal system of justice. But as he thought this, he felt a tingling in his hands. Blinks of images appeared and dissipated. A sensation of disaster and completion entered the room. He took in a quick breath and held it.

Jaguar eyed him. "Shaking your web again, Spider Magus?" she asked.

He attended the feeling until it was gone and then he shuddered. "More like the web is shaking me," he replied.

"Anything I need to know?"

"Just—do what they said. Kill the vent."

"And events will occur," she added. "Or at least, I hope they will because if they don't, my ass is grass." She looked at her clock. "You'd better get back to your cell—oh, hell. We sent Scott away. We'll have to retrieve him. Poor guy."

He put a hand on her arm, shook his head. "Not leaving," he said.

She turned her gaze fully to his. "I'm fine, Alex. Really."

"*Not* leaving," he repeated.

She scanned his face. His wolf eyes flashed fire somewhere in their depths, something she'd come to recognize as a signal of Alex at his most determined. "Is that from my lover, my supervisor, or the Adept?" she asked.

"All of the above," he answered.

"Elaborate, please," she requested.

"The Adept says stay until the artificial dawn, and needs no reason why. And a good supervisor knows when to give his Teacher a break. You can sleep, and I'll keep watch."

Mischief shone in her eyes. "What if I'm not quite ready for sleep?" she asked.

"Then a good lover knows what to do," he said, moving over her to show her how devoted he was to all his roles in her life.

* * * *

Adrian spent much of the night staring down at a sleeping Marie, wishing she would wake and go back to her own room. When he finally fell into an uneasy sleep he felt her tugging hard at his arm.

"Adrian," she complained. "I have to go home. Walk me back."

He groaned, got up and dressed, dragged himself down the hall after her, mumbling incoherently in response to her cheerful chatter. At her door she kissed him. "Maybe we can do this again tomorrow," she whispered, and he had everything he could do to keep from saying, "Fuck, no." She was smart and good-looking, but her extra-curricular conversation revolved mostly around shoes and TV shows. The waters were warm only because they were very shallow.

He escorted her to her room, and on his way back to his own he was looking forward only to his own bed, occupied alone, but sleep wasn't in his stars tonight.

"Adrian? Is that you?" a bright voice called to him, and he cursed softly before he turned and showed a smile.

"Hey Jamie," he said. She had her briefcase slung over her shoulder and all her rings and make-up on.

"You're up early," he noted. "Still another hour 'til lights up."

"Oh, I love the morning. Best time to get work done. You, too?

"Not," Adrian said. "I'm getting home late."

Jamie laughed. "That doesn't surprise me. Hey—you hear the latest?"

Adrian shook his head, not much caring.

"That mutoid—the one they say killed Diane. He's a goner."

"What?" Adrian asked, suddenly alert. "I though they couldn't execute him yet."

"It's not that," Jamie said. "They took him to the infirmary."

Adrian frowned. "Is he sick?"

"I don't know. But it's the infirmary. They go in, and they don't come back out. I suppose that'll quiet things down a lot, right? Something to be said for that."

"Right," Adrian said. "Something."

Jamie chattered on and Adrian let her, not listening, glad when they got to the turn off for his room and he could leave her.

He went to his door, stood outside it and counted a minute. Then he turned and headed back to the hallway, going fast toward Jaguar's room.

This was news he had to get to her. Something she'd definitely want to know. And it gave him a bad feeling about their continued residence in this place.

As he rounded the corner for her corridor, Scott, who apparently never slept, caught hold of his arm, stopping him.

"Hey," Adrian said. "I'm heading to Jaguar. News."

"I wouldn't bother her right now," Scott said. "She's, um, resting."

Adrian eyed him. "Not alone?"

Scott shrugged.

"Okay," Adrian said. "But she'll want this. Francis is in the infirmary. Word is he won't come out alive."

Scott took this in. "I'll tell her," he said. "And just so you know, things are heating up. You might want to pack your bags."

"Good," Adrian said. "I'll go ahead and do that. Find me if you need me."

Scott watched him wander back to his room and thought through this recent development. Adrian was right. Jaguar would want to know this. So would Alex. Still, he could give them another hour. He planned on making himself available to get Alex safely back to his cell, something they apparently forgot about. But Scott hadn't forgotten. He knew his job, and would see it done.

He leaned back against the wall, and kept an eye on Jaguar's door.

* * * *

When the lights of the bubble dome began to rise in Planetoid dawn, Alex got himself dressed and moved toward the door. Jaguar, waking with the sound of his motion, rose with him.

"Wait," she said before he left. "Let me check first."

She wrapped a robe around herself and opened the door, looked up and down the hall. As she did, Scott, who hadn't obeyed the order to get some sleep, appeared across the way.

Keep him inside, he said, speaking subvocally, urgently.

She took a step back, but not fast enough. A security guard appeared, apparently sliding out from the walls, and flashed his badge at her.

She motioned Alex back, smiled at the guard. "Something wrong?" she asked politely.

"Reports of a mutoid missing from his cell," he said, and stepped up to her quickly enough to see Alex before he could duck into the bathroom. "Hey," he said sharply. "Stop right there."

Alex stood still. There was nothing else he could do.

The guard brushed past Jaguar, went to Alex and took hold of his arm. "What's he doing here?"

"Hmm," Jaguar said. "Let's see. He's a man, I'm a woman, we had access to a bed. . . ."

"What?"

"You want details?" Jaguar asked.

"It's illegal for staff to have—interactions with prisoners."

"Good thing I"m not staff, then," she said. "Just visiting. Teacher from Planetoid Three, and I requested his presence. Not something he could actually refuse, is it?"

He looked appalled. "Jesus. You didn't—Why would you?"

"You got a tape measure on you?"

His eyes opened in wide shock. "I'm a Christian," he said.

"Does that apply in this context?" she asked.

He turned and left before she could taint him further, pulling a grinning Alex with him.

CHAPTER 22

After Alex was gone Jaguar spent half an hour pacing her small room, determining her next best moves. She'd seen Scott trailing after Alex and the guard, and she trusted him to keep anything horrible from happening. She also doubted Alex would get in much trouble since she'd said she dragged him into her lair. Still, she still didn't like it. Not with what she had planned for the day. She'd have to get Scott to spring him, send him back to Planetoid Three as soon as possible.

And Scott would have to get in touch with Adrian, tell him to get the hell out of Dodge. It was one thing to have minions, another to have people she cared about in danger on her behalf. But she had to take care of the ventilation system first. That was her final obligation here. After that, she was done with this place for good.

She got dressed and made herself ready to go. As she did, she went through some options on how she might also get the proof they needed to complete this assignment, but no bright ideas were forthcoming. She'd have to figure that out somewhere between wrecking federal property and getting a shuttle seat. Or maybe Alex, the Adept, was right when he said events would occur.

She was about to leave when she felt the tingle of telepathic contact from Scott. She stopped, attended to it.

Something? she asked.

Yes, ma'am, he replied. *A report from Adrian. Francis was taken to the infirmary last night. Adrian thinks that means—*

I know what it means, Jaguar said. And she did. It meant Francis was a dead man, without the bother of hiring an executioner. Now she'd have to do something about that, too. She cursed silently, forgetting that Scott was still listening.

Yes, ma'am, he said. *All that.*

Yeah. That and more. Stay with Alex. I'll take care of Francis. I'll be in touch.

She closed contact and had her hand on her door when her intercom buzzed. She tensed, expecting to hear the only voice that ever called her that way. This time, however, it was a living voice. Regina.

"Jaguar?" she asked.

She moved to it, pressed the button. "Here," she said.

"I need you in my office. Now."

Angry, Jaguar thought. Regina was angry. So, in fact, was she. But this was good. She might learn something about Francis from Regina. Might get permission to visit him, which would save her the trouble of breaking in.

"Sure thing," she said. "Be right there."

She moved quickly, before she could think about how she'd face this woman right now. How she'd look at her and pretend she didn't know. But she couldn't give it away yet. Couldn't get into that fight. She had no proof, and she needed to get to Francis, needed to take care of the vent. She had a day ahead of her, and she had to stay focused to meet it.

Meantime, Scott would take care of Alex. And she had to be ready to leave. She wasn't an Adept, but she had a feeling they wouldn't stay much longer.

She knocked on Regina's office door, heard that woman's voice inviting her in. She took one deep breath, put her game face on and entered.

"Hi," she said. "I know you want to talk to me, but I hear Francis is in the infirmary. Had some kind of breakdown. I want to see him."

Regina, who looked pretty grim, shook her head. "We don't want you disturbing the sick people, Jaguar."

"That's not my intent," she said. "Why is he there? Do you know?"

"Of course I do. I keep track of all my people. And there's nothing wrong. He's just giving blood."

Jaguar's heart beat a little harder. "Now?" she asked.

"They give on a regular schedule. He's scheduled for today."

Before she could stop herself words spilled out, and she was unable to keep the bitterness from her voice. "You make a pretty penny on that, don't you? Blood money, Regina?"

Regina pinched her lips in tightly. "If you're accusing me of something—"

"Not at all," Jaguar said quickly, trying for a save. She couldn't do this now. No confrontation. Not yet. "I'm just worried. Francis was a little shaky last time I saw him. Maybe a check on him would be in order."

Regina relaxed. "I'll look into it," she said. "Meantime, that's not the issue at hand. Jaguar, a security guard reported a prisoner leaving your room early this morning. A mutoid, who'd gone missing from his cell. He seemed to think you two were . . . . well, you weren't, were you?"

That, Jaguar thought. Always that. Why did everything have to hinge on her sexual preferences?

"Having sex with a mutoid?" she asked. "Why not? You're not prejudiced, are you?"

Regina drew herself up. "It's not prejudice. It's the rules. You can't take a new prisoner out of lockdown and keep him in your room all night."

"Actually I can," she said. "I'm a Planetoid Teacher. I've got security clearance to get a prisoner, and keep him in my charge as I see fit. Or did you forget who I am?" This last said too forcefully, with too many jagged edges in her voice. She made herself quiet. Waited.

Regina lifted clear blue eyes to her. "No, Jaguar," she said. "I wouldn't make that mistake. Not ever."

Brief silence. Both women absorbed what they'd heard, text and subtext. Regina was the first to move on.

"However, you're here as a visitor. Your clearance doesn't cover our prisoners," she said. "Even if it did, surely you know better than to—to take advantage of someone like that."

"I think," she said, "all advantage was mutual."

"Jaguar, tell me you're joking."

Jaguar told herself to stop this, stop baiting her. It was her anger speaking, sharp as her absent knife, and it should shut up now. But it wouldn't. Neither would she.

"Why? You always said a relationship would be good for me."

"Relationship? Nobody wants to—to—"

"Fuck a mutoid? I thought you believed they were equal to any other human on or off the planetoid. Besides, he's kind of cute—and really vigorous. Quite appreciative, too. You can't underestimate appreciation in bed."

Regina made a fist, hit it against her desk. "Stop it," she said, her voice too high, ready to break. "Stop this, right now."

Silence followed, and Jaguar let it play out. Then she shrugged. "Sure," she said, quiet now, her own anger temporarily appeased. "Where is he, anyway?"

Regina stayed composed. "It's also his day to donate blood. When he's done, he'll be interviewed." Her heart skipped a beat in rhythm. None of that was good. They'd drain him, assuming he'd be weak, a fragile mutoid. He'd survive, but then he'd face an interview, where anything could happen. Prisoner trying to escape. Mutoid, suddenly dead.

"What're you asking him?" she said, trying to stay cool.

"We'll inquire as to his state of mind, to make sure you haven't hurt his adjustment here."

"The whole thing was my idea, so don't take it out of his hide, okay?"

"We don't do that," Regina said crisply. Back in control of herself.

In spite of her best intentions, Jaguar decided to shake that control one more time. "Of course not," she said. "Anyway, you've got more important matters to deal with."

"What do you mean?"

"That blood money," Jaguar said. "It's about to catch up with you."

Regina's face showed concern, surprise, all of it false, deliberately produced. "Jaguar, I have no idea what you mean. Ever since you got here you've been . . . . angry. Understandable, given the stress you're under. But you're just not yourself."

"No," Jaguar cut in. "Very much myself. And wondering about all the things you never told me."

Regina made placating gestures with her hands. "I've only held back on what's important for the continuing function of this Planetoid."

"Not true. You never mentioned you had a child, Regina. In all the years I've known you, you never told me or Diane about that, or about what happened to him."

The skin around Regina's lips went pale. She stared at Jaguar, who met her gaze fully. For a count of one to ten, neither woman said a word. Jaguar waited for Regina to explain, to say something, anything, about her past. Instead she remained silent, while her face worked hard to keep itself composed.

Jaguar understood. This was the source of all she'd done since then. The source of her fear and her crimes. She ducked her head down, brought it back up. Out of deference to their history, to what she owed Diane, she'd give her one more chance to do the right thing, one more chance to slide away clean.

"You ready to send me back to Planetoid Three?" she asked quietly.

Regina spoke coldly, clearly. "I am not," she said.

Jaguar nodded. That was all she needed to know.

As she walked out of Regina's office, she was aware of eyes on her back, colder than anything she'd felt in a room full of ghosts.

CHAPTER 23

The Cleaner called in sick to his cover job that morning. He didn't want to go anywhere, except maybe taking a fast shuttle back to the home planet, something he was making arrangements for.

He hadn't slept, nor did he expect to ever get any sleep in this place again. What happened was beyond his ken, and for the first time in his life, he didn't know what to do about it. He hadn't felt this level of panic since his grandmother died, and he'd seen—well, what he'd seen then was clearly a moment of delirium, brought on by stress, by the emotions of the moment.

So he'd always thought. Now he wasn't so sure.

He'd been present at his grandmother's deathbed, a little boy who didn't completely understand what was going on, except that she was sick with cancer, had been sick for some time. And as she breathed her last breath, an energy had emerged from her broken body, hovered in the room and touched him lightly on the face.

He could still feel it, the touch cool and gentle as a morning in April.

He'd sat in his chair, very still, and waited for it to go away. It wasn't something he wanted to feel. Maybe it was soft and kind, like she had been, but it came from a place that was too big. Bigger than the night sky, bigger than the ocean he'd seen for the first time last year, the endless blue making him catch his breath with fear.

After it was over, he'd explained it to himself in a variety of ways, from the emotional overload to the general theory of energy produced by death. When he went on to create his own ghosts, finding how easy it was to do so, he'd dismissed it as just one of those things, an event that occurred around death, meaningless and ultimately unimportant.

What had just happened made him question all of that, and he didn't like questioning what he knew. He liked reality solid, something he was in charge of. Something he either lived in or created for others. He certainly wouldn't put up with anything else when he was on the job, and that meant it was time to leave.

As he opened his notepad to book a shuttle seat, he saw another message coming in, from the client. He opened it, read it. The client wanted one more shot at Addams, and gave details on how to get it done this time.

His first response was hell, no. His second response was no fucking way. But a part of him hated to leave a job unfinished, and as he read over the message one more time he realized the plan was a good one. Simple. Quick. And it left the client with the burden of any aftermath. He considered, and with his business head on, in the bright lights of the dome, he remembered something else.

Dr. Addams was an empath, and a powerful one. Maybe she'd done something to mess with his equipment. Added her own psi capacities to the mix. He'd worked with empaths in the past, and knew they could do shit like that. If so, he had nothing to be afraid of at all.

He gave it more thought. That, of course, was the most rational explanation, and he was the most rational of men. Also not the kind of man to put up with those tricks. He wouldn't let her get away with it. He wouldn't leave until he finished her.

He punched in a message to the client, saying he was on the job. When he was done he went into high gear, organizing all he had to do. He booked a later shuttle, one that would take him out as soon as the job was done. Nobody messed with him the way she had and got away with it.

He raised a hand, flexed it, lowered it again. For a moment he thought of what the General said, about getting her heel in his eye.

"Not this time," he muttered, and went on with the business of his day.

CHAPTER 24

When Jaguar left Regina she decided to go back to her room and grab a few items she didn't want to leave behind, thinking she'd better do it now. As she strode quickly forward, she felt a shift of motion around her, in her, and it stopped her in her tracks.

She wasn't an Adept, and she couldn't see ahead, but she was clairvoyant, and she could see through. Someone was headed to her room. Someone who had their own plans for her immediate and long-term future. Unpleasant plans. She considered.

The situation presented both risks and potential benefits. The risk was to her life. The benefit was the possibility of gathering evidence.

"What the hell," she said to herself. If she couldn't make it better, she'd make it worse. She continued on her way, back to her room. Once inside she stood and waited.

For a while, nothing happened. Then, unexpectedly, a communication from Scott.

Ma'am? he asked.

I'm listening. What is it?

Supervisor Dzarny. They took him—

—to the infirmary. You have to—oh hell.

She cut off contact when she saw an unusual motion in her room. The knob of her door was turning. Slowly. Steadily.

She readied herself. The door opened and Clyde stepped inside. He smiled at her, and closed the door behind him. She didn't smile back.

"How'd you get in?" she asked.

"Your door was open," he said.

"No it wasn't," she replied. She saw that he kept one hand behind his back.

He laughed nervously. "I'm hearing all these rumors and I was worried about you."

"No you weren't," she said.

He shrugged, then showed his hand, which held a gun. "Okay," he said. "So you're right."

"I always am," she said.

He took one step forward. She thought through her moves, and kept him talking.

"Surely you're not going to shoot me," she said. "That'd be way too obvious."

"Don't worry," he said. "It's covered. All part of the plan."

Interesting, she thought. There was a plan. Before she could ask about it, she saw more motion. Her doorknob was turning again. Someone else was about to make an entrance. She'd stall as she could.

"What plan?" she asked.

"None of your business," he replied, still smiling.

"What about the surveillance camera?" she asked.

"Also covered," he said. "That footage'll be deleted." He pointed the gun toward the bed. "Go over there and lie down."

"Why should I?"

"Because then you can close your eyes, and you won't see what I'm doing. You'll make less noise that way."

She backed toward the bed, going slowly. "That doesn't seem like your style. Regina's idea?"

"A good idea," he said. Then he shrugged. "I usually like to be more subtle," he admitted, "but I'm in a hurry today."

"Scared of ghosts?" she asked.

"I don't believe in them. I create them," Clyde said.

"You didn't create the ones I saw last night. That must've come as quite a shock to you."

"On the bed," he said.

She sat on the edge, and behind Clyde, the door opened silently and Scott appeared. She moved her head a quarter of an inch.

Not yet, she told him. *I need more info from him.* He stood very still.

Clyde frowned, moved slightly as if to look behind him. Jaguar feinted forward and he startled, turned back to her.

She grinned. "Boo," she said.

His face showed anger, then smoothed itself. "Cut the crap," he said. "It won't work. There's no such thing as ghosts."

"Depends on how you define ghosts," she noted. "For instance, Regina's looking pretty damn haunted lately. You trust her to hold up?"

"That doesn't matter. I get paid up front."

"I hope she made it worth your while."

"They always do. Lie down, face up, and close your eyes. You might as well. It'll be easier on you, and you'll be that way soon enough."

He still hadn't said anything that constituted proof. She had to get more. She thought through her next words. "Sure. Something else I want to know first. Why does Regina need me dead?"

He laughed. "Too many reasons to count," he said.

"Okay. Why did she need Diane dead?"

"She knew too much."

"About the blood donations? The dead mutoids? The smuggling?"

"All of the above. And we're out of time for Q and A. Say your prayers."

An inevitable pain washed through her. Corroboration, sure and clear. She let it go.

"Okey-dokey," she said. Then, she nodded to Scott. "Take him," she said.

Clyde chuckled. "That's the oldest one in the book," he said, taking aim.

Scott came up quickly behind him, got an arm around his neck, gave one hard jerk and held on. Clyde's eyes rolled back and he crumpled to the floor.

* * * *

"You're useful," Jaguar told Scott.

"When you broke contact I figured I'd better check." He stared down at Clyde. "This is his first failure to complete," he said.

"You know him?"

"I'm not supposed to say. But I wish I'd gotten a punch in before I took him down."

"Sorry. No time for fun. That was a nice move, by the way. Do you know the telepathic one, where you send out a quick signal about a bullet in the heart? I was thinking of using it before you showed up."

"I'm not familiar with it, ma'am."

"Works like a charm, but it takes some finesse. I'll show you sometime." She kicked at Clyde's leg. "I think we should tie him up and leave him here."

"Hogtied?" Scott asked hopefully.

"Beautiful," she agreed, and went to her bed, tore off the sheet and started ripping.

As they trussed him, Jaguar spoke. "I can finish this," she said to Scott. "You go tell Adrian to send the camera footage from my room to Rachel before it disappears. We've got all the evidence we need there. Then you and Adrian get Alex, and haul ass to a shuttle out of here."

Scott hesitated, looked to her. "No, ma'am," he said, politely.

She returned his gaze, surprised. "What's the problem, Scott?"

He met her gaze fully. A SEAL about to speak his truth. "I promised two men I admire I wouldn't leave you until you were safe. I won't break my word to either one."

"Alex is one," she said. "Who else?"

He cleared his throat. "Before I got here I received a communication from General Durk."

"Oh, really? What did he have to say?"

"He said, 'Cover her ass, soldier. It's an ass worth covering.'"

Jaguar grinned. "Did he now, the old son of a bitch? I hope he doesn't think that'll make me like him."

"I don't think the General cares if anyone likes him," Scott noted.

"Probably not. Okay. Here's the deal. I have to mess with the ventilation system for a bunch of ghosts. But we also have to get Francis and Alex out of the infirmary before they end up dead, and we need the camera footage from this little tete a tete before it disappears. So I'll take care of the vent, and you do the rest. Clear?"

Scott considered, then shook his head again. "I'm supposed to take care of you, ma'am."

"And I just told you the best way to do that, Scott. If you don't, I'll be worried and distracted. Could be dangerous."

He considered some more, shook his head one more time. Jaguar tried a different approach.

"That's a direct order, soldier, and I think, in Planetoid terms, I'm your boss."

Scott understood a chain of command much better than Jaguar. "Ma'am," he said, still polite, "Supervisor Dzarny gave me this assignment. And in Planetoid terms, he's your boss."

Jaguar sighed. She always forgot about that. "Maybe he is," she said, "but love trumps all hierarchies." She took his hand and brought it to her forehead. He wasn't an empath, but he was a good enough telepath to feel empathic space when he entered it.

For a moment, she let him feel the motion of her heart in this matter, showing him the ways in which saving Alex was the same as saving her. The ways in which his well-being was of primary importance to her. For a moment, his world shifted into places more startling than watching ghosts, plural. For a moment, Jaguar let him take that in. Then she dropped his hand.

"The thing is," she said, "I won't be happy if he's not alive, and he wants me happy. That's his prime directive. You know that."

He chewed on his lower lip. "But if—"

"There's no if. There's only the job, and I have to complete it," she said quietly. "Alex knows that, too. So you just do your part, for me, as you've been instructed. I'll find you as soon as I"m done with the vents."

One more hard look at her. One more moment of thought. Then, "Yes, ma'am," Scott said.

They completed trussing their recent quarry, and he left her to her next task.

* * * *

As soon as Scott was gone Jaguar moved toward the lower levels of the bubble dome, to the place the ghosts had shown her, where one of the main controls for the ventilation system was housed. Nobody paid any attention to her and she returned the favor.

The downstairs halls were quiet. One maintenance man walked toward her, jangling the tools on his belt and whistling. He nodded at her and moved on. She kept going until she came to the door marked "High Voltage. Unit 30B."

That was the place the ghosts showed her. She took in a breath, put her hand to the door. It was locked, but she broke that easily enough, and entered a grey room where pipes and switches sprawled in what looked like random patterns across the walls and ceilings. She closed her eyes for a moment, remembering what she'd been shown. It was simple, really. A small switch to flip. A few wires to rip out. That was it. But she had to get the right switch. The right wires.

As she moved forward, she felt a now familiar energy behind her, cold and clamoring. The dead were with her, waiting for release.

"Don't rush me," she murmured at them. "I want to get this right."

She found a wall that looked like what they'd shown her and viewed the many switches on it. Again she closed her eyes, counting on memory to lead her right. Then she opened her eyes, looked to one particular switch and flipped it. Below it was a twisting of wires, two of them labeled A and C, as she'd been shown. She put her hands on them and gave a hard tug. They came loose.

Immediately, there was a shrieking of alarms. She jumped, not expecting that, and took a moment to breathe, let her heart settle down. Then, quickly, she moved out of the room. She didn't want to risk meeting anyone else in here.

As she went back down the corridor, she felt the cool and persistent motion of the dead behind her.

"Hey," she said. "It's done. You can leave. Have a good time on the other side."

They continued to linger, though she wasn't sure why. Nor did she have time to attend to it. She went as swiftly as she could, making her way toward the infirmary, which was closer than the shuttleport, hoping to meet up with her minions there.

Around her, lights flickered on and off, and alarms sounded. A soothing female voice spoke over the PA system. "Master Bus B failure," it
said quietly. "Master Bus B failure. Alert. Alert."

Soon it was joined by another female voice that said the same thing
about Master Bus A. Cold and hot air blew through the halls in alternate
rhythms. Something rumbled under her feet and over her head. All this
from flipping one little switch, ripping out a few wires? Surely the rest
of the system would provide enough backup to keep it all running. Even
if it didn't, someone should figure out what was wrong quickly and fix
it. As she thought this, she was aware of a cooler presence sliding by her
shoulder, laughing as it went.

She stopped, looked around. Saw threads of motion, shadow and
light, snaking through the ceiling, around the walls. The dead were still
with her.

"Hell," she said. "You're doing this, aren't you?"

They didn't answer, but they didn't have to. She got it. Now that
the system was open, many ghosts were running through it, sucking out
energy, breaking shit as they went. The dead, getting their revenge.

She had no reason to argue with them about it. As far as she was
concerned, they were doing the right thing. "Go ahead," she told them.
"Knock yourselves out."

She felt more laughter, something like unfettered joy. The demure
female voice spoke over the PA.

"Begin evacuation procedure for Dome A," she said.

Jaguar would do so, as soon as she found Alex. As the voice talked
on, and people began pouring out of offices, she kept herself pointed
toward the infirmary and walked fast.

CHAPTER 25

Scott trotted down to the lower levels, found Adrian in his cubicle in the computer area, and tapped his shoulder.

"Something?" Adrian asked.

"We need footage from the surveillance camera in Dr. Addams' room," he said. "Get it fast. It's about to go away."

Adrian frowned. "All of it?"

"Just the last hour."

Adrian touched his ear and spoke quietly. "You hear that?" he asked.

He listened for a moment, nodded. Worked his computer. Then he turned back to Scott.

"Consider it done," he said.

"Okay," Scott said. "Time to leave."

Adrian didn't ask any more questions. He stood and followed Scott out of the offices and down the corridor toward the infirmary. Scott filled him in on the latest developments as they moved, but he hadn't gotten far when alarms started going off. Something about Master Bus A. Then something about evacuation procedures.

"Holy shit," Adrian said. "What the hell did she do?"

"Keep going," Scott said quietly, and they did so.

By the time they approached the infirmary doors people dressed in scrubs were pouring through them, leaving fast. Scott and Adrian kept going forward, into the infirmary, where no guard sat at the door. Ahead of them, a nurse wheeled a gurney with a patient on it toward the door.

"Hey," Scott said. The nurse didn't stop. Scott went to her, grabbed her arm. "I said hey," he repeated.

"Hey," the nurse replied. "Don't you know an evacuation order when you hear it?"

"Yeah," he said. "I have to get Durero out. Francis Durero. Security issues. You know about him?"

"Who doesn't?" The nurse shivered. "Go ahead and take him. I don't want him."

"Where is he?"

"Blood Donation. Check at the main station. They'll know which bed."

Scott released her and moved briskly down the hall, Adrian trotting to keep up. Nobody was at the main station, so Adrian did a quick check on their files and found the charts for both Alex and Francis, still present and accounted for. They followed the arrows directing them through ICU, where nurses and orderlies were scurrying to wheel patients toward the evacuation shuttle. Nobody stopped them as they went through the final set of doors, to the last room at the back, the place where they were not to be admitted under any circumstances. The blood donation unit.

Once through these doors they stopped, held still by what they viewed ahead.

The room was clean and white. It held more than a hundred beds, and each one was occupied by a mutoid. Each mutoid had an IV in their arm. Each IV led to a bag that was slowly filling with blood. Their blood.

No nurses or orderlies moved through this room. Nobody was getting these patients to safety. Nobody wanted them safe.

"Now that's ugly," Adrian said quietly.

"Yeah," Scott agreed. He looked around more, and at the back of the room he saw motion. Alex, standing, bending over another hospital bed. His arm was bloodied, but other than that he looked okay. Scott moved to him.

"Sir?" he asked as he approached.

Alex looked up, blinked. His face was tight with anger. "We have to get them out of here," he said. "Fast."

He removed the IV from the mutoid he was bent over, then moved on to the next bed. As he released them, he talked to them. "Get to a shuttle," he said, "Get out of here."

Scott and Adrian followed his lead, going to beds and releasing mutoids from their bondage. Some of them stared blankly. Some of them nodded and moved. Alex spoke to the ones who understood, saying, "Take care of the others. I can't move you all, and there's no time. Take care of each other."

They began to do so, the more able ones nudging or pulling at or simply lifting those who couldn't walk. In short order they formed a slow but persistent procession heading toward the door. Dead men walking, Alex thought.

They found Francis at the back end of the room, still in his bed, shivering, his eyes closed. He'd killed seven women, but right now he looked like nothing more than a pitiful, injured animal. And he still clutched his bear.

While Scott removed his IV, Alex touched his shoulder and he opened his eyes. "Francis, I need you to come with me," he said. "I can't carry you. You have to walk."

His native strength served him well. He managed to stand and once up, he walked steadily. Alex turned to Adrian and Scott. "We need to put him on a shuttle to Three. Just—stay with me."

They made their way out of the infirmary, moving more quickly than the rest of the patients, Alex nudging Francis along at his rate of speed. They were nearing the gate for the emergency shuttles when Alex spotted a paramedic and led Francis to him.

He nodded at Scott, who flashed his badge, spoke with authority. "This is Francis Durero. He needs to go to Planetoid Three. It's a security issue. Can you get him there?"

"Can he walk?" the paramedic asked.

"He can."

"Then I'll get him there," he said. "We got a shuttle headed that way." He eyed Alex. "What about that one?" he asked.

"I got him," Scott said. "Take care of Durero."

The paramedic took hold of Francis's arm, but he turned to Alex, trusting him.

"Go with him. You'll be okay," Alex said. "I'll see you soon."

He lifted his broad, dark hand, touched Alex's face, dropped his hand to his side. "Thank you," he said. Then he shuffled away.

They watched as the Paramedic led him toward the gate with a group of others, some walking, some being pushed on gurneys. The voices still spoke over the PA system. Alarms continued to go off. Strange cracklings could be heard all around and lights flickered on and off.

To Adrian's surprise, Alex turned to Scott and showed him a glare. "Why aren't you with Dr. Addams? You're supposed to take care of her."

"I am, sir," he said, not blanching or backing down.

"What the hell does that mean?"

"Sir, it'll be faster if you just—see for yourself."

Alex made a sound of impatience, but he raised a hand to Scott's forehead, and saw what Jaguar had shared with him.

As he took in the persuasive argument she'd used, something in the region of his chest tugged hard. What Jaguar was, what she felt and what she chose, always entered his blood stream like a celestial storm. He breathed into the feeling, asked it to subside for the time being. Later, he'd show her what it meant to him. Now there was work to do.

"Okay," he said tersely. "You—you did the right thing. I'll find her. You two get to a shuttle."

"Yeah," Adrian said. "As if."

He looked at Scott, who only shook his head.

Before Alex could argue with them, Adrian gave a yelp. Scott and Alex turned to him.

"What the hell is that?" he demanded, pointing ahead.

Something coming at them, a dark cloud, filled with lightning, flying at them head on. Scott, who already knew how to name it, braced himself. Only Alex stayed relaxed.

"Hello, Damon," he said. "Something you wanted?"

* * * *

Jaguar didn't get too far toward the infirmary when she was aware of a presence at her back, a particular and well known energy. She stopped, closed her eyes and opened them again.

"Diane," she said. "Forget something?"

She felt laughter, then heard a voice speaking within her. *You did. Regina.*

"We've got the proof we need," Jaguar said. "Clyde gave it away."

Is it enough?.

That, Jaguar thought. What they had on tape were the words of a hired killer, which would have to stand against Regina's years of service.

"It's what we could get," Jaguar said, a little testy.

No. You could get Regina.

Get Regina, before she disappeared in the chaos. Face her down, take her in as the world fell down around her. "It's damn risky," she pointed out.

Diane's soft laughter. *As if that ever stops you.*

Diane had her on that one. It wasn't the risk that made her hesitate. It was something else. A petulance born of too many demands on her time and her emotions, made by those who never had her back. A yearning to get away from here.

"Here's the thing," Jaguar said. "You're dead, I'm not, and I'd like to keep it that way. Besides, I already saved your ghostly asses. Can't you let Regina go?"

Can you?

Let her go. Just walk away. It wasn't in character for her, but she still resisted completing the job. And that went beyond petulance or simply wanting to leave. It was more about not wanting to face this particular betrayal, with all its attendant pain and anger. Mentor, role model, mother, friend, all gone at once.

"The last thing I want to do here is go get Regina," she said.

She felt the concordance of Diane's sorrow. A recognition of loss, and the inevitable necessity that followed.

Yes, she agreed. *The last thing you want to do here. The last thing you need to do.*

Jaguar sighed deeply. There were so many reasons why she'd been friends with Diane, and that kind of clarity was just one. In her best moments, she shed light on what was dark. In her worst, she ran from darkness, hiding in the light. But in her death she no longer had anything to fear from the darkness. No longer had anything but light to shed.

And what she said was true. They had been friends, she and Regina and Diane. Three powerful women working to transform evil into good. Now Diane was dead and Regina had betrayed all they believed in. Jaguar was the only one left standing. The only one left to throw light on the darkness Regina had created.

Then, Diane's voice again, kind and warm. *It's what empaths say. See who you are. Be what you see.*

Jaguar felt her jaw twitch. Diane, who hated her for an empath, hated herself for loving her anyway, dared use the empath's ritual words to convince her. Not right. Very not right, in many ways. And Diane had yet to acknowledge that.

"You didn't like that so much when you had me kicked out of here," she noted.

A rueful assent. A long-held regret.

I was afraid of what I felt for you. Afraid of something I didn't understand. I've learned better since then. Can you forgive me?

Her words washed over Jaguar like cool water on a festering wound. They were a gift she didn't hope to receive, and one she'd wanted for a long time. They dismissed ancient pain, and allowed her to move toward what she had to do next.

"Yes," she whispered. "That I can do."

Something warm entered her. Something like old friendship, the meeting of two women who each lived close to their principles, their errors meaning much less than the quality of their souls, which were both now entirely visible. Jaguar let it settle in, then turned her face back to business.

"I'll go to Regina's office, get some evidence, and get her if I can, but after that I'm out of here," she said. "If I can't find her, she's all yours. And do me a favor, would you? Let Alex know what I'm doing. Make sure he's okay. And tell Scott not to worry. Tell him he did the right thing."

She felt a soft brushing of energy against her cheek. Felt the ending that went with it. All between them was complete.

Diane's ephemeral form drifted away. Jaguar moved on.

* * * *

As Alex stood his ground, Damon's form moved closer, and others like him followed close behind. Adrian swore with reverence and Scott stayed silent.

Follow us, Damon said. *Now.*

An urgent command. No time to waste. Jaguar was in trouble. They knew where she was, and it wasn't close by. Damon's form sped forward.

Alex followed quickly, his long strides breaking into a run as he tracked the static charge that coursed swiftly in front of him. They had a lot of ground to cover and they had to cover it fast. Behind him, Scott and Adrian hesitated. Alex paused just long enough to turn to them.

"Well," he said. "Run."

As he moved toward Jaguar's light, Alex created a whole new set of pejoratives for her obstinate, if embodied, soul.

CHAPTER 26

When Jaguar got to Regina's office it was dark and empty, with no sign of Regina's presence. She was caught between irritation and relief. She'd prepared herself for a showdown she didn't want, and now she wasn't going to get it. Well, she thought. Oh well. She could still gather evidence, and that would have to be good enough.

She moved to the computer on Regina's desk. Most of them went automatically to a backup power source, and she hoped that was true here. If it was, she faced another problem. It would be coded to Regina's fingerprint, probably a retinal scan as well, and she'd have to override that. She went through the moves in her mind, and held her breath as she pushed the start-up key. When it actually lit up she allowed herself to breathe again.

"Regina Hawthorne?" the computer voice asked politely. She focused, put her face to the screen and the index finger of her right hand against the print pad, blanked out everything of self and brought to mind all she knew of Regina.

The machine made its noises, and the voice spoke again.

"Confirmed," it said.

"You bet," Jaguar answered. She punched in Rachel's number on the telecom function and waited. Then Rachel's surprised face appeared on the viewscreen.

"Jaguar?" she asked. "What the hell?"

"Hey," Jaguar said. "Very glad to see you, too, and no time to explain. I'm on Regina's computer and I have to find stuff on it. Tell me how."

Rachel frowned, but didn't miss a beat. "What kind of stuff?" she asked.

"Um—everything?"

Rachel rolled her eyes. "That'd take a few years," she said. "Listen, just go to the info icon and open it."

Jaguar did so. "Now what?"

"Give me the serial number and ID code," Rachel told her.

She read them out. "What next?" she asked.

"I'll take it from here," she said. "You get out of there. Fast. Adrian told me what's going on."

Jaguar hesitated. Was this enough? Should she stay and hope Regina returned? Start looking for her? No. She couldn't hang around, and she couldn't run blindly through the bubble domes looking for a woman she didn't really want to find, with no idea if she was even still here. Wanting to do so was just ego and the remnants of anger. Nothing she needed to hang onto.

She shivered, pushed the thought away, grinned at Rachel. "Adrian looks forward to meeting you in person."

"Don't start," Rachel said.

"I won't, only because I don't have time. See you soon."

"You better. Oh—I got the camera footage from your room. Now go, would you?"

Jaguar nodded. Now, in all good faith, she could leave. "A thousand blessings on you," she said.

Rachel signed off and Jaguar stood to leave the office. As she did, the lights in the room flicked on and off wildly, strobelike. She squinted ahead, trying to adjust her obfuscated vision as she made her way to the door. She was just in front of it when she realized that, for the second time in one day, someone was aiming a gun at her. She blinked at it, around it, until she could see the face on the other side.

"Hullo, Regina," she said. "How's that mutual respect thing working for you?"

Regina pushed the gun at her. "Show me your hands, and they better be empty," she said. Her voice was thick and rough. She was close to the edge, Jaguar thought. Like the Planetoid itself, a complex system held together with lies, easily dismantled by too many ghosts.

"Very empty," Jaguar said, holding them up, keeping her own voice neutral. "In fact, I'm totally defenseless, just like you made sure I'd be. Though I still wonder why the hell you wanted me here. You could've walked away clean if you left me out of it."

"No," Regina said. "You kept talking about us. You wouldn't shut up. Sooner or later someone was bound to listen."

Jaguar nodded. She'd been a threat for a while, with all her noise about Planetoid One programs. And Regina would want to manage her as she did all crises—with a plan that was subtle and thorough and complete.

"You're right," Jaguar admitted. "I get that. But I don't get the rest of what you did. When did it start? All the killing here, I mean."

Regina's head jerked to the side, back again. "There's been no killing," she said. "The mutoids—they just—they die. They're fragile. They would die anyway."

Jaguar looked at her with some amazement. Did she really believe that? She held eye contact, looked closely at the calm assurance in her mentor's cool blue eyes as well as the tension in all the small muscles of her face. A quick slide into the surface of her thoughts told her the rest.

Regina had worked hard to convince herself she wasn't responsible for the deaths of the mutoids, that somehow, sucking their blood dry to smuggle out drugs was different than killing them. But her belief was growing fragile, crumbling within her as her system crumbled around her, and she was desperate to hold it together. It had supported her for a long time, starting well before her work on Planetoid One.

Jaguar felt the confluence of fears, old and new. As she'd seen before, everything Regina did here started with her son, doomed from birth. The horror of watching him die slowly was too much for her, and so she'd managed his death as she managed everything else in her life since then. Through the power of her words, the strength of her intent. That was her training ground, and the source of her fear. In spite of danger, in spite of her anger and sorrow, Jaguar felt the thrill she always had when she reached a prisoner's core and knew how to proceed next.

"Fragile, like your son?" she asked.

Regina stepped forward, pushed the gun into Jaguar's chest. "Stop it," she said. "Don't try your Teacher tricks on me."

Jaguar breathed out, releasing old friendships, old contracts of mutual respect. "So," she said, "shoot me."

Regina shuddered lightly, her neurons firing too hard, her hand not entirely steady. She composed herself, stepped back.

"In front of my office?" she said. "I don't think so. Turn around and walk."

Jaguar did as she was told, taking time to think through her next moves. Those depended entirely on what she was trying for. Saving her own life seemed high on the agenda, and that would require only a quick whirl and kick, something Regina wouldn't expect and wouldn't be prepared to meet.

Then again, there was Diane's mandate, her own mandate. Bring her in. Bring this one home. Diane, who loved her and betrayed her and was dead. Diane, whom she owed nothing. Diane, who was right.

Hell, Jaguar thought. Rat fuck and hell. Then, she started talking. "Tell me about your son, Regina," she said, and felt the gun twitch. Very reactive. Had to watch that.

"You already know, don't you? He was sick. My husband killed him."

"Not without consensus," Jaguar said. "You wanted it, too, and I understand why. You saw how much pain he was in and wanted to end it."

She kept her tone clear of judgement, which was easy because she truly didn't judge Regina for this. Wanting to end the misery of a child who would never heal was understandable. A complex human dilemma

Regina met in the only way she knew how. A tragedy rather than a crime. Making someone else carry the burden of it for you was something else altogether.

The lie inherent in that choice had wrecked Regina for good. Made it impossible for her to ever love again, ever do anything but relive the same act over and over, because the lie had to be justified, had to be made true in some essential way. But it couldn't, because it was still a lie. That's what Jaguar had to deal with. She had to find a way to help Regina barter her dearly prized illusion for the truth. And that, she thought, was probably one of the most difficult tasks in this and any world.

Regina's next words only confirmed Jaguar's thoughts.

"I never touched him," she said firmly.

"No. Of course you didn't. You keep your hands clean. But you're a woman of integrity and sustaining that kind of deception would just about kill you. Then, to come here and do it all over again with the mutoids. Seeing them every day, knowing their condition. Knowing what the blood donation did to them. Regina, that's gotta hurt."

Another twitch of Regina's hand as the truth flicked at her flesh. But when she spoke her voice was both sorrowful, and firm in its conviction. "It's not been easy," she admitted, "But it was a mercy, really. They had none of the suffering they'd face if they lived."

This was good, Jaguar thought. Regina was talking, letting her in to a place no one else had seen before. She was still lying to herself, seeing herself as a hero who released the weak from their pain, but it was one layer of deception down. Only a profundity of others left to go.

"That's why you do it, then," Jaguar said. "To relieve their suffering. Just like your son."

A moment of hesitation on Regina's part, and then she ducked back into denial. "I told you, I didn't touch my son. And I'm not responsible for what my husband did."

Okay, Jaguar thought. It always took more than one try. So she'd keep trying.

"That's the story you told the world, but you're too smart to believe it fully, and it's eating you alive to keep trying. I see what it's doing to you, Regina, and it worries me."

Behind her she heard laughter, low and a contained. "You're worried about me? *You*? Please. Give me credit for some brains, and spare me your feeble attempts at playing Teacher. You never cared for anything or anyone beyond your own ego. Not for any lover or friend. Not whether your prisoners live or die. Next life cycle, you say. They mean *nothing* to you."

And that, Jaguar thought, is that. Compassion and connection clearly wouldn't work. She'd have to go for the back of the neck, find a skull to crack.

"You'd rather play that way? I'm good with that," she said. "Then let's remember I'm not the one using prisoner's blood to smuggle drugs out. I'm not the one hanging on to their ghosts. What the hell was that for, anyway? Fun or profit or both? Did Clyde give you a discount if you let him keep them in his zoo?"

The pause that followed told Jaguar she'd got that one right. But Regina quickly found the words she needed to justify that as well.

"Ghosts," she said, derision in her voice. "If you care about their lives, then the afterlife will take care of itself."

"And if you kill them, they'll come back and take care of you," Jaguar noted. "Lots of trouble with your systems lately, right? Strange occurrences at meetings? And the thing about ghosts is they've got time. They keep coming back until you send them on."

"Don't start that nonsense," Regina said, pushing her forward. "I never killed anyone. *Never*. Do you hear me? I gave the mutoids the best care, and the possibility of doing good in the world. They died because they were sick and suffering already."

"They died because you needed money," Jaguar shot back. "Jesus, Regina. Aren't you even a little sorry about the smuggling?"

A small tension, dissipated quickly. "You have no idea what it's like here. Nobody cares about the mutoids. Nobody funds what we do. I— I'm not proud of my method, but it was the only way to help them. The only way to keep the programs running."

"The programs that keep the place running so you can kill more mutoids to keep the programs that kill them running?"

"My programs save many lives," Regina insisted. "The ones who died—well, we choose our blood donors very carefully. I'm not—not a cruel woman."

"I never thought you were. But you've certainly fallen into some essential errors, and you won't continue in them. We've got evidence of what you did. The money trail will lead right back to you."

"No it won't," Regina said, her voice prideful. "I took no profit. It all goes to the programs."

Of course it did, Jaguar thought. She should've guessed that. Regina might be a maniac, but she wasn't mercenary. "What about everything I just got from your files?" she tried.

"Got from my files or put in them? I saw you illegally breaking into my system, a federal offense. And lots of people will confirm you've been more than a little strange since you got here."

Jaguar offered a silent curse to all her gods. This was going west fast. She had to bring it back somehow. She dug into her nonexistent pocket and found no senators, but there was one more ace.

"Not all the money went to the programs. Some of it paid your Cleaner to take out Diane," she said.

"Not traceable. And Diane is dead through her own folly," Regina said, and now her voice was thick with bitterness. "She started asking questions when some of the mutoids died. *Her* mutoids, she called them, as if she held their patent. I told her they were weak. They died young. She wouldn't accept that. She kept digging, got hold of the blood donation records. Then she was arrogant enough to confront me with them, as if she was pure and holy and I'd done something wrong. And you're as arrogant as she was, thinking your life is more important than the work we do here. Would I let all this disappear, just because you say I should?"

"It will now," Jaguar noted. "I'm not the only one who knows you killed Diane."

"No," Regina said curtly. "My hands never touched her."

"Like they never touched your son?"

If she could bring her back there, dig in at the source, she could still turn this around. But she didn't have much time, and absolutely no safety net.

She tried for empathic contact, a small touch, but Regina, brittle as frozen glass, felt it this time. She raised a hand and slapped hard at the side of Jaguar's face.

"Don't you dare," she said through her teeth.

As she spoke, the PA system, which had been blaring the whole time, suddenly went dead silent. The lights, which had been flickering on and off, went out for good. Regina shoved Jaguar forward.

"Move," she said. "And keep your mouth shut. After everything I did for you, you pay me back by trying to wreck my life? You have *nothing* to teach me."

They walked the empty corridors, and this time Jaguar kept her peace. She couldn't find her way in to Regina. Couldn't find the right hook, the right words. Not yet. That happened sometimes in an assignment, but on Planetoid Three she had more resources, more time to figure it out. Now she had only the cold of a gun against her flesh, held by a volatile woman who had every reason to prefer her lies to what Jaguar was offering.

As they walked, Regina said nothing except to tell Jaguar when to turn left or right, until Jaguar knew where they were headed. To the room where she'd made puzzles with Francis. The only room without a camera. The interview room. As if that mattered anymore. But it did to Regina, lost in her fantasy and her fear.

They drew closer and Jaguar made one of the few moves left to her. She reached out empathically to Alex, telepathically to Scott. At first all she got back was static, any message she sent lost within the wild and random energy shot out by the collapsing systems of the bubble domes.

But when they got to the interview room and Regina reached around her, opened the door and shoved her inside, she became aware of thoughts brushing against hers. Alex, chasing her light. He used no words, but he didn't have to. She felt his determined flight toward her, with minions.

However, she couldn't tell where he was coming from or how long it would take him to get here, and guns could go off pretty fast. Back to work, she thought, and started talking again.

"Why here?" she asked Regina. "Because there's no camera?"

Regina stayed behind her, kept the gun close to the back of her neck.

"No. Because we'll have evidence you used this room for trysts with your mutoid lover. The one you kept in your room. But you know how unstable mutoids are. This one shot you, then killed himself."

In the darkness, Jaguar grinned. That's what Clyde meant when he said it was covered. She was supposed to be shot in her room, with the mutoid probably brought in later to join her in death. Not a bad plan, and Regina's improv on it would probably work just as well, except for one small problem.

"My mutoid lover," Jaguar said. "You mean Alex?"

She couldn't see Regina's face, but she felt her cognitive dissonance. "Alex?" she asked. "What's he got to do with it?"

"He's the mutoid," Jaguar said.

Jaguar heard the sharp intake of breath. "No," Regina snapped out. "He's a—a prisoner."

"He's *Alex*. An Adept with enough smarts to figure out how to get here. Did you really think you could keep him away from me?"

A pause, and when Regina spoke, her voice crackled with anger. "You *lied* to me. You told me you weren't lovers."

"Jesus Christ," Jaguar muttered. "That's what you're worried about?"

Immediately she felt a sharp punch in her back that shoved her down onto her knees. A moment of instability. She could use it to take Regina down. Or she could use it to try one more time to make Regina face the truth.

Rat fuck, Jaguar thought. Rat fuck and hell. She dropped to her side, rolled over flat on her back, so Regina could see her face.

Do it, she said, speaking into her. *Kill me, with your own hands, your own intent. Look in my eyes, remember everything, and then kill me.*

Regina's cool blue eyes were full of static as all her conflicting motives, all her lies and all her truth, met in this particular moment. Jaguar's sea green eyes showed her every good thing they'd ever shared. Every moment of friendship, everything she'd ever felt about her, about Diane.

Look at that and pull the trigger, she insisted. *Do it, and own it. Your hands. Your murder. No killer but you this time.*

A half a minute passed, and nothing happened.

"You can't," Jaguar said gently, speaking out loud. "Just like you couldn't kill your son. You could only talk your husband into it, because that's what you're good at. Talking. But you can't talk your way into killing me."

Silence. A long silence. Regina's hand quivered lightly.

"You're not a killer, Regina," Jaguar said. "Put the gun down. I'll stay with you. We'll see it through together."

A shudder passed through Regina and then she jerked back into awareness. "You want me to give myself up?" she said, her voice a storm of rage and fear. "Then what? I'm one of *your* prisoners? The ones you kill?"

"No," Jaguar said. "The ones I heal."

"My programs—they'll be tainted. Destroyed. All my work gone. It's my *life*, and you'll wreck it. I *won't* have it."

Hearing this, Jaguar realized she'd made the worst possible error. She'd imagined that Regina, in some part of herself, wanted to be saved, maybe even brought Jaguar here to do so. As a Teacher, she'd found that spark of possibility in pedophiles, assassins, spree shooters, and con artists. She couldn't believe she wouldn't also find it here.

Okay, she thought. A mistake. An essential mistake, the kind that get people killed. But not today. This was still recoverable. Or so she hoped.

"Roll over," Regina demanded. "Your face on the floor."

As Jaguar considered whether it was better to stay where she was, or use her motion to end this, a chill moved up her arm, and the lights in the room began to flicker dimly. Jaguar sensed a shift in the air, a building of pressure, approaching like a line of thunder storms.

Stall her, a familiar voice said within her. *Almost there.*

Alex. He was, Jaguar thought, even more reliable than death.

Regina pushed the gun closer to her face. "I said, move," she spit out harshly.

"Moving," Jaguar said, and took her time in doing so, rolling onto her side, putting her hands and knees firmly on the floor. She felt the gun at the back of her neck again. "Can I say something first?" she requested.

"Go ahead," Regina said tightly.

"Maybe you'll have the satisfaction of knowing I was stupid enough to get you all wrong. But I'll have the consolation of being one more ghost haunting you."

"I don't believe in ghosts," Regina said firmly.

Jaguar felt the pressure drawing closer, and grinned. "You may have to rethink that position," she said.

And as she said it, all hell broke loose.

The floor rumbled with the imperative of an earthquake, and the lights began a strobe-like dance, hissing out sparks. Regina tipped, righted herself, and Jaguar felt the pressure of the gun retract. She scrambled to stand but the floor shook under her, she lost her balance and came down heavily again on all fours, while the door blew itself open and the room filled with swimming, swirling motion.

From her position Jaguar saw shadow filled with crackling light, drawing close. Someone she knew. Someone who tried to kill her. Someone who had amends to make.

"Damon," she whispered. Behind her, Regina gasped, stumbled further back.

Now. Now she could take her down. She tried to rise and whirl back toward her, but Damon's energy flowed over her like heavy water, shoving her down, banging her face against the floor. A bright flash of pain stopped her vision and she blinked against it, pushed herself up again, looked ahead. Through the throbbing in her eyes she saw someone enter the room.

Alex, moving to her fast, Scott and Adrian close at his back. And other ghosts, Diane's among them, flowing through the room like rising floodwaters, bringing cold and a flashing of lights and strange rumblings and the taste of forever.

Alex shot a glance her way, raised a hand to hold Adrian and Scott back. They stopped at his command. He shifted his wolf eyes back to her, his will for her life a sparking of fire within them, his fixed intent holding her still.

Look at me, Jaguar. Only at me.

It was a tribute to her trust in him that she complied. She lifted her eyes to his, saw his face as if it was the center of the universe.

The gun fired.

She heard it. Felt the blast. Felt wet blood on her skin as she was pushed down by the heaviness of death and vastness of eternity. She was a body dragged to earth, something heavy at her back. Alex will never forgive himself, she thought. Never, never.

Flat on the floor, she stared up, saw Alex approaching fast as she waited for death to find her. She wanted to tell him it wasn't his fault. Wanted to say she was sorry they wouldn't have more time, more sex, more fun. But no words came. She just stared, waiting for her heart to stop beating, her lungs to stop breathing.

Alex.

Here, Jaguar. Here.

Then he was with her. He grabbed her arms and pulled her out from under the weight on her back and somehow she was on her feet, standing, and her heart continued to beat and she kept breathing. Alex wrapped his arms around her and sheltered her face in his chest. In her peripheral vision she saw wispy figures exit the room, the Planetoid, this world.

Damon and company, leaving for good.

For a long moment there was only silence, and the relief of a storm that had recently passed. The air was clean, the room still.

"Jesus," a voice said at last. Adrian's voice. "That's messy."

She lifted her head and saw Scott and Adrian standing behind Alex, at first staring beyond her, then turning away. She looked at Alex.

"Alex? Did she shoot me?"

He regarded her as if she was insane. "Would I let that happen? No, Jaguar. Not you. Not you."

She pulled away from him, turned and looked behind her.

Regina was splayed on the floor, face down, the back of her skull shattered and blood pooling around her. Jaguar went to her and turned her over. The hole in her forehead was small and her eyes were open. Her mouth was caught in a grimace of something that combined satisfaction and pain.

Jaguar knelt and spoke to her so softly Alex couldn't hear what she said. A farewell, an absolution, or a prayer of her people for a better journey than before.

Outside the interview room, he heard the sharp crackle and hiss of many systems failing all at once. He touched her shoulder.

"Sorry, but we better get a move on," he said.

She stood, faced him. "Okay," she agreed.

"Anything you need in your room?" he asked.

She thought of Clyde, hogtied there. Once they got on the shuttle she'd have Alex call Durk to go pick him up. For now, she'd leave him. There might be a ghost or two in the vicinity to keep him company while he waited.

"Not a damn thing," she replied.

"Then let's go," he said.

EPILOGUE

They ran into Susan at the shuttleport and she charged up to Scott, fury in her face.

"Arrest her," she said, pointing at Jaguar. "She did this. All this. Destroyed an entire Planetoid. And—and she was having *sex* with that mutoid."

Scott looked to Alex, who shrugged, went and put a hand on Susan's shoulder, leaned close to her ear. "I warned you not to let her stay too long," he said.

She turned and gaped at him. She recognized the voice, but it didn't go with the face. Alex grinned, spoke to Scott. "You got cuffs on you?" he asked.

"Yes, sir," Scott said.

"Use them."

Susan was quiet after that.

* * * *

On the shuttle back Alex put a call in to Durk, telling him where he could pick up his package and advising him to hurry. Durk only grunted, and signed off. Alex figured he already had a minion or two of his own on hand to manage it. Then he turned to Jaguar.

"There'll be hell to pay. You know that, right?"

"All they can get me for is opening one vent. That didn't do all this damage." She mulled it. "But I suppose I can't really tell them how it happened, or why I did it, can I?"

"Sure you can," he said. "They just won't believe you."

"Then I opened it figuring it'd set off an alarm, and I wanted to create a distraction so I could save you and Francis. And I don't have a rat's ass clue about the rest. How's that?"

"Exigent and urgent situation. Good enough," he agreed.

After that, Jaguar was also quiet, resting her head on his shoulder, closing her eyes. He could still see bruise marks on her throat. Rough.

It had been rough.

When they got back to Planetoid Three the days that followed weren't much better. They were sequestered away from each other at night, thoroughly guarded to avoid any chance of the media getting to them. Administratium wanted no interference with their spin.

During the day they went through long interrogations separately and together, in the company of Planetoid officials, legal reps, and some very nervous insurance representatives. Scott, made invisible through Rachel's careful planning, was the only one who didn't get snared. The others were asked seemingly endless questions at proceedings from which Paul Dinardo was decidedly absent.

When Jaguar and Alex had a minute to talk between interrogation sessions her first comment was about that.

"The greasy bastard slipped the noose," she said.

"I'm guessing that's not the case, Jaguar," Alex said. "He's just stuck in a different one."

They had no time to discuss it at length, because the questioning went on. And on and on.

For some time they focused on Clyde, who was completely gone from Jaguar's room by the time the authorities looked for him. Did she know anything about that? Did she have anything to do with it? She answered no and no, and kept saying that, keeping herself well reined in.

Though Alex took some pleasure in thinking about what Durk was doing with him, he was concerned about how they'd use this against Jaguar, and the absence of corroborating evidence for Regina's involvement. He supposed they had the camera footage from Adrian, and everything Rachel retrieved from her computer, but they weren't mentioning either, and Rachel and Adrian were questioned separately, so he could only hope that would pan out in their favor.

When they wore out their questions about Clyde they returned to pounding Jaguar about opening the vent, insisting she must have done more. She repeated her story enough times that Alex could see she was losing patience.

"Dr. Addams," an attorney for Planetoid insurance said at last, "Our technical experts are certain that opening the vent and pulling two wires couldn't possibly have caused the level of damage we saw. You must have done something else."

"I did not," she said crisply. "I pulled out the wires labeled A and C and opened a vent. The alarm went off, and I left."

"Then how do *you* explain what happened?"

She lowered her head, raised it again, always a danger sign, and Alex paid attention.

"Ghosts," she said succinctly. "The place was filthy with them. You want details?"

Alex stifled a groan, and the others whispered among themselves. One young man in a suit got on his cellcom and did more listening than talking, then moved to the insurance attorney and whispered something in his ear. The attorney raised an eyebrow, then shrugged.

"I understand some of the information is classified," he said. "Thank you, Dr. Addams. That will be all for now." And he turned back to Alex to bug him about the blood donation program.

"What the hell was that?" Jaguar asked Alex when they had a break in proceedings.

He nodded toward the young man who'd been on the phone. "He's military," Alex said. "One of Durk's legal team. I think it means you're off the hook."

"Rat fuck," Jaguar said. "I'll never get rid of him now."

Finally, word came through that Ned Tackerson and Derek Rhinehart had caved, giving full statements about their part in the citrozine smuggling in return for sentences on Planetoid Two rather than Three. Anything, they said, was better than ending up with *her*. Jaguar took this as the compliment it obviously was.

Susan also caved, though she claimed to know nothing about smuggling. Her only interest was getting rid of that Addams woman, who was, she said, pure evil. She'd worked with Clyde Holmseby on that, arranging to get her drink drugged with Praxoline, arranging to lower Francis's meds in hopes he'd kill her, and she was still pissed he hadn't because she certainly deserved killing.

"People keep saying the nicest things about me," Jaguar said to Alex, who only smiled.

When the interrogation was completed they were all exonerated of wrong doing, and then put on display at a press conference where they were publicly praised for doing their duty. Paul showed up for this, went immediately to Jaguar, took her hand in his and shook it hard as cameras clicked around them..

"Don't kill me, okay?" he requested nervously. "I told them I sent you, but they wouldn't let me anywhere near you."

"Get any closer right now and I'll rip your lips off," Jaguar offered in return.

Later, she found out he was telling the truth. He'd been stuck in his own interrogation room, explaining his part in the meltdown of Planetoid One, and they wouldn't let him speak to Alex or Jaguar until they were sure their stories all meshed. Jaguar decided to forgive him, and maybe even to tell him so.

When it was all done and the spin doctors went to work, refashioning this story into something other than the hell it truly was, Jaguar stalked back to her own apartment and locked the doors against all except her known minions, living or dead.

Alex, not so lucky, had to go to the home planet with Paul and explain things to the Senators who funded the Planetoids, because Paul said they liked his style.

"I won't lie for you," he told Paul. "I'll tell them exactly what I know."

"Yeah, but the way you tell the truth, people think it's a good thing," Paul noted.

"Then I take it you don't want Jaguar to come along?"

"God forbid," Paul said. "Any god at all."

* * * *

When Alex returned to Planetoid Three, he went first to Jaguar's apartment. She'd be on rest leave for another week, but he knew her. She wouldn't actually rest until the story was complete.

He found her lounging on her couch, reading an old book, in an old hard copy version. *To Kill A Mockingbird.* He knew the title, and the substance, and the fact that she still read books in hard copy was just one more thing that endeared her to him.

As he entered her apartment she put it down and offered him a tired smile. He moved to her, bent down to kiss her lightly on the forehead. then perched on the arm of her couch.

"How'd it go?" she asked.

"Tediously," he answered.

"Meetings," she said. "Brrr."

"You bet," Alex agreed. "However, the politicos decided the smuggling was an isolated act of desperation to support an outdated and underfunded system. The main thing, they say, is to rebuild One with mass generator and replica cities like those on the very successful Planetoid Three."

"Hecate," Jaguar said. "How the hell did they get there?"

"Got me," Alex said. "But there's worse places they could've gone. And by the way, the Senate's starting a committee to review the new plans for One. They want you to consult on it."

"Me?"

"You and me, with Paul Dinardo."

Jaguar frowned down at her book, back up at Alex. "I don't think I can stomach it," she said.

"Not now, you can't. But by the time they call you in you'll be ready. You've got a thing or two to tell them about how to get it right."

The corner of her mouth twitched up into a smile. "Your accuracy rate is almost as high as mine," she noted.

He heard the mischief in her tone, as well as the lingering sorrow it couldn't mask. He smoothed a hand over her face. Between the interrogations and his trip to the home planet, they hadn't had much time alone to go over what happened.

"Talk to me," he said quietly.

Jaguar's expression moved between anger and sorrow. "The whole place was rotten," she said, "and nobody wants to look at how it got that way. Through expediency, and short term thinking by a bunch of rat fuck pencil-pushers who prefer their well padded lives to the truth. Regina only got away with it because it was so fucking convenient to let her deal with the mutoids, far away from home planet eyes."

"Some of them know," Alex said. "But right now they're all circling the wagons against the media, hoping they won't catch on and make a stink."

"They won't. There's no way you could fit this into a sound bite." She peered up at him quizzically. "You ever worry about that kind of corruption happening with us? We color pretty far outside the lines sometimes."

Alex understood. Issues of identity were involved. "You won't become her, if that's what you're worried about," he said. "Your pride is all about rehabbing prisoners. Regina's was about ego, and fear. You know that. You saw it for yourself."

"I did," she admitted reluctantly. "What are they saying about her?"

"Lots of head shaking and not much else," he said. "But they're ashamed—of her and of themselves. You'll notice there's no memorial service for her."

At this, Jaguar shifted uncomfortably. One of the worst things you could do in her worldview was deny a dead person their memorial, deny the chance for their stories to be told. That was the equivalent of wiping them out, as if they'd never been born. As if all they'd done was meaningless. And that, she knew, was Regina's worst nightmare.

Jaguar gave Alex her direct gaze, full of insistence. "She shouldn't be dead. She should be here, doing her program. But you saw she was going to kill herself, and you let her."

He'd wondered when they'd get around to that. Never mind that it saved her life. That was nothing compared to getting the job done, for a woman who would have gladly seen her dead. The Tango of their work together. He called to mind a move called *arrastre*, where the leader's foot drags the follower's into a new position.

"That's right," he said. "And you knew Scott was supposed to stay with you, but you sent him to me. Are we going to fight about any of that?"

She considered, shrugged, and was still.

That's what he thought. But he wanted her to understand his position, since he already understood hers.

"It was over for Regina the minute she put you on the case," he said. "She saw it drawing in. And the only way she could salvage her heroic delusion was self-sacrifice. If you tried to stop her . . . . " His hand moved in a small gesture, flicking away the disaster that might have been. "We take a lot of risks, Jaguar," he concluded. "That one just wasn't worth it."

Her jaw worked hard for a moment. "I still wanted another shot at her," she said.

He ran a hand through his hair. "You say that as if I don't know you. And I'd be sorry you didn't get it, except I'm too damn glad you're alive to bitch about it."

At this, she showed a flicker of a smile. "Okay," she said. "You're probably right."

"No probably about it." He put a hand on her arm, stroked it softly. "She gave you what you needed when she could still give it. But you're the better person, Jaguar. You might as well accept that."

Pain moved across her face. Not easy, Alex knew, to accept that you've grown well beyond those who taught you. He watched her struggle with it, and was relieved when she breathed in, breathed out, moved on.

"Okay," she said. "What'll happen to the prisoners?"

That, he thought was pure Jaguar. Eye on the prize. He was glad of it. "Most of the mutoids go to home planet programs, where they should've been in the first place. The rest are being shipped here or to Two."

"Francis?" she asked.

"He's staying here. I'm taking his program."

She raised her eyebrows at him.

"Supervisors are required to take on a prisoner program once a year. I'm taking Francis," he said.

Jaguar nodded, leaned back and let her arm rest across her closed eyes. She remained quiet, and Alex knew she was gathering her thoughts. He waited in silence.

"Thank you," she said at last.

"For what?"

"For being that kind of man. I wish there were more of you. If some-one—anyone at all—had the guts to name what was really wrong with Francis in the first place a few more women might still be alive."

"He's a mutoid," Alex said. "Everyone saw that first. Everyone except you. Jaguar, have you taken any time at all to consider what *you've* done? Saved his life, saved God knows how many other lives, not to mention sent a lot of dead folk to a better place. Even Regina, who couldn't bring herself to kill you in the end. You gave her the only redemption she'll get, at considerable risk. And you ended an ugly chunk of corruption in the bargain. Have you thought of that at all?"

"That's my job, Alex," she said. "And I didn't do it alone. I had the best help possible. I had you."

A piercing warmth spread from her words to his heart. Who she was. What she did. To be loved by a woman like this. What good deed had he done that justified such a reward? If he could figure it out, he'd do it again and again.

"We work well together," he said quietly. "In many ways."

She ducked out from behind her arm, looked at him briefly, retreated again. "We do," she agreed, "Though I wonder what you'll do on the day I pull some shit you really mind."

"I think we've been there and done that. Besides, do I mind rain being wet? The sun being hot? Jaguar, I love you. As you are. Impossible to deal with, honest to the core, smart as all hell and beautiful as any creature from heaven you'd care to name. I trust that to hold true when the going gets rough."

She didn't move, didn't speak, but he could feel her taking this in, processing it through the continually evolving mill of her heart and mind. He'd leave her to it for now. He brushed a hand across her cheek, kissed her forehead one more time. She closed her eyes, enjoying the feel of his lips against her skin.

"I have to go the office, fill out more paperwork," he said. "Get some rest. You'll be back to work in another week."

She kept her eyes closed, and felt the breath of air that washed over her from his passing. He was so good at knowing when to leave her alone. But as she heard the door open, she stopped him.

Alex, she said, speaking into him.

Yes, Jaguar?

Come back later. Stay.

She felt his assent, the heat of his intentions toward her. Heard the door close behind him.

Tonight, she thought, she'd remind him that the light they shared went well beyond work, and was filled with pleasure. She considered that pleasure, and smiled.

Then she turned on her side and fell into a deep and restful sleep.

www.ingramcontent.com/pod-product-compliance
Lightning Source LLC
Chambersburg PA
CBHW031424250626
47155CB00004B/1620